"What do you think? I'm an animal?" asked Andreas.

The mood between them had become serious. "You have nothing to worry about," he declared.

If only he knew how wrong he was. She had everything to worry about. In the tight, faded jeans, his physique was muscular, and he looked as tuned to physical response as any jungle creature. Kate warned herself to think rationally. "I'm not some hot-to-trot tourist woman."

"Maybe you are," he returned. "Maybe that's why you brought it up."

"I brought it up because of the way you're looking at me."

"I'm a man, and you're a woman.... How the hell would you expect me to look at you?"

"With respect."

"Then maybe you should respect me. You think I'm just—"

"A playboy," she inserted.

"Yes ... well, you're wrong. I'm not a man who plays with any woman who comes along."

"Oh, no. Not you." She looked at him hard.

"You know," he said, "you are a very difficult woman."

Dear Reader,

Sophisticated but sensitive, savvy yet unabashedly sentimental—that's today's woman, today's romance reader—you! And Silhouette Special Editions are written expressly to reward your quest for substantial, emotionally involving love stories.

So take a leisurely stroll under the cover's lavender arch into a garden of romantic delights. Pick and choose among titles if you must—we hope you'll soon equate all six Special Editions each month with consistently gratifying romantic reading.

Watch for sparkling new stories from your Silhouette favorites—Nora Roberts, Tracy Sinclair, Ginna Gray, Lindsay McKenna, Curtiss Ann Matlock, among others—along with some exciting newcomers to Silhouette, such as Karen Keast and Patricia Coughlin. Be on the lookout, too, for the new Silhouette Classics, a distinctive collection of bestselling Special Editions and Silhouette Intimate Moments now brought back to the stands—two each month—by popular demand.

On behalf of all the authors and editors of Special Editions,
Warmest wishes,

Leslie Kazanjian
Senior Editor

JENNIFER WEST
Greek to Me

Silhouette Special Edition

Published by Silhouette Books New York

America's Publisher of Contemporary Romance

To Bobbis Alexioy of Mykonos, with love
and appreciation for sharing his beautiful
world with me.

SILHOUETTE BOOKS
300 East 42nd St., New York, N.Y. 10017

ISBN: 0-373-09432-9

First Silhouette Books printing January 1988

JENNIFER WEST

was born into a family of concert artists and mad inventors in Brooklyn, New York. After her studies in the dramatic arts, she enjoyed a career in musical comedy. Her current hobby is tracing her roots to see if she has claim to any European throne. In the meantime she writes novels, television scripts and short stories. Jennifer's husband, son, two Akita dogs and an indeterminate number of goldfish share a busy residence in Irvine, California.

ALBANIA
GREECE
AEGEAN
SEA
TURKEY
Athens
N
ANDROS
TINOS
SIROS
MYKONOS
DELOS

Chapter One

It was a standoff, clear and simple, a case of the mysterious East meeting the pragmatic West in a contest of wills.

There were two women: one armed with the heavy artillery of a computer, the other with self-righteousness and fluency in English—which in the end didn't count for a lot because her opponent understood no more than every other word of the enraged pleas for assistance, and remained undaunted by the caustic observations of heartlessness and inefficiency.

After both parties completed another rapid-fire round of bored bureaucratic explanations, foot-stomping and gesticulations, the victor deployed the ultimate weapon...silence. The West had been overcome. And Kate Reynolds had been made to understand, if not accept, that she was not going to get a plane out of Mykonos to Athens.

Yes, finally, that was clear enough.

It didn't matter what she said or what she did. There *were* no planes flying from Mykonos to Athens. There was no promise of any plane flying that day, the day after, or the day after that. Only God knew when the planes were going to fly, and He had not communicated His schedule to her adversary behind the airline computer terminal.

Kate understood all that. Still, she could not understand how it was that the sky looked calm, and the sea reasonably steady, and yet no planes or boats could leave or enter the island.

Mostly she could not accept that no one else seemed particularly concerned by the situation. In America someone would have at least said they were terribly sorry for the inconvenience. She understood, also, that Greece was not America. There were differences. Vast differences. For instance, in America if you complained enough, someone was bound to do something eventually, even if it wasn't exactly what you wanted. But you got the satisfaction of action, at least. Here, in the crossroads of civilization, they just looked at you. And sometimes they didn't even do that.

But if there was anything Kate Reynolds had come to understand over the past year, it was defeat.

She knew defeat in its every variety and infinite nuance. She knew how sometimes the winner might even let you walk away thinking you had triumphed, knowing you'd be two hours into the sky on your way to another country, before you realized you'd been charged double for the leather jacket you were told was such a bargain; or, when in a moment of weakness, brought on by wine, moonlight and a foreign accent, it was possible to pay for a lavish meal ordered by an Italian poet who had said one's beauty made his heart soar and his head dizzy. Like praise had made her wallet thin. Ah, such were life's lessons this past year.

In essence, there was nothing all that complicated about defeat. To Kate, defeat was defeat, any way you cut it, and the only thing she'd found that could possibly assuage the sting of losing to a tougher or wilier opponent was to fade from the battleground with a strong parting glare that stood for "I shall return."

It made no difference that you both knew the truth: that you were a miserable worm and you'd never dare show your face within a mile again. For the time being, a glare saved face.

Kate glared malevolently across the airline counter.

Unfortunately the fury of her look was wasted. The object of her undisguised wrath had been hated before, many times and by people far angrier. In consequence, the young Greek woman seated behind the airline computer terminal merely shrugged, and turning to her co-worker, asked to have another cup of coffee brought over.

Kate retreated several steps to where her son waited by their luggage, three bags lumped in the center of the sparsely furnished airline office. With sudden and passionate clarity, she understood the madness and satisfaction of Mediterranean vengeance. She'd drink to vendetta anytime.

"This can't be happening...." Kate muttered into the space over her son's head. "This is all just a crazy, bad dream. This isn't happening...."

"It is, Mom. It's happening."

Further annoyance. "I know it's happening, Jason. The point is, it shouldn't be."

"You're taking this all personally, Mom."

"Of course I am. It's a plot to ruin what's left of my life, not to mention my sanity," Kate intoned wearily.

"It's only inefficiency," he went on stoically. "The world's full of it. You may as well accept it."

"When you're older and you've been kicked around by life, you'll understand, Jason. Sometimes, even if all you can do is rise to your knees and whine, you have to take a stand."

"You took it. Four times now. Four days it's happened, Mom. It's probably been going on like this for years. There's nothing you can do. When the planes don't fly, they don't fly. She's not God, she just runs the computer. Come on, Mom, let's go." Jason Reynolds tugged gently on his mother's sleeve.

Both mother and son wore identical three-quarter-length, navy blue parkas. The padding was heavy enough for winter in New York or a trek into the Himalayas, and both locations had been visited by them within the last eight months. Colorful mismatched fabric patches and irregular stains gave testimony to former adventures, and even the leather on their expensive trekking shoes bore the patina of more than a few misadventures. Three fat, green duffel bags were dumped on the floor, looking like monster sausages gone bad.

Kate herself had changed greatly since they had set out on their flight from Chicago eight months before. Even on that day, she probably had given the appearance of an innocent. Although she was thirty-one, with her delicate bones and slender figure, she could have passed for twenty-five. Easily. Her complexion was smooth, glowing as in a soap commercial. Her wide brown eyes had a softness and vulnerability that reeked of naiveté, a woman who had existed untouched by life's unpleasantness. At the beginning of her journey, her hair had been cut into a neat bob, falling to just above her shoulders. Now her hair was past her shoulders and somewhat shaggy, making her appear much like a left-over flower child of the sixties. Even her cheekbones appeared more pronounced, as if pieces of her softness had been whittled away by the trip's various experiences. No one could deny that she was pretty, and some might speculate that she could be beautiful if she didn't look so tired and angry.

"Jason, no... I'm not budging from this spot!" Kate tugged back, standing her ground. "This is one time I'm not giving in, I'm not giving up, I'm—"

"—going paranoid on me, Mom. You're getting looney-tunes over this, and it's all because of the—"

"Don't say it...."

"Dad and The Claw," Jason finished resolutely.

Kate stared into her son's gray eyes. They were the eyes of an eleven-hundred-year-old man, the eyes of a guy who lives in a cave and contemplates the mysteries of the universe, not those of a boy born a mere eleven years ago in a Chicago hospital to a woman who was—then, at least—generally considered in all ways to be ordinary and normal. She couldn't say if those really were the good old days. It was hard, anymore, to get a clear perspective on her life with Michael.

But even in her turmoil, Kate had to wonder how a person got to be like Jason: so old, so wise, so fast. Maybe the answer lay in that breakfast cereal he used to eat three times a day until he was six and went on a health kick—the cereal with all the stars and spacemen and sugar.

And she? She was a thirty-one-year-old, pushing the emotional age of three; a splendid living example of devolution of the species.

"This situation has nothing to do with The Claw," she answered. A lie if there ever was one. "There's a principle involved here." If they had been home, she could have sent him to his room. But since they didn't have a home anymore, she had to resort to reasonable discussion.

Of course Jason was right. The Claw was largely responsible for her present rage.

There had been a time in her life when she had never made a big deal about anything. She had just flowed merrily along with life. She didn't even need paddles for her boat, the stream was that smooth. Everything in that serene world of hers was predictable and whatever wasn't, Michael always seemed to handle.

But Michael was handling things for another woman now—as if The Claw needed any help. Ha! The Claw could very well fend for herself, as she had certainly proved by grabbing Michael away from her and Jason.

So, at thirty-one, she—formerly suburbia's most perfect wife and mother—was learning how to paddle in what quite suddenly had turned out to be the harsh white waters of life.

Jason had not changed his expression.

"Okay, it's true, Jason," she conceded grudgingly. "Indirectly, The Claw might possibly be a prime motivating factor in much of my anguish."

"You know you'd like to kill her, Mom. It's perfectly normal."

"Oh, well . . . in a passing dark moment I might have entertained the barest, the most fleeting thought of ripping her heart out with my bare hands."

"You'd break your nails. So let's go, okay?"

The small, wise face looking up at her with a universe of compassion, had freckles and reddish-brown hair. Who was this kid? she wondered. He didn't look like her; he didn't look like Michael, either. Jason looked like Jason. Her heart, hardened as it was at that moment, gave a small leap and remembered how it was to feel good. Softness, that crippler of hard fortitude, overwhelmed her.

Damn. She wanted everything to be so nice for him. She wanted things to be like she had once believed they were—

perfect. Big, pretty house in an upper-middle-class neighborhood, cookies baking in the oven, Scouts in the afternoon, a dad to defer to on important issues like camping equipment and keeping the stray dog.

But all of that, and a lot more, not even material in nature, was gone now. Gone with The Claw . . .

As Kate looked down at her son, whatever love was left in her, she felt for that face with freckles and for the ancient soul lying beneath.

"Jason, you are wise beyond your years," she said with a catch to her voice. "Maybe even beyond my years. But Jason, shut up now. I'd like to enjoy my misery and anger in peace."

Jason sighed.

"And don't sigh. It makes me look bad. If I've lost control and I'm a horse's ass, let *me* convey that to the world. There are still some things I can do for myself. Okay?"

She moved from Jason and leaned back against the counter. She would have liked to have been cool. Oh, yes. She would have liked to have been devastatingly hard. But she wasn't. Maybe that took high, chiseled cheekbones and cold, gray eyes, which she didn't have—her own face being slightly round and her eyes being the warm brown of an animated Disney fawn. All she could manage, therefore, was fury and frustration, and it took all her energy to fight back tears that would humiliate her before her arch enemy, the airline reservationist.

"Excuse me," she began, at the same time feeling Jason efficiently sidling up, most likely to claim her broken ego when the debacle had ended. "But maybe you haven't heard . . . we are now in the twentieth century."

The young woman glanced up. She took a sip of coffee, waiting with a neutral, or blank expression, depending on point of view.

Kate continued. "There must be someone connected with this operation who has some sense of responsibility, some accountability to the public, which it so loosely serves."

"Mom," Jason whispered, nudging her. "I don't think she cares about the history of the world. I don't think she speaks English much."

Kate sent Jason a fast, debilitating look. Later she would kill him in his sleep.

To the airline reservationist, she said, "It may interest you to know that today, right at this very moment, there are people flying from New York to London faster than it takes to cook a turkey in an ordinary oven. And all I want is to take one simple, short, half-hour plane ride off this island to Athens."

The reservationist put up a Closed sign. She rose from her post behind the counter and sauntered off with another Greek woman, both seemingly in animated discussion over a watch one was wearing.

"Okay, Mom? Great, you've taken your stand. Let's hit it now. We can watch Petros eat fish, and maybe get some cheese pies. You like cheese pies."

"You needn't humor me. I am not a child, Jason. You are. Try to remember that. It makes things less confusing."

"Mom," he said, "everything's going to be okay. You worry too much. Life's got a way of working out, you'll see. We're here, aren't we? Nothing really super bad has happened yet."

It was his hopefulness that finally got to her. Adversity and disappointment she could handle. Misery shored her up somehow, kept her going. But it was looking into the innocent, hopeful, well-meaning face of her eleven-hundred-year-old son that undid her at last.

The tears came. There, in the middle of the airline office on the island of Mykonos in the far-off country of Greece, on a particularly gray and damp Tuesday afternoon in the middle of February, the seemingly impregnable dam of emotion finally gave way.

One after the other, they came: large hot tears of helplessness, tears that had incubated within her for over a year, tears begun on the day when Michael had told her he no longer required her services as a wife, tears she had pushed away on train rides through Japan and on elephant rides in India. They were there now, the lot of them, monster tears that had just been waiting all along to wipe whatever was left of her away.

Jason was there at once. He swept his arms securely around her and held fast, his head providing a platform for her chin as her body quaked in short, tight spasms of grief.

"I'm sorry, Jason. I'm sorry," she sobbed, and gasped for air. "I know I'm making a spectacle of us. It's just—"

"...The Claw and Dad and—"

"The Claw and your father..."

"...and we don't have hardly any money left, and—"

"I've got to get to American Express in Athens to get some money for us..."

"I'm not worried, Mom. I know you'll handle everything. Remember that time in China? Now that was scary."

"But I can't even get us the hell off of this island."

"Excuse me."

Both Jason and Kate looked up. Except for an old man and woman waiting on a bench against the wall, the room had been empty during the last few minutes.

Now, a foot away, a man stood before them. He carried a pouch filled with newspapers and envelopes.

"I couldn't help but to hear," he said, with what Kate took as exaggerated gravity.

Kate sniffed, trying to think back to what exactly she had said. Pride was one of her few last remaining possessions.

But under the man's green-eyed scrutiny, it was difficult to recall the exact content of her recent verbal hysteria. Had she mentioned Michael casting her off for another woman? Had she sounded pathetic and desperate? Probably, judging by the way he was looking at her.

It was *that* look.

She knew that look well enough. She'd seen it on the face of a cheap Italian poet and a deceitful, married French count. It had been worn by a lustful Egyptian camel driver, and a Japanese computer manufacturer.

The look was sincere enough, but misleading. One had to learn to read behind it. It said, "You are a female American pigeon; a sitting duck; easy prey for those who would dabble in amour for the space of an afternoon or an evening or two or three."

Those sporting the look would offer a tour of their city. They would offer help with luggage. In two blocks they would say they loved you, but with an accent. Naturally, even a naive American dodo wouldn't believe a man could love her after the first glass of wine; although certainly the notion would give one pause for thought. But such initial rejection was okay with these fast-track romancers because after the second glass of wine they would say they loved you and cry, or get furious that you didn't believe them, and then even an American dodo *had* to believe it was true love. Did grown men cry?

In Omaha, no. In Madrid, yes. They cried if that's what it took to get into someone's hotel room, euphemistically speaking.

But grudgingly, Kate had to admit the Greek was particularly attractive. She might go so far as to allow the adjective "handsome." His hair was black, thick and wavy, worn shorter in front and longer behind the ears. It was a style adopted by many of the Greek males, who, because of their generally hard lives, were unusually masculine no matter what their age. The unique hairstyle, therefore, provided a contrast of soft vulnerability that was particularly romantic. Another nationality would be hard-pressed to pull off the same style—a further compliment to the combination of angular cheekbones and dark, full brows. And, annoyingly, the man before her was a splendid prototype for the modern Greek ideal. She tried to overlook this.

"My son wasn't feeling well," Kate said, placing her hand firmly on Jason's shoulder, a warning to keep his mouth shut for once. "It's terribly upsetting to me when he gets these sudden attacks. I just seem to...to overreact." Thus explaining the red nose and puffy eyes, she hoped.

"Ah," the Greek said, nodding. "I thought so. Then let me take you to a very good doctor."

He threw the pouch of papers and mail over the counter, then immediately, and with great purpose, bent down and lifted two of their bags, placing the third beneath one arm. Kate watched, amazed; it was a Herculean feat.

"Come!" he commanded with the same degree of enthusiasm, and was marching toward the door with all their worldly possessions before Kate had the presence of mind to yank back one of the duffel bags and halt his progress.

He turned, surprised. "Yes?"

"No," Kate said firmly.

"But you needn't worry. This man is very modern, an excellent doctor. He was educated in America, at one of your fine schools."

"We don't believe in doctors. It's a religious thing," she said inventively, not having the energy for yet another clash of wills that day.

"I see," the man said, nodding as he took in the information. "An excellent philosophy! It saves money."

"It does," she said, relieved she had gotten off so easily. But she hadn't. For in the next breath he had retrieved the duffel bag she had dislodged and was backing toward the door again.

"So," he announced, "we will skip the doctor and go directly to the cheese pies."

"What?" Kate said, keeping a step or two behind her luggage, although she doubted he could get far with what they had to weigh. Anyway, at her question, he stopped.

"I understand you like cheese pies," he said with the barest smile, explaining, of course, that he had overheard at least part of her conversation with Jason.

His tone was also slightly skeptical, and Kate realized he did not believe a word about the doctor. Probably he knew there was nothing wrong with Jason, too. He simply refused to give up. Well, he was going to have to.

"No," she said firmly, and with direct eye contact. "That is, I do like cheese pies. But I don't want a cheese pie. I don't want anything." She was about to add that she would like to be left alone, when Jason preempted her.

"She would like to leave Mykonos," he volunteered far more diplomatically.

The Greek looked aghast. "To leave Mykonos? But Mykonos is a good place. People from all over the world come to Mykonos. There is magic here."

"But no planes," Jason said.

"When the gods want there to be planes, they will come." He cast a humorous look at Kate. "And then your mother will be able to escape back into the world she misses so much."

"Why don't the gods want them to come now?" Jason asked.

"They like to play with mortals sometimes. To arrange their lives. Why not? We are their television!"

Jason laughed. Even Kate responded to the imagery, smiling for a moment before she remembered her current plight and settled down again into her funk. Gods and cheese pies and cute, pushy Greeks aside, she had to find them a place to stay. The hotel they had spent the past week in had closed that morning to be painted before the tourist season began. There was almost nothing else open—maybe nothing at all. The Mykonian merchants were smart. And, from what she had heard, rich. Eighty thousand people a day on a little patch of earth in the Aegean brought in a lot of currency. At the end of the season, around November, they, along with the tourists, all fled the island for the real world—as she had longingly come to think of it. She also had very little cash left.

"Where do the gods live?" Jason inquired in a rush.

His eyes had become very bright, and Kate could tell he was off on what would certainly turn out to be another passionate quest of intellectual discovery.

"The gods—where do they hang out now that we've got bombs and jets, and all of that?" Jason pressed on, hungry for information.

"They live on Delos." The Greek turned slightly, hitching his head in the direction of the window that overlooked the harbor. Kate looked also, catching sight of small white crests against the gray sea. "Always they've been there," the man went on to explain. "That's what makes Mykonos so attractive. We get the fallout of the spiritual energy."

Jason's eyes misted over. Kate didn't need a crystal ball or contact with a muse to see into the future. Shortly, Jason would be poring over the tour book she had bought, describing the history of Delos, the nearby island that was once the religious center for the entire ancient Mediterranean world.

"Please," Kate said, her eyes making contact with the Greek's, "he takes all of this very seriously. He's imaginative enough as it is. I'd just as soon he studied his math book than indulge in myths about things that never existed."

"And then he could learn to build faster jets?"

"Why not?" She felt challenged and could foresee the beginning of a political argument. The Greeks were very big on pointing out the failures in all political systems, their own included. Such discussions ended in a lot of yelling, and there was no way to win.

The Greek shrugged. "Jets are fine. For some people. The world needs them!" he conceded expansively. "But for others, there are better things, more important things."

Kate felt as if she were battling for her son's soul, as if the forces of fantasy and reality were swirling about, and she and Jason were likely to get sucked into the Greek's outrageous view of life. She felt, also, as if she were in danger of losing herself to what his presence in her life promised.

Physically, he was a beautiful man, and after the split with Michael, she hadn't wanted to be close to any male. First there had been the pain. And after there had been the anger and self-doubt. The world trip she and Jason had embarked upon was to mark the end of one life and the beginning of another. The trip wasn't over yet, and neither was the pain and lack of trust in herself or anyone else.

But lately there were emotions surfacing that pushed against the walls of her loneliness. Once again there were faint but familiar stirrings—the desire to touch and the need to be touched. There was that occasional yearning to love.

Now, in the presence of this man, she warned herself to be careful. If she was ever to love again, it would be a good love, a real love, not a brief encounter on an island whose chief sport during the high season was rumored to be horizontal bodies.

Her ego was too fragile for romantic game-playing; after all, she had been thrown away by one man. It wasn't as if she was filled with a lot of personal confidence in herself as a woman, and a one-night stand with a Greek Romeo certainly wouldn't do much to improve her self-image.

Jason's ever-sensible voice intruded upon her ruminations. "It's not silly to believe in things you can't see, Mom. You can't see atoms, but they're there anyway. You can't see radio waves, or television waves, either, but when you've got the right receptor, you hear stuff and see people on the screen. So why should it be so crazy to believe in gods?" Jason said defiantly. "At least we can give them a chance. Think of it as an exploration into the science of invisible things."

"Not only that," the Greek said, his glance taking in both Kate and Jason, "it's fun."

And in that one sentence, Kate realized her son had been captured and would reside for the duration of their stay on Mykonos in the realm of cheese pies and the mythology of ancient Greece.

"You are very wise, very clever. There must be some Greek blood in you," said the man, smiling at Jason, who beamed in response.

In the look, Kate read the gentleness of an older male for a boy just on the brink of manhood. There was the telegraphing of masculine camaraderie, the code of which no woman could break. Something in her heart clutched. Michael should have been looking at his son this way—not a stranger on the make for Jason's mother.

Her face must have reflected her thoughts, for the man said suddenly, "Come, you don't have to be afraid of me. You don't have to tell me anything, either. Pretend what you like, hide what you want." He was looking past her outer shell, into her.

She wanted to hide. She was vulnerable to a thousand hurts and susceptible to any kindness. He knew it already, and she felt ashamed and foolish and slightly panicked that if she didn't get away now, at once, she'd be stuck with the Greek forever—or at least, God willing, until the first plane took off.

"Thank you," she said, one word running into the other, "for all your concern and interest, but my son and I have things to do and...well, we've got to be off, doing them, you see..."

At this, the man's expression changed again, radically. A smile appeared, dazzling, overwhelming in its charismatic appeal. It was, thought Kate forlornly, the smile of a thousand rogues.

"On Mykonos?" the man said, laughing. "On Mykonos in February there is nothing to do but drink and gossip and make love."

"And eat cheese pies," chimed in Jason, his mood having become as merry as the man's.

"This is Greece," the stranger said. "You may as well enjoy it while you are here. Our cheese pies and ouzo, our music and our jokes."

"Mom?" Jason looked pleadingly up at her.

She had been trapped, of course. No consideration or deliberation was necessary. From the moment the seductive Greek had cast his eyes on Jason, the future of their afternoon had been ordained.

"Okay, cheese pies, it is. Lead the way..." she said resignedly, capitulating to the army of freckles.

"To the cheese pies!" Jason roared, taking off for the front door.

She looked quickly to the Greek, who was watching her, and not Jason, with amusement.

"You think you're very clever, don't you?" Kate said.

He lowered his eyes briefly, then smiling his peculiar half smile, said, "I'm Greek, what do you expect? It's my duty to make visitors to our land happy."

"I'll bet," Kate returned.

Jason had returned to the door and was rapping on the glass for them to come out.

The Greek opened the door, and hoisting the luggage, allowed her to pass before him. Their bodies brushed as she squeezed by the duffel bags, and in his soft melodic accent, in a voice as deep and smooth as the Aegean had been on her first day on Mykonos, he said, "Before you leave here, you will see the gods . . ."

Kate looked at him disapprovingly.

Laughter shone from his green eyes, but beneath the surface humor there was a serious promise. And she knew, as she left the building in his company, that she would have to be very careful around this man. If not, she just might be seeing Pan and Poseidon and the rest of their gang coming around the bend some moonlit night.

Chapter Two

The taverna was one of the few to remain open on the island during the winter.

The Greek dropped the three bags into the corner of the room, and as if the host in his own home, led them with a proprietary air to a table that he insisted was the best, being far from what he called the "dangerous" cross drafts. But rather than joining them, he disappeared immediately into the kitchen where he was gone for a brief time before returning with a platter heaped with warm cheese pies and several small bowls of Greek condiments.

"Ah, this is the best!" he proclaimed. He positioned himself at the table and began to portion out their food. "Good food, good company!" A carafe of red wine was brought by the owner's wife, and pouring two glasses, their cheerful new acquaintance handed one to Kate. With a grand flourish, he raised his own wineglass. *"Viva!"*

Jason clinked his water glass, participating fully in the gaiety, his face filled with something bordering on wild gladness. "Mom," Jason urged. "*Viva*, Mom..."

"*Viva,*" Kate intoned, but without vigor.

The Greek's happiness made her sad, and her sadness made her even sadder, and then guilt set in for being a spoilsport. There was something so honest and simple about his joy, just as there was in Jason's, and she felt mean and selfish that she could not enter into it. But then the Greek could afford his cheer; he was not emotionally bankrupt, as she was. He had not been dumped by Michael for a blond, blue-eyed vulture in a dress-for-success suit.

"Don't be sad," he whispered to her across the table, reading her condition perfectly. "Please," he cajoled. "This is a celebration."

Their eyes connected. Again she felt him physically enter her, roving through the dim, shadowy corridors of her inner world, places where her wounded feelings cowered, ashamed and alone. "A celebration of what?" she asked sarcastically in a blind attack at him. She resented him, felt his sensitivity as a weapon rather than concern.

"Of Tuesday," he said lightly, seemingly unoffended by her tone. With more seriousness, he added pointedly, "And of our meeting."

His green eyes glittered, boring into her like twin emerald drills, and before she could look away, she'd glimpsed more than she'd wanted to of the personality lying beneath the flamboyant exterior. It was as if, for a flash of an instant, she had entered the deep stillness where his soul resided and found another side to his character. With sudden clarity she understood that he had earned his infectious laughter through his own knowledge of grief. He had experienced his own Michael, or Mary, or whatever. He had wept and raged and felt the disgrace and the disbelief, just as she had. He understood.

The intimacy stunned her, and she recoiled from its effect. She did not seek closeness with anyone. It was too soon.

And, anyway, this man was not the right one. She would know when that man came, if he came—the right man who would take Michael's place in her life and Jason's; the man who would be her lover and her friend, and who would never, never leave them. The man sitting with them was a lover all right, but of the roving variety. And yes, being honest, she *could* imagine a night of wild passion in his arms; but she could also project the morning after when with a yawn and a stretch he would slip out of bed and out of her life. She'd heard the same story repeated by more than one tourist woman.

"Our meeting was an accident," she returned crisply, in a voice destined to make an end to the fantasy he was trying to weave around their association.

"But you see, there are no accidents. They only appear to be so if someone does not understand," he replied, undaunted. He nibbled on a pie, and put another one on Jason's plate.

"Interesting belief. I'm sure it makes life a great deal more fun."

"And easier."

"But a scientist might differ with that opinion."

He leaned forward. "What matters is not opinions and what a pen scratches on paper . . . the measurement of life's mysteries is found in what a man feels in his own life is true."

"I'm glad you're so tolerant. Because if I want a philosophy lesson, I'll enroll in a course when I return home."

He nodded, bowing to her wish to change the topic. "Where is home?" he went on cordially.

He *is* a clever bastard, Kate thought again. He had ignored her antagonism, and had instead seized the opening to discover more about her. She wondered how much to tell him, and then had to wonder why she would even wonder. With other people, she would just digress immediately and the topic would become buried beneath conversational trivia. She didn't like feeling like a freak in a sideshow, and that is precisely how she felt when she discussed the background of her current rootless status.

"We don't have one anymore, no home, nothing. Just Mom and me and our suitcases. We're vagabonds," Jason answered for her, pieces of crisp filo dough flaking from his fingers and chin.

Listening to him, Kate wasn't certain if he had made the two of them sound fabulously glamorous or like two tawdry bums drifting through life. God only knew what the Greek thought. He probably fancied her a loose woman; wasn't that true of roamers of either sex?

"But we used to have a home," Jason went on. "It was real big, with a game room, and everything. Video games, even."

The Greek was stunned. "This is something impossible to imagine."

"We had a pool table."

"A swimming pool?"

"Yeah. And four televisions."

The Greek became quiet. "I would never want to leave such a place."

Kate had been listening in horror as the conversation unfolded. This last was a deliberate question posed as an innocent statement.

"Jason...do you want some milk?" Her voice was harsh, cutting him off, cutting, period.

Jason stared, surprised.

For the past few minutes Jason had seemed mostly involved with his food, fading in and out of whatever they had been saying as he picked and prodded the unusual fare set before them. His awareness had surfaced at exactly the wrong time.

The happiness in his eyes faded.

She was sorry immediately. Sorry. Sorry. Sorry. That was her middle name. She was sorry she was sharp. She was sorry she couldn't give Jason his televisions and game room anymore. She was just plain and miserably sorry.

But the damage was done and now she had to explain to the Greek or he would think God only knew what. She would explain, but with as little disclosure as possible. "We've sold our home. Before we resettle into something permanent, we decided to become adventurers for a year."

It sounded fine, she thought, lighthearted, light-headed; just the sort of thing an upper-middle-class American would do who was bored with a life that had become too easy and good, who wanted to "feel" the pulse of the "real" world. Hadn't she met her share of that variety of world voyager during her travels? Then, appalled at the poverty or inefficiency of a Third World nation, they would scurry off to the nearest Hilton or Marriot, where, from a perfumed suite on the twentieth floor, they could watch the masses who really *did* have to live the drama of danger or poverty. So let him think she was of their ilk, rather than know the truth, that she was just a thrown-away woman with a kid, no funds for spiffy hotel suites and nothing much else to do in life but run from her hurt feelings.

She was steeled for more of his prying, but rather than ask another question related to her personal life, he backed off from the subject and volunteered his own dreams.

"I have always wanted to travel. I've wanted to see everything in this world. Everything! But," he added with a note of genuine sadness, "I've never left Greece. For one thing, it's too expensive for a Greek—unless our last name is Onassis, or such—to go many places. And for another thing..." And here he stopped, as if he, too, had reason to keep parts of his life in shadow.

"I can send you postcards," Jason offered expansively.

"It's not the same, though. Not like really being there."

"Maybe it's better. I can travel in my mind. Then things will always look the way my heart sees them." The Greek took a long swallow of his wine. His eyes closed briefly, as if he were contemplating the drink's flavor. But he wasn't, he was hiding.

Kate had used that ruse herself many times over the past year, escaping into some busy physical activity when she felt she was in danger of exposing the secret, too soft underside of herself. When you were intensely aware of your own limitations, you became intensely aware of those of other people around you.

His delivery had been jaunty enough, but Kate noted the flicker of hurt in the green eyes, the spasm of longing to have something that was forever out of reach.

Like the past, she thought, *like the past, which looked so warm and safe and sunny when you lay awake at night in a third-rate hotel room in a distant country. It was so hard sometimes to believe that all of her memories were just that, memories, things that were forever out of reach.*

So, of things he did not care much about, the Greek might joke, and of things he did care about, he would also joke. But there was a thin wall through which a discerning eye might detect the pride of a man who was forever denied his most cherished dreams. And she had breached that barrier. She wished she had not. She did not want to feel sympathy for him or anyone else. All emotional involvement was debilitating.

Suddenly his eyes were open again and he was staring into hers, seeing her interest. She felt tricked. She felt that he had purposely manipulated her into his psychic space. Who was watching whom?

She looked quickly away, her hand reaching for her own glass of wine.

"We've been everywhere," Jason was saying enthusiastically, his humor restored. "I've been on an elephant. And a camel. And guess what? I climbed one of the tallest mountains in the world."

Good, Jason, Kate thought, *chatter on. Leave me to exist in my nice, safe, emotional vacuum, where piercing green eyes cannot pierce.*

Jason obliged, holding his own conversationally, while Kate looked about their surroundings.

It was a place she had not found before, somewhat off the beaten track. The establishment was small and rather shabby, the only decor being a few Greek travel posters hung with tape on the walls, but it had a cozy quality, too. Kate attributed this to the animated conversations of the owners—a husband and wife who fought good-naturedly with themselves and customers alike. Whenever Greeks spoke in their own language, it sounded like an argument. This was sometimes true, Kate knew, but often the actual content of the conversation consisted of no more than an exchange of casual pleasantries. The perceived strife lay in the harsh inflection of the language.

The other customers consisted of a solitary, sad-eyed, Greek Orthodox priest in his long black robes, eating a dish of white beans and boiled lamb, and two tables of fishermen who argued loudly as they slammed cards on the table, only to laugh uproariously in the next play. In the few thousand years since their first dramas began as religious festivals to thank the gods for their bountiful harvests, the Greeks had lost none of their flair for putting on a good show. Present personal experience confirmed as much.

"Was it really a shark?" Jason was asking. Trembling with anticipation, he leaned forward on his chair.

"Two sharks."

"Wow. And you killed them both?"

"Only the larger one. The smaller one swam off quickly. He was smart."

Jason howled in delight.

And so it went, from cheese pie to cheese pie. The stranger who had adopted them was a mesmerizing wizard, his words painting a vivid world in which he was always the featured player.

Even before the first crusty triangular pie filled with feta cheese had been consumed, Jason had found a new hero; perhaps his first, thought Kate, observing the scene. Even Michael had not elicited such pointed attention from his son as the man sitting opposite them.

It came out that the Greek's name was Andreas Pateras. He admitted readily that he was thirty-three years of age, the information volunteered, Kate guessed, as a preliminary to setting the stage for the colorful tales he had to tell of those years. He may not have traveled the world, but he knew his country. More so, it was clear he knew life.

Besides being influenced by his physical attributes, Kate was discovering with ever-increasing annoyance that she was also not entirely immune to the charm of Andreas Pateras's personality.

If Jason were transfixed, she had to admit that she was sliding into a state of mild enchantment. There was an effervescent jauntiness about him that was contagious and irresistible. It was impossible not to respond on some level. And also, although his stories were mixtures of fact and outrageous mythology, there was, underlying every wild tale, a serious undercurrent. Small lessons of human fallibility were recounted with a biting accuracy, but each example was also cloaked softly in humor. Kate was left with the feeling that in every person's folly, he recognized his own.

Hoping to find something mean and small in him, she found nothing, yet...there was an indistinct, mercurial sense of the devil about him. From moment to moment she felt herself off balance; whatever decision she had firmly made about his character or intent would dissolve in the next instant. And that was it, she suddenly realized: Andreas Pateras lived purely by impulse, in his emotions.

And she, Kate Reynolds, preferred to stay as far away from the territory in which the heart was king as was humanly possible.

"We've got to go," she said suddenly, just that and nothing more. The desperate quality to the statement surprised even her. Both Jason and Andreas broke off their conversation, and with raised brows, appeared to wait for some additional comment from her. None was offered. Standing, she slipped quickly into her jacket, anxious to be out of the Greek's net. "It's cold, Jason," she said, "put yours on, too. And button up."

Jason stood, reluctant to obey. "Do we have to go now, Mom?"

"Yes. Now."

"Your mother has an appointment," Andreas said with irony.

She was fiddling with the zipper, her head bent in avoidance of whatever yearning or lust or amusement she might find in the Greek's expression. Nevertheless his eyes were on her again, the green, impudent, invasive eyes, and clearly they were laughing at her. "It so happens I do have something to do. I've got to find a place to stay tonight."

"I know a place," he said.

"Thanks, but no thanks," she returned, at last trusting herself to look into his face.

"With an old lady," Andreas said, with that cattish smirk he would adopt when she had assumed too much.

Refusing to give him any satisfaction, she said, "Thanks, but I'm sure I'll find someplace on my own."

Andreas rose slowly from his seat, his attention directed to the proprietor to bring the check for their refreshments.

"Thank you," Kate said, "for the...hospitality."

"It is nothing." He gave her a deep look, then quickly turned his attention to Jason. Holding his hand out, he said, "You must take good care of your mother."

Kate watched as the two males shook hands. A powerful sense of sweet sorrow seemed to accompany the act of their simple parting: the boy who was beginning his life, who had already seen great vistas, for whom the horizon yawned infinitely vast; and the man whose destination in life was to be marooned to his imagination on a small Greek island.

Both the man and the boy held too long to each other, and when they finally released their grip, it was as if they were being jerked apart, torn by some force outside of themselves.

"Maybe the planes won't fly tomorrow," Jason said.

"Come, Jason..." Kate urged before plans could be made.

Andreas Pateras studied her, looking hard, as if trying to figure something out. But he only shrugged slightly, as if answering himself, and turning without another word, left to settle the bill with the taverna's owner. With his back to them, it was as if a door had closed. Their connection to each other's lives had been severed. It was what she'd wanted, this freedom, and yet as she took a last parting glance his way, she had not expected to experience the sudden emptiness of feeling.

Jason was already at their bags, making a display of lifting the heaviest, one that Andreas Pateras had handled as if it had been a feather. Jason was taking care of her, of course, and she would be careful to let him do what he could.

Walking toward the corner, Kate felt the "dangerous" cross drafts against which they had been warned by Andreas. She had laughed at the description, the way Westerners do who find all folk wisdom of less technologically advanced cultures quaint and not to be seriously considered. But they were there, narrow flowing streams of sharp, icy air that seemed to seep from some other source more frigid than the outdoors. Certainly there had to be some scientific explanation.

But maybe, she thought, there was none. Maybe, she thought, as she and Jason dragged the bags to the front door, she would find a god—Pan, perhaps—lounging around the corner. Really, she didn't much care anymore. All she knew for sure was that the bags were heavier than they had ever been.

Andreas did not turn to watch them leave. She knew because she was watching him through the glass window of the door. Her last sight of him was as he threw back his head and laughed. She could only see him in profile as he spoke to the proprietor. But the face of Andreas Pateras was alight and his own body alive with that curious tight energy he brought to his every gesture. He was a man, through and through—a man who was totally a man, and Kate knew somehow, the way a person glimpses something that is actually quite outside their own experience, that there was more to loving, so much more to making love, than she had ever experienced with Michael. But she would never unravel this mystery. Like the glass through which she looked, their lives were separated. A night of the kind of passion promised in his glance, in the way his body moved, would shatter whatever serenity remained in her life. She was moving on, and he was staying. Stepping away from the window, she was caught by the wind full force.

The scent of approaching rain was in the air although the sky had not darkened sufficiently to pose an imminent threat to their search for quarters.

"Which way, Mom?" Jason asked, his hair fluttering wildly.

"I don't know." The narrow street—if it could be called a street, being no wider than five feet and only navigable by walking—seemed as vacant of life as the most desolate of African veldts. "Let's try that way...to the right." And going against the wind, and at a slight upward climb, they set off with their bundles.

Around every new corner, she half expected to see Andreas waiting. But if she had expected the Greek to follow them, to again offer his house or a friend's house to her and Jason, in a self-serving effort to remain connected long enough to satisfy his male impulses—or her own!—she was very wrong.

The only people out were a few elderly women wearing black dresses, black stockings, and black scarves over their heads. None spoke English, and all looked quickly away when approached, unable or unwilling to engage in even sign language. A couple of rough fishermen were trundling home, but these men offered no sense of security to Kate, and she avoided their glances as the women had avoided her own.

And so it went, Jason and she trudging through the labyrinth of stone pathways for an hour, every so often knocking on a painted green or blue or brown door to inquire about lodging. There was no lodging available, nor was there any sign of Andreas Pateras.

The storm began with a few harmless sprinkles. By the time the first real drops of rain splattered in dark splotches over the whitewashed stone, Jason was voicing aloud what she knew already.

"You should have gone to Andreas's friend, Mom."

"Why, Jason? Don't you think this is fun? Drowning together?"

"I'm tired, Mom. And I'm cold. Why didn't you let Andreas help you?"

"Because. I didn't."

"Let's go back and find him."

"Andreas is gone, Jason."

"We'll find him."

"No. He's gone. It's finished."

"What's finished?" he asked, sputtering through the deluge.

The water was pouring down their faces in buckets. They were shouting at each other to be heard.

"Whatever it is that didn't begin," she said, and turned her head away, hiding the tears that may or may not have been from feeling lost and tired and afraid in a strange land. Saying nothing more, she took off with the two bags, leaving Jason to struggle behind with the third. There was a fork in the pathway, and looking at both alternatives she decided not to take the "right" path. For once, she would deliberately take the other direction. Being right never seemed to get her anywhere. As she saw it, the worst that could happen is that they wouldn't find any place and eventually they'd be washed downstream into the Aegean and that would be that. And so what?

Chapter Three

Andreas Pateras had never realized how terrible the sound of a door closing could be until that moment when the American and her son departed the taverna. And his life.

At the click of the door's latch, he had tensed, willing himself to remain as he was, his back to the woman and boy with whom he had just spent what to him were magical moments without compare. But he was a fine actor, and Dimitri, owner of the taverna, continued on with his jokes, never sensing the anguish raging through Andreas's soul.

As Andreas peeled out the eight hundred drachmas, nodding on cue to whatever Dimitri posed, responding by brief comment when necessary, another part of him was poised to race after the departed foreigners. His desperation was such that he was on the verge of breaking the cardinal rule in the unwritten code of all Greek males: never admit to a woman your truest, deepest feelings. One could play the game of baring one's soul to a potential female conquest, but such disclosures were only theatrics necessary for the goal of physical pleasure.

Had it not been for the interference of Eleni, Dimitri's wife, who attached herself to him just as he was ready to bolt, Andreas might have succumbed to carrying out this impulsive gesture of honesty.

"When are you going to get married?" she shrilled, her voice shattering the image of the American woman he held in his mind.

It was an old litany of Eleni's, stirred to the surface by her preoccupation with his continuing bachelorhood. Two or three times during the past year she had dragged him off to meet a young woman of marriageable age and status, only to have Andreas escape the net of her intent with the ease of a slippery eel. Yet he could never escape her efforts to marry him off for very long. Eleni was a stubborn woman, and possessed, it seemed, of energy enough to run the lives of innumerable people, he being one of her chosen projects.

"Soon, Eleni, soon..." Andreas said, and as he did, something leaden sank from his heart into his gut.

He was not fulfilling his destiny. His life was dissolving into a mist around him. For some time now this had been his feeling, and it was becoming more difficult as the months rolled on to ignore the urgency that would well up within him when his guard was down. It was time to commit himself to someone and something. But he was adrift.

At first the pressure was subtle. He would attend this wedding and that, of other young men he had known, feeling only a slight pang of remorseful separation as they stepped from the careless pleasures of single life into the seriousness of family life. Eventually a sort of low-level panic set in. It seemed that one by one the associations of his youth were becoming the victims of an enormous biological clock that only he had managed to evade. A sense of loneliness, of being faintly out of step with other people, began to pervade his quiet moments of reflection.

He wasn't consciously set against marrying and having a family; it merely seemed wrong for him. In fact, nothing in the present scope of his life offered any appeal. He felt as if he'd fallen from the sky into this small island and was trapped here, unable to leave and live out his proper destiny—a life that should have been spent in Paris, or Los Angeles, or any other place than where he actually was.

And he wanted to do something. But there was nothing to do. On Mykonos one had to have Mykonian ancestors with land at their disposal on which to build a discotheque or hotel or restaurant, and thereby make a fortune from the tourists. Otherwise one toiled as a slave in one of these same establishments, earning a mere 1200 drachmas a day—a sad joke when converted into its American equivalent of nine or ten measly dollars.

His grandfather had been a Mykonian fisherman, but he had been killed at sea during a storm, and his grandmother had gone on to the mainland afterward with his mother, who had married a poor farmer from a village on the Peloponnese. It was only ten years ago that his grandmother had returned to claim her original house in the village. He'd come with her to help her get settled.

They'd found the building in sad shape, a hovel of crumbling decay, and Andreas had stayed on, helping her to redo the upstairs into a separate dwelling, and converting the lower level into secondary quarters suitable for renting to tourists during the high season.

But from the moment Andreas had set foot on the island, he had felt the excitement pulse in his veins, experiencing the rhythm of Mykonos as if it were a second heartbeat. From that first day, he had never wanted to return to his parents' small village, where there was no work anyway but to tend the olive trees and the few sheep they owned, scratching by from day to day and year to year as best they could.

On Mykonos, however, there was a constant flux of colorful humanity, and Andreas studied the ceaseless parade of exuberant foreigners with as much interest as a scholar might invest in a formal education. He marveled at the sophistication brought on by money and mobility. He grew to expect, if not to accept, the outrageously hedonistic behavior of the visitors, for which the island had become famous.

Most alluring of all to a hot-blooded young Greek, was the constant stream of beautiful women flowing through Mykonos during the summer. To his increased delight— abetted as he was by the island's amazing quality of light, by the lulling effect of the crystalline blue waters of the Aegean, and hypnotic pounding sensuality of the music pouring from the discos—these equally magnificent specimens of nature were easy targets of seduction. With a natural aptitude he and his friends boasted as being genetic, plus with the practice afforded by the sheer numbers available, the young Mykonian males had perfected the art of the fleeting romantic encounter to its highest form.

They billed themselves as *kamaki*, the Greek word for the three-pronged fishing spear. A true *kamaki* could exercise his powers merely through a glance across a crowded dance floor, or while passing in a street. By an intense, dark look, a *kamaki* worth his title could draw his female prey to him without so much as moving his big toe in her direction. It was attitude, and the marshaling of male energy, that gave the *kamaki* his specialized ability of seduction. There was talk at one time that Andreas, himself, had earned the exalted title of king of the *kamaki*.

Over the past ten years he had known his share of women. Within the first two years, he felt he could judge a woman at fifty paces, know everything about her, from how her body would look unclothed to how she would move in bed, to how her voice would sound. Like an expert swordsman, he could feint and parry with never a wrong move. The hunt and conquest of a woman was in some ways a religious experience, bringing forth emotions bordering on the poetic.

But after each success, there was always the faint remnant of disappointment. When he was new to the game, there was little regret, but later, as the years wore on and the bodies mounted in numbers, every triumph carried with it the tinge of slight loss.

The woman today, the American named Kate, had touched him deeply in some way that he could not understand. Pretty she was, but beauty on Mykonos was almost inconsequential it was so abundant. A man began to look more for a special quality than the surface flash of a perfect body and stunning face.

He had wanted to make love to her. He had wanted to touch her, to know her completely.... And he could have.

He might have pursued her. He might have played the game unfairly, pulling out the full strength of his summer charm. How simple it would have been to make her his captive for a night. And when she left, she would remember him, the passionate words, the smile, the body that could move in a hundred different directions at once, pleasing her beyond her wildest fantasies. She would have sailed off, or flown away from the island, keeping the single memory of him intact, never realizing that for a *kamaki*, a woman off-season was merely a gray day's diversion—a time, a face, a body, a name forgotten even before the first rush of tourists had invaded Mykonos in the spring.

He might have had her in his bed that night, only he had not wanted her that way. He had wanted more—more of her, more of everything—and to have taken her by guile would have brought no satisfaction. She had not wanted him as a man, as he was, and that was that. That was also, he suddenly realized, why he felt so lost at that moment. He had offered her that part of him that was without sham, the genuine side of himself, and she had rejected what was on view.

As he glanced toward the door through which the American woman had just departed, he encountered the barren grayness of the day, seeing it symbolically juxtaposed against those sunlit days of his youthful summers.

How low the mighty have fallen this day, thought Andreas somewhat whimsically as he tried to extricate himself from the mounting harangue of Eleni.

"Your parents will cry," shamed Eleni with feminine despair. "No grandchildren!"

"He'll give them grandchildren!" Dimitri exclaimed with a wicked grin. "Just without the wife attached!"

"I promise I will marry," Andreas said with passionate and false sincerity. "But first I must find a woman exactly like you."

This form of light flattery did nothing to deter Eleni. "Good! I'll find you a woman exactly like me—better than me. By next week!"

"Impossible!" crowed Dimitri, who had gone off to the kitchen to chop lamb into stewing pieces. His cleaver came down with a sharp thud. "Impossible that any woman could equal you, my fabulous flower!"

"I will find a wife," said Andreas more seriously, as he knew it was the only way to put an end to the dialogue. "But first I must find myself. I must have something to offer her."

"Let her offer you something. Find a rich woman and sit on your ass like I do all of my days," Dimitri shouted.

At this Eleni took off after him with a snapping towel. Howls of laughing protest accompanied the attack.

Seizing his chance, Andreas backed off, departing the fray with a wave and voiced hopes that their marriage would survive another fifteen years of such ardent bliss.

Outside, the dampness chilled him to the bone, and he hunched his shoulders against the wind that had picked up since he and the Americans had entered for their refreshments. The sky had turned a threatening shade of slate, and as he walked along the wide expanse of the harbor he made out the small caïques of the fishermen racing into port. Their return meant safety, but another day without income.

He should pity himself, thought Andreas. His work during the winter consisted of the odd jobs he picked up here and there, mostly construction work and his duties as courier to some of the establishments that had special mail to be delivered to or from Athens. It was in this capacity that he'd been in the airline office that morning and came upon the American woman.

He had sailed on the last ferry from Piraeus, the harbor just outside of Athens, on a boat that had arrived in Mykonos but could not depart until the harbormaster gave his approval. The American woman was incensed by the caution his countrymen exercised, but she did not know that five years before, a ferry had sunk three miles beyond the port in rough waters, taking to the bottom of the Aegean several passengers also anxious to go about their lives.

No, the American woman did not know about Greece, and he did not know about the rest of the world.

In this state of suspended melancholy, he continued to walk by himself, stopping occasionally to chat when he came upon a friend. During the winter, most of them had gone off to find work in Athens, returning at times to their villages to pay respectful and loving visits to their families.

Andreas himself should have gone home, but if he did there would be ten times the amount of pressure for him to marry, over and above that which Eleni had levied against him that day.

His excuse was his grandmother, whom he pretended needed his help to exist. Nothing, of course, could be further from the truth. His grandmother was a cyclone of energy, able to rush up and down the seventeen narrow steps leading to her apartment faster than a weasel. In fact, she insisted upon the upper level for her quarters, as the exercise kept her joints oiled. So she claimed.

Personally, Andreas always secretly maintained his grandmother was a creature like himself, discontented with her lot, a woman who might have had a wildly wonderful life full of extravagances of all variety had she been born to wealth or to another nation.

During the Second World War, his grandmother had been selected by the government to study languages: French, Italian, German and English. She was quick in the mind, his grandmother, and there was talk that she would be used in some capacity for counterintelligence. It did not come to pass, however, due to the ending of the war just as she was prepared to step into her role as the Greek Mata Hari. For his grandmother, at least, the end of the war was not a joyous occasion; it marked the end of the beginning of a life of adventure unknown to Greek women of her day.

So Mykonos, with its transient population, allowed her—as it did him—at least a whiff of the delights contained in the outer world. He and his grandmother were kindred souls, two voyeurs on a global level. It was as if they had always had their emotional bags packed for a great trip into the universe but could never afford the price of the ticket. From school he had learned some elementary English, from his grandmother he had perfected and expanded his vocabulary, and from the tourists he had fallen into its cadence. Yes, and as in his grandmother's case, his skills were for naught, other than flattering the silly tourist women who found his accent so fetching.

Three people had warned him to return home soon or be caught in the storm. Andreas reluctantly heeded the advice.

He did not want to be alone with his thoughts, but as those remaining in the village battened their dwellings, the streets became as lonely as his soul. He went first to his grandmother's, but she had disappeared on some mysterious errand. Without her presence in the apartment, even those rooms brought an ache to his being. He waited for as long as he could bear the silence and inactivity, then restlessness drove him home.

Home was a small villa reached by a tired junk of a car he had bought the previous summer. One came upon the dwelling by following the road from Mykonos to Korfus Bay, and there at the exact point where the tide washed in at its greatest rate between two bands of land jutting out on either side, was the small crumbling farm house he rented for the drachma equivalent of one hundred and seventy-five dollars a month.

There was little to it, the whole of the structure consisting of only a main central room off of which two other rooms extended from either side. One room was a kitchen, the other his bedroom. A small bathroom had been added on to the kitchen—it was inconvenient to the bedroom but took advantage of the plumbing available on that side of the house.

However rustic his surroundings, he kept them spotlessly maintained. He had just enough glasses to offer three friends a glass of room-temperature coffee frappé—he had no refrigerator—or a shot of Metaxa, and enough room in his living room to hold a somewhat shabby sofa, a bookshelf, and two end tables, along with a coffee table he had made himself. His bedroom consisted of an armoire in which his few clothes were hung neatly, and a double bed covered in a beautiful lace spread made by his mother.

His dream was, of course, the same as every Greek's—to someday have a good home. Until then, he would make do with his present circumstances.

But as he turned on the two lights in his living room, the glow was not bright enough to dispel the overriding inner gloom that had followed him from the taverna.

He stood in the center of his living area and cursed aloud the gods whom he had called upon earlier that day in conversation. How loyally he had sung their praises, upholding their interest in the disbelieving age of modern man to the American woman. Well, where the hell were they, these wonderful, omnipotent gods? Could they not see that Andreas Pateras, just below them on the Island of Mykonos, could use the intervention of a god or two, to change the course of his rotten, go-nowhere life!

As if in response, an outburst of thunder resounded overhead, shaking the ground on which he stood. Well that was all right with him; let the earth heave and quake—any change in the dullness of his life would be welcome. At least he would know he was alive.

The rain began slowly, gathering force with every passing minute and finally pounding on the ancient tile roof in earnest fury. From the window where he stood, Andreas watched the angry sea flow toward his home. His mind drifted inward as well, thinking of the woman and the boy, and he wondered who had taken them in and wished again it had been him.

* * *

"Come...come..." said the elderly woman in black stockings, black dress, black coat, and black scarf.

It seemed she had appeared from nowhere. Suddenly she was before them, her feet seeming to glide on invisible wings, such was the momentum of her purposeful advance. Even the raindrops appeared to part in deference to her presence.

With a shove, the woman motioned Kate along. "You come..." she ordered, and whirling around, she commanded Jason to do the same.

After the initial lurch forward, caused by the woman's unexpected push, Kate stopped and stared, trying to make some sense out of the assault. Through her dripping bangs and the wall of gray liquid between them, she examined the woman for signs pointing to dementia or what might simply be compassion for two semidrowned foreigners.

"Come, come!" the woman repeated with a sort of urgent aggravation, as if they were two dolts who weren't applying themselves to a necessary task.

Jason remained where he was, looking to Kate for a decision. But the woman gave him a tug and pulled him with her, and Kate, thinking that anything might be better than dropping dead from exposure in the streets of a Greek island, fell into step behind them.

Her arms ached painfully from the weight of the bags she still hauled, and her feet felt frozen and sloshy as she trudged forward, ever forward to God only knew where. And all the while, the woman who led them moved swiftly ahead in stout rubber boots, her squat, compact form safe against the veritable wall of water rushing down the narrow passageway. Jason splashed resolutely along, his small body drooping from the long bundle he hefted.

Seeing him so, Kate's heart went out to him, and at the same time she muttered a billionth curse on Michael, whom she had come to blame for anything and everything that went wrong in their lives. She had found that hating Michael always proved an excellent diversion from any immediate problem. At least he was good for something—mental target practice.

Yet in spite of the elements raging about them, the woman's spirits seemed fine. Kate even caught the unmelodic strains of what had to be some Greek tune being hummed jauntily—all notes ringing in the minor keys—as she and Jason fought against the miserable torrent. There was no song in either of their souls.

"Come...come...we go still," the dark apparition would coax periodically, hustling them onward to their unknown destination.

When they had taken several twists down the serpentine byways of the village, and Kate felt that surely, in ten paces, she would drop against the stones in exhaustion, the woman came to a triumphant stop.

"Here," she said, and pushing Kate aside, nimbly approached a shiny green door on the bottom level of a high, whitewashed stucco building wedged between two almost identical buildings. All buildings inside the village were attached by common walls. In this way, Kate had learned, the ravaging effect of the winds were lessoned, and also, from previous history, marauding Turks or pirates from Italy could be trapped in the narrow lanes, having no way to escape.

With a twist, the door opened easily and the woman disappeared quickly within.

Kate and Jason followed.

"For you," the old woman said. That was all the conversation necessary to impart her invitation. Instantly she became a whirlwind of activity, rushing from room to room as she checked through the small apartment, which at a glance showed no signs of current habitation.

"Thank you," Kate said when she understood that the dwelling was being offered to them for the night. "Please...how much do I owe you?" Kate spoke slowly and loudly. She did not know how well the woman spoke English, or if perhaps her hearing was faulty. With accentuated gestures, she made a show of pulling her wallet from her dripping purse, further pantomiming the financial transaction.

"Whatever you want," the woman said. "Later." She brushed the money aside, and made quickly for the front door. Just before disappearing, she turned back, and with a girlish grin erupting on her wrinkled face, announced, "I speak English fluently. I was trained as a spy, you see, during the big war." And with that, she was gone.

Jason was staring after her, his gray eyes wide in wonder and relief. "What was that?" he asked.

"An old spy. You heard her."

"I think I'm dead," Jason moaned.

"Die later," Kate ordered. "Now you've got to get out of those wet clothes and into a hot bath." She stopped. "Do you think there is a hot bath?"

"Mom, if there're gods, there's got to be."

An investigation into the matter brought forth a shower of sorts with hot water, but no bathtub.

It didn't matter. Looking at the small hose dangling from the small hook on the wall of the tiny bathroom, with its drain in the middle of the floor equidistant from the toilet and washbasin, Kate felt she had been transported to heaven.

"Look," she said with tears in her eyes, "isn't it wonderful? Have you ever seen something as extraordinarily, fantastically beautiful?"

"It sure beats drowning out there," Jason agreed, and began to strip out of his wet clothes.

While Jason showered, Kate went about investigating their new quarters. It was actually small, their place, but gave a more spacious appearance in that there was a particularly long and narrow hall leading from the front to the back of the apartment. There was one door opening to a bedroom located immediately off the front door, and where the hallway ended, a living room opened up. Off of this was a small kitchen and the minuscule bathroom from which she could hear Jason singing and splashing about. Above the living room, a small, partially open loft could be reached by an attached wooden ladder. There was an assortment of furnishings, comfortable and shabby. For one night, it was home; and it was wonderful.

When Jason had finished his bathing, he crawled up the ladder to explore the loft, and Kate went off to experience the wondrous pleasures of hot water and soap for herself.

She was lathering for all she was worth, and singing at the top of her lungs—in a decent major key—when a glance through the frosted glass of the bathroom door brought a dark shadow into focus.

At first she was frozen in fear; then she thought that it had to be Jason, his body somehow magnified by a trick of light and space into an enormous optical illusion.

"Jason?" she called tentatively.

But Jason did not answer.

She heard, instead, a cough—one that was deeply masculine.

"Who's there?" she challenged, reaching for the thin terry towel. Her eyes darted around for some sort of weapon, finding only a small drinking glass. She picked it up and, brandishing it, screamed "Jason!" as she came wheeling out of the bathroom in a primal panic to protect her child.

Her trip was cut short by an immovable wall of masculine bulk. The glass she'd held found a target accidentally, and a cry of pain ensued. At the same instant a crash sounded, and she felt warm liquid oozing down one ankle and between her toes.

Chapter Four

Y ou?" Kate said, her body trembling in the aftermath of psychological terror.

"You?" echoed Andreas Pateras, whose own voice registered no less shock. The heavy, red, fisherman's sweater he wore was dripping a thick brown liquid.

Between them on the floor lay the broken pieces of crockery from what had been, until a minute before, a large serving bowl. Chunks of broad white beans and portions of meat rose amidst the dark stain like small mountain peaks in a thick sea. A separate portion of the warm, viscous fluid had left a trail down's Kate's leg. But it was the scarlet half circle gradually taking form on the cheek of the Greek that claimed most of Kate's horrified notice.

"Oh, no..." she gasped, for the first time making the connection between the smashed glass she had wielded and his wound. *She* had done that to him. "Oh, my God," she said, "it's blood."

But to her further distress, the Greek seemed disinterested in the damage he had incurred from her hand.

"It's nothing," he said casually, as if she had merely bumped against him. He made no move to check if that were true, even as small trickles of blood escaped from the open cut.

"You're bleeding," Kate insisted. "Bleeding is something. I'm so sorry... You've got to do something."

And yet nothing was done. A spell might have been cast over them. Neither of them made any move to organize the required medical attention. Andreas merely continued to stand there in bafflement, and for her part, she was only able to stare back, locked in a state of inertia. The whole atmosphere had become gluey and thick with indecision.

"I never thought I'd see you again." He spoke wondrously, as if some magical feat had been performed. Then, as if realizing he had given away too much of himself, he stiffened slightly. A different note entered his voice. "I came to visit my grandmother—to make sure she was all right. The storm," he explained further. "Sometimes it's hard to fasten the windows."

He paused, possibly to allow her to express some comment that might relieve his discomfort. But suspended in her crazy trancelike state, Kate said nothing. She was, in fact, as overwhelmed by his presence in her life again as he seemed startled to be in it. In the apartment's shadowy, filtered light he might have been the most beautiful man she had ever looked upon in any country, at any time in her travels, or in her entire life.

Andreas Pateras was not terribly tall, but tall enough; a shade beneath six feet, Kate judged. He had a body that gave the impression of being both lean and powerful at the same time. His shoulders were square and broad, and his chest, beneath the red sweater he wore, appeared muscular, as did his arms. There was an unconscious elegance to his movements, and at the same time an awareness of his male power—as if, Kate thought, he considered his body an attribute to be used much like a toy for his own pleasure—and to give pleasure. A heated question followed immediately upon the thought. What might it be like to be his playmate? The answer that arose was dangerous. She was glad when Andreas broke the silence, continuing his explanation.

"My grandmother said to bring this down here." He gestured to the broken pottery. "I didn't know it was for you. Really," he stressed, as if at a loss to convince not just her, but even himself that what he claimed was factual. "It could have been anybody here. It often is. Anybody...tourists my grandmother meets in the streets. During the summer months, she rents these rooms out. Don't think that—"

He broke off, a frown creasing his forehead. He looked as if he had just been thrown a fast curveball in a game he had been playing—and had missed the pitch.

Anyway, it pleased Kate somewhat to see him disoriented. For the moment she was relieved of having to take up her bent, war-torn shield and rattle it around to show how impregnable she was; she could just relax and watch him go through his own paces.

But then again, it also worried her, this show of vulnerability. It was far easier to withstand his physical appeal when she was certain he was just shucking and jiving and handing her a well-worn line, than when this note of sincerity became a prominent ingredient in his conversation. The display of true emotion was thoroughly unbalancing and sent her mind skipping frantically ahead in search of some defect in his character, something obvious and convenient to the situation, something mildly loathsome that might stem any wayward good feelings she entertained. Why was it that her bad attitude always deserted her when she needed it most?

Then, feeling a draft and shivering slightly, she remembered she had nothing on but a towel—a fact that in turn, translated into the understanding that she had been caught in a somewhat compromising position. Wonderful. He had done this to her! The beast. Indignation was in order. Accordingly, she summoned what she hoped was a cold glint to her eyes. It was going to be hard to maintain it.

"Excuse me," she said, and turned to find something more substantial to cover herself with. She walked through the kitchen to her bags in the living room and noticed Andreas following. The blood was still trickling down his face. She thought twice, and a third time about displaying righteous indignation. She didn't know if that was really fair. Was it the proper time to take a stand for her honor? There was a certain amount of guilt involved in such an attack. It would be like kicking the already downtrodden. But, she figured, better to live with a little self-remorse for being a crummy person, than with a broken heart, not to mention the humiliation of being just one more marcher in a long parade through his bedroom.

Her short, terry-cloth robe was the first thing she came to that was easy to throw on, so she tied it quickly around her—towel and all. Then she turned to face him and cast her blow. "And I suppose you never thought to knock?"

The sentence held a world of accusation and inferred his low motives and general caddishness—not to mention that what he claimed was fundamentally an out-and-out lie to begin with. The tone said, also, that she was a lady, not only a lady but close to being a vestal virgin in terms of her sanctity. Maybe, she thought, her delivery was a tad overdone.

He looked at her as if she were slightly mad. "But I did knock. I banged! Hard."

"Oh?" she commented, a universe of disbelief edging the single word. She remained prim. "I didn't hear you."

"I wonder why that was?" And with a glance, he made reference to her damp hair and robed body.

Of course he was right. She had been showering. How could she have heard anything? It was also hard to remain dignified attired so skimpily. "Oh."

"Oh," he mimicked, self-satisfied.

"Jason!" she called, seizing upon a new angle to give her a safe upper hand in the relationship. If he had knocked, then why hadn't Jason answered the door? Ha! She had him now. He was a scoundrel, this handsome, smirking Greek standing before her, and would soon have to admit it. She felt clever, and let Andreas know it, too, matching his smug smile with one of her own. Her heart felt much safer.

"Good," said Andreas enthusiastically, carrying out his charade of innocence with aplomb. He started toward the bedroom area. "Where is your son? Get him. He'll tell you. Jason! Jason!" Andreas's voice rang through the quiet hall.

They waited, both eyeing the other with a look of anticipated triumph. When no reply came, Kate backtracked to the living room and climbed the ladder to the loft, the only other place where Jason might be. Andreas moved after her, holding the ladder steady as she ascended.

"You didn't need to do that," she said testily. "I've climbed mountains and lived to tell about it."

"I have a vested interest in your safe journey," he returned. "And I've fallen down ladders. It hurt when I told about it."

There, in the loft, she found Jason. He was totally out, curled into a ball on a mattress placed on the floor. He was always such a staunch little trooper, it was hard to believe he was as exhausted as he now appeared. Her heart went out to him, and she wished, as always, that she might be a better mother—wiser, stronger…and all the rest of the things she felt she was not. Once she'd thought she was okay in that department. She'd gone buzzing about her life, and Jason's and Michael's, too, feeling that she was handling her end of the domestic deal just swell. But with Michael's defection to the enemy camp of The Claw, a wide gap had formed down the middle of her personal confidence.

"Well?" Andreas quizzed as soon as her face reappeared over the loft's half wall.

"He's asleep," Kate whispered down. "So your story's safe. Lucky man."

"Yeah. Zeus was pulling for me."

She was halfway down the ladder when she remembered that she had nothing on besides the short robe and a single towel under it. She'd come to realize this because the eyes of Andreas Pateras were practically burning her skin with the heat of his glance.

Stopping cold, she brought her legs together tightly and looked down at him. "Do you mind?"

"I don't mind at all," he said, his tone all friendliness.

"Could you please—" she waved her arm, "—step away?"

Andreas grinned, and obliging her, abandoned his hold on the ladder to move to the center of the room.

The geography might have changed, but even so, she could sense his desire against her flesh just as certainly as if his fingers caressed the length of her body. It felt good. She experienced the fleeting thought that even when Michael had made love to her it hadn't been quite as exciting as this glance from a stranger. Feeling that good frightened her.

She peered over her shoulder to where Andreas stood. He was still eyeing her with unconcealed interest. "Jason's right up there," she reminded him from the safety of the ladder.

"What do you think? I'm an animal?" This time Andreas did not smile. The mood between them had become tense and serious. "You have nothing to worry about."

If only he knew how wrong he was. She had everything to worry about. In the tight faded jeans, his physique was muscular and natural, and he looked to her as tuned to physical response as any jungle creature. It wasn't as if she hadn't been subjected to all the usual metaphors about wild, animalistic, sexual abandon. It would be so easy to give in . . . so tempting to become a living metaphor. . . .

Steeling herself against these feelings, she warned herself to slow down and think rationally. Lust begat lust and nothing more . . . unless she included heartache and self-recrimination.

Hadn't she seen other women, seen what had happened? Their lives became a series of one-night stands with strangers who cared nothing for them. God! And she'd had a husband who'd cared nothing for her! The women would wake from their romantic tryst the next day feeling used and empty, and in order to compensate for the previous night's experience, seek comfort in yet another pair of emotionally uninvolved arms. It was a merry-go-round she did not want to ride, for fear she would never get off. It was hard enough to heal the wound in her ego without having salt thrown into it.

"And I'm not some hot-to-trot tourist woman," Kate returned as she stepped onto the dangerous terrain of the floor. Her fingers drew the lapels of the terry-cloth robe securely across her bosom. Beneath the words, she heard the haunting, faintly seductive refrains of a calliope.

"Maybe you are," he returned, giving her back a dose of her own snideness. "Maybe that's why you brought it up."

"I brought it up because of the way you're looking at me."

"I'm a man, and you're a woman, and you hardly have anything on. I'm not blind. How the hell would you expect me to look at you?"

"With respect, with a sense of decency."

"Then maybe you should respect me. What makes you think I have no pride of my own? You think I'm just—" He thought for an instant.

"A playboy," she inserted in a sugary voice accompanied by a smile.

He considered the label. "Yes, yes . . . I know the word."

"Oh, I'll just bet you do."

"Well, you're wrong. I'm not a man who plays lightly with any woman who comes along."

"Oh, no. Not you. Of course not." She looked at him hard, willing a level of honesty between them. Maybe in absolute emotional openness the mystery each perceived in the other would dissolve, and with it any romantic notions either of them entertained. She could leave the island in the morning unscathed.

"I've . . ." He had to stop, obviously wrestling with the question of how much truth to tackle. "I've known my share of women. But that doesn't mean that some women, that a particular woman, might not be special."

"Why do I think you're speaking hypothetically? Not from a historical perspective."

He looked momentarily caught. She should have felt good at having been right, but the emotion just wasn't there.

"A man can change," Andreas said in his defense, and in doing so, remained in the arena.

"Really?" Kate countered. "For how long? One night?"

"You know," he said, "you are a very difficult woman. How would I know for how long? Life moves along. Things happen. Things don't happen. Many things, I think, are out of our hands. We might as well enjoy what comes, when it comes. If love—or passion—leaves, then we can cry if that's the case. But until then..."

Kate sighed. "So we should cast our fate to the winds...excuse me, I forgot, this is Greece—you've got your gods up there meddling around, rearranging our destinies to amuse themselves."

"In some things, we don't have any choice."

"A convenient philosophy. Meaning, of course, that you, then, don't have any responsibility."

"And if I fell in love with you? Would you stay with me, or go off on a boat to be in your rich country with your microwave ovens and your big cars?"

She had never thought of it in that way; this notion that one of these schemers and plotters for the physical favors of visiting females, could have their own hearts touched, even broken in the disappointing aftermath of an affair. The man before her was too attractive physically as it was; she didn't want to think of him in such human, vulnerable, identifiable terms. It was a far safer concept to maintain that she was an innocent tourist woman, and he was an exploiter of same.

"I've always been fond of electrical gadgetry," she said. "So I guess a five-minute potato takes it hands down over a five-day affair."

"Too bad. There are better things to give yourself to in this life."

"Let me guess! Like to you . . . for a night of wild pleasure."

He laughed. "Pleasure, anyway. I don't know how wild." But the smile faded and was replaced by a perceptible sadness seeming to Kate more real than ingenious.

"Look," Kate said, "within the last eight months, I've heard every line ever cast in this universe. And this particular plague of insincerity is rampant in the Mediterranean."

"Would you know the truth if you heard it?"

The question surprised her. More than that, it troubled her. Would she know the truth if it walked up and sat down beside her? Maybe not. Michael had turned her sense of judgment upside down and inside out. To Andreas, she answered, "Absolutely."

"Well, then," Andreas said, "I'm not interested in taking you to bed."

"Oh?" Kate sent him an incredulous glance.

"I wanted only a friendship."

"Sure." And she realized at that moment that if he had only wanted a friendship with her, she would have felt impossibly rejected, unbelievably disappointed and miserable to the core.

"To get to know each other," he said, piqued. "You're too suspicious. What?" he said. "You think I couldn't have caught you today, if I had wanted? You think I'm so desperate for love—"

"I think it's called sex."

"Sex, then. You think I'm so desperate I would—"

"Yes," Kate said. "I think you would."

"Okay." He relaxed and allowed a soft smile. "That is the truth. You see, you do know it." In deference to her accomplishment, he nodded; then, raising his eyes to hers, their green darkened. "But maybe not the whole truth. Sometimes the truth comes in layers—" Breaking off, he moved from her to look out the window.

Thin droplets of rain streaked against the panes of glass. The sound, the whole scene, was lonely, and she was seized with the desire to run to him—for her sake or his, she couldn't be certain. But of course, she didn't move. How could she? They were nothing to each other, and it would stay that way. Tomorrow she would leave the island and in a day or two the charismatic Greek would be as much history to her as the Parthenon.

Reflected by the window, Kate saw his expression as pensive and somewhat tortured, even as he carefully kept his back to her. She felt embarrassed, as if a voyeur, and thought to look away. She couldn't. Perhaps the power of revelation held her transfixed. Touched by the sensitivity she read in his face, she was compelled to see him as a person, not merely in the original characterization of a cartoon Mediterranean lover.

"But?" she said, urging him to take up the conversation again. Somehow there seemed less danger of intimacy in their banter than in their silence.

Andreas turned to her, remaining pensive. "You're a beautiful woman. I'm a man. It's raining outside. It's warm in here. I would naturally like to be in your bed with you. Why not? It's very romantic. This is very simple. This is life. Why must you make everything so complicated?"

"Why?" She shook her head, momentarily at a loss. What he proposed, and in the manner it was offered, certainly held a certain degree of attractiveness. "Because..." She backed away, and headed toward the bathroom to get another towel to stop the blood from dripping over his clothes. The rain was pattering against the window of the bathroom. *It was romantic. It was wonderful. It would feel good to have his body against hers, inside hers...oh, my...*

She returned and held the towel tightly against the cut, trying to apply enough pressure to stem the bleeding.

"Because," she continued, now having to deal not only with the sweet, sad music of the calliope in her mind but the very real sound of the rain outside, each drop now an invitation to a night of pleasure. "I don't consider a romp in the hay with a stranger all that romantic."

"After we sleep together, we won't be strangers," Andreas said, his smile infinitely seductive, infinitely knowledgeable. "I can promise you that, at least." He reached up and took her hand in his, kissing the tops of her fingers softly.

To her humiliation, goose bumps began to claim the surface of her body. There was no way to hide her arousal, undressed as she was before him, and besides, she knew very well that his every move was premeditated, a well-choreographed routine guaranteed to deliver rave reviews. She was merely tonight's audience.

"Tomorrow I'm going to leave," she said. It was a reminder to herself more than information for him.

"Perhaps not." He kissed the side of her neck lightly.

Kate jerked her head away, ignoring him outwardly while inside chills moved like exploding skyrockets throughout her body. "Then the weather will improve the next day, and I'll leave."

The green eyes twinkled. "We'll have had two nights then."

"Two nights of what?"

"Whatever we want it to be."

"I want to be left alone," Kate returned, and backed several steps away, careful to hold tightly to her robe.

Andreas sighed and shook his head. "All right," he said resignedly. "I will leave you to yourself. And tomorrow maybe the boats will sail, the planes will fly, and as you like, you will be gone from Mykonos. *Yiásas!*" he said in

Greek—goodbye—and tipping his hand to his forehead, saluted her.

Abruptly he turned and started toward the narrow hall-way leading to the outside.

"I don't like my passion on the run!" she called to his back.

He looked over his shoulder. "So don't run. No one says you must go. Stay." Turning fully around, he stood with his legs spread apart and sent her another of his looks that dissected her, heart and soul. "You have no home to go to anymore. You have nowhere that you belong, and no one that you belong to. So why not belong to your own heart, your own mind for a while? What have you got to lose? You've lost everything already."

The look, the words... She withered beneath the truth in both. Having nothing to say in her defense, she could only retreat; but there was nowhere to go, except to her role of the perfectly well-bred American woman, a woman totally above and beyond the passions and sorrows of flesh and soul—those thorns in man's existence that seemed so grand and noble to Andreas Pateras. Curse him, anyway. "Tell your grandmother thank-you for the food. Tell her I'm sorry about the bowl. I'll replace it in the morning."

"Don't worry about it," Andreas said with a coldness to match her own. "In the morning you must go quickly to see about your plane. Or your boat. It's important that you get out of here at once," he finished dryly.

"Yes," she said, but could not summon much force to accompany the word. "I can assure you I will."

Turning, he left her with the last word. She had won. She would be alone for the night, there would be no sorrow of parting, no remorse of humiliation at daybreak. And to-morrow she would leave the island. In Athens there would be an envelope from her attorney with the support payment from Michael, and soon afterward she and Jason would depart, on their way to another destination.

Yiásas, Mykonos...yiásas, Andreas Pateras... Soon both would be forgotten.

Jason slept through the cleaning of the kitchen, as well as her second shower. When she felt she was too exhausted to fantasize about what might have been with the Greek that night, she turned off the lights and found her way to the bedroom off the front entrance.

The sheets felt as cold as her soul as she slipped between the covers. The sound of the rain was a sad refrain accompanying her memories, each drop beat a minute in days already passed. It took no time at all for physical longings to arise. Cell by cell, she felt the desire spread, filling her with an agony that became as much spiritual as it was physical. She saw the face of the Greek, could imagine the warmth of his breath on her skin, could imagine...so much...too much.

She had not won at all, unless her prize was this loneliness. She thought of him then, wondering if he lay in bed alone, thinking of her, too. Or did he sleep with another woman, their limbs entwined, warm bodies, warm feelings....

At sometime she must have drifted off to sleep. When she awoke, it was with a start, and into a world the color of pitch. Her eyes flew open, and for a moment she did not know where she was. Then with a jolt her heart took up the pace of an engine racing out of control.

Panicked, but not knowing why, she pushed herself up from the pillows. The covers slid away and the room felt as cold and damp as a coffin. She shivered as she looked about her, wrapping herself in her own arms as much for security as for warmth. The blackness in the room gradually lightened to an identifiable environment of fuzzy gray, and her thoughts, likewise, began to form a more recognizable shape.

Something was wrong.

And then, no sooner had she thought it, than Jason's name flooded her mind.

Jason!

Moving like a rocket, she flew from the bed and across the room, stumbling against a piece of furniture, then scrambled down the hall, searching along her reckless path for a light switch, found none, but knocked over a lamp that she did manage to locate. Righting it, she snapped its switch and brought light into the small living room. Her eyes fixed on the loft above, and with dread she made her way across the final few feet to the ladder.

A moment later her amorphous fears became hard reality.

Chapter Five

"Please," Kate begged, "please..." She could hardly speak, her voice choking on every syllable. Before her, rumpled and groggy from sleep, Andreas stood in the doorway of his grandmother's apartment. He wore the same tightly fitted jeans, but was without a shirt or shoes.

His face took on an expression of alarm. "What is it? What's the trouble!"

"It's Jason," Kate gasped. With every breath, her heart constricted. She could barely hold herself upright, and leaned against the doorjamb for momentary support. It was as if she were living out a terrible dream. She could not move fast enough. Her body seemed weighted by thousands of pounds, and her mind spun crazily, making it impossible to formulate clear thoughts.

"Has someone hurt you? Hurt Jason?" Andreas demanded in alarm, tensing as if to spring upon the attacker.

"No, no," she said, realizing that the wildness of her inner state must have been reflected in her appearance. She had fled the house in her long nightshirt, already drenched from the downpour. Likewise, her rain-sodden hair was plastered against her face and dripping down her back. On the way up the steep stairs to the old woman's quarters, she had slipped in her bare feet. Her knee had hit the stone hard, and she'd banged herself severely, managing to scrape both palms in her effort to save herself. In attempting to avoid further harm, she had also managed to put a severe rent in the front of the garment's fabric.

"Tell me, tell me..." Andreas said, stepping back as he pulled her in out of the rain. His eyes had widened in confused apprehension.

"He looks like he's dying! What if Jason dies? What if...what if...I can't help him...can't stop it, can't—"

He grabbed hold of her shoulders and shook her gently. Tears flew from her eyes, and she gasped, on the verge of hyperventilating, just as Andreas appeared to be on the edge of slapping her. She would not have minded. Hysteria mushroomed within her, and she was helpless to control the paralyzing feelings.

Pulling her against him, Andreas stroked her hair, her back. "It's going to be all right...just quiet now, quiet..."

The softness of his touch dissolved some of the panic. Eventually thoughts began to assemble themselves into a cohesive order, and with her face nestled against his warmth, she could at least speak haltingly. "My son...Jason...he's very sick. Oh, I don't know what to do...there's a doctor? Someone who—"

"Yes, yes...of course there's help," Andreas said. He was backing off in the direction of the sofa where he had apparently been sleeping, as evidenced by the blankets and pillows. Speaking to her all the while as she stood taking short, hysterical gulps of air, he pulled on his shoes, then his sweater. "There's a good doctor. We'll go at once."

"He's so hot. He won't even wake up!" Kate cried, desperate fear again arising as the image of Jason filled her mind again. "He won't even open his eyes or talk. Oh, God...Jason, he's burning up!" And then she was crying, sobbing in the middle of the room, unaware of anything more than the sheer sorrow and terror she was experiencing.

Vaguely, she saw Maria, the old woman, come to the room, but at the same time she found herself being bundled into Andreas's arms and led out of the door, down the stairs, and into her own apartment.

She knew almost nothing from then on, moving through the night with Jason in Andreas's strong arms, her entire being in a state of shock. A thick blanket covered Jason, and she was dimly aware that at some time or other a blanket had been given to her and remained draped over her body in a haphazard fashion. The rain had not let up, but continued to downpour in a steady cadence, sounding to Kate like a million drums.

"Come, come quickly now...." Andreas urged her as he moved more swiftly ahead, even with the weight of Jason in his arms.

At last they reached the darkened building. Over the doorway hung a white sign with a red cross painted in its center. The doctor's name and hours were etched into a sign by the portal.

Andreas pounded on the door, calling frantically, his voice a trumpet against the rain. A light went on, then another, and finally, in what seemed to Kate as an eternity, the door was swung open.

"Quickly. This boy is very ill," Andreas said.

Without further comment, the doctor led them into the warmth of his home.

An hour later Kate listened as the doctor spoke gravely in English almost as good as her own. "He must have had this for quite some time, a mild case of viral infection that finally took hold and became serious."

"I should have known...done something..." Kate said solemnly.

"Oh, probably it came and went. These things are hard to recognize at times for what they are. Anyway, we have caught it now. And I've given him an antibiotic. He must rest. Rest a great deal. He is to be kept warm and comfortable, and if he becomes hot like this again, you must let me know at once. Such fevers can be dangerous."

"He almost died."

"Yes," the doctor said. "He might have, if he had not come." He looked from Kate to Andreas, then back again. "You were lucky to have this man take care of you."

"Yes," Kate acknowledged, but could not look at Andreas. Her gratefulness to him was beyond any human expression she had at her command. If she were to look at him, she feared they would be forever bonded, so intense was her present feeling. Instead, she addressed the doctor, to whom she also owed her gratitude.

"Thank you, doctor," she said. "Oh, thank you." Her voice was so stricken with grief and relief, it was all but inaudible. "He's such a good little boy. He's so, so good and sweet."

"Tonight he must stay here," the doctor said, rising from the chair opposite Kate. "The rain is not good for him. And tomorrow you can come early and see him home." The doctor smiled at Andreas. "And you will see that the American gets into dry clothes and perhaps I recommend something for the nerves—a glass of brandy, some Metaxa.... And pleasant dreams.''

Andreas gently placed his arms around her shoulders, and began to withdraw her from the doctor's home. Kate held back, her heart full, overflowing with emotion. "He's all I have, doctor...." Kate said, as if to impress upon the man the preciousness of his charge. She noticed the doctor exchange a glance with Andreas. It said that she was as fragile now as the boy. In response, she felt Andreas's hands tenderly rub her damp shoulders, and again there was that surprising comfort in his touch.

"He will be good here, madam, very safe. And soon he will be well," the doctor assured her, and looking into his warm, dark eyes, Kate knew with the same instinct that had awoken her to Jason's dangerous condition that the words were true.

Andreas opened the door to her apartment. "Come," he said to her, "you will do exactly as the doctor ordered."

There was no opportunity for protest as he guided her into her bedroom. He hit the wall switch, overlooked in her earlier madness, and a dim overhead bulb brought light into the room.

"Thank you," she said wearily, and not without some sense of wariness.

With one danger gone, the old one had arisen again. The man in her bedroom was no longer her champion but the object of earlier heated fantasies. She did not know if she was in a position to resist her own desires, much less any advances he might make.

Saying nothing, but wearing a look of seriousness, he brought her gently down to sit on the mattress. "First, get out of those wet clothes." There was no innuendo attached to the tone, nor did he make a move to ravish her. Instead he turned and looked about the room. "Where are some dry ones?" Before she could answer, he was on his way to the open duffel bag on the floor.

"I'll be fine," she said, but found herself ignored. On bent knee, he rummaged through the bag's contents.

"And so will this," Andreas said. He had discovered a long flannel shirt she had worn on treks in Nepal.

"Put this on," he ordered, tossing it to her, and then marching to the door, said, "I'll boil some water, and you will have hot tea with honey and brandy."

"It's not necessary—" she began in protest, but he gave her a sharp look and she knew that necessary or not, she would be served tea.

She changed as she had been ordered, feeling mildly childlike and strangely safe under his care. She did not mind at all, and knowing that Jason was also in good hands, actually found herself relaxing into a rare state of contentment. It was as if for the first time in a very long while there was someone there for her, another person to carry the burden of her life, which had become so terribly heavy.

There was a small warped mirror on the wall, and as she stood before it, brushing her damp hair, pulling it away from her face and tying it in back with a scarf, she was surprised to see a light behind her tired brown eyes and the ghost of a smile playing at the edges of her mouth.

She had heard Andreas leave the apartment, listened as his footsteps flew upstairs to his grandmother's place, and again heard him in the back of her house, making busy noises in the kitchen.

"Time for your medicine," Andreas said. His voice behind her came as a surprise, and she turned from the mirror to find him standing in her doorway with a tray.

Their eyes collided across the expanse separating them. Kate felt herself reeling from the impact his presence had on her. He looked stunning. The image of him in her doorway, standing with the tray, was anything but domestic. He was the most incredibly masculine, yet tender man she had ever encountered.

"You look beautiful," he said softly, as if his mind spoke her thoughts.

She did not know what to say. "Thank you" was not the response to match the sentiment she read in his eyes.

He had expressed more than an idle compliment, more even than a statement of physical fact. His heart had spoken. She felt as if in those few words, he had managed to enter her, to touch her true self, and the intimacy made her want to cry, made her want to thank God, or the Greek gods of Andreas Pateras, or whatever force it was that made such an experience possible. In that strange meeting between their two souls, she did not feel so terribly alone anymore. There was someone who knew her, whom she in turn knew—at least for that flash of an instant.

"Now I am the doctor!" Andreas said, his face registering more emotion than he could contain privately within himself. "First you will get into bed."

She was glad to break the emotional intensity with physical activity and, for once, did as she was told without an argument.

Andreas moved to the bedside as she slipped under the covers. "Now," he said, placing the tray on the nightstand, "you will drink this, and soon you will be warm and able to sleep well."

He handed her the cup and saucer. The china clattered softly as he made the transfer to her hands. But her own fingers could not stop their shaking, either.

"I'm cold," she whispered, her eyes downcast so that he might not see the truth.

"Yes," he said with an irony that was meant to be recognized. "And so am I." He sat at the edge of her bed, his face turned so that she could not see his full expression. But she felt it, knew that his eyes were burning with the same intensity of feeling as his voice held, as his heart held, as his body would display if—

Kate closed her eyes tightly, wanting so much to say what she felt, but was afraid that these few words from her depths might unravel and unravel and unravel until there was nothing of her left. There was so much feeling stored there that the spillage from within might drown them both. She took a swallow of the brew. It was hot and strong, creating a pleasant sensation as it flowed down her throat.

The Metaxa he had added to the tea gave her courage, or perhaps only gave her the excuse to be brave because after the drink was half downed she said, "You were wonderful tonight." She even dared to meet his green glance once more, decidedly more dangerous now that they were within an arm's reach of each other.

This time it was Andreas who looked away. His profile was that of a Greek statue, poetically masculine, a balance between pagan sensuality and thoughtful sensitivity. He seemed to weigh the wisdom of expressing his own feelings. Kate could monitor the passage of ideas, the flicker of contrary notions, in the slight muscle spasms registering on temple and jaw.

Finally, reaching some decision, he turned his face partially back to her, but spoke softly into the room's empty spaces. "I felt tonight...something...like you were my wife...and Jason, my son." Then he was still. She saw him close his eyes against rising emotions.

"That was nice," Kate said quietly, too overwhelmed by his honesty to think of anything more appropriate to say. "That you felt that way was really...nice." She had wanted to say "beautiful." She was truly touched and didn't know how to handle it. If Michael had been there, he might have dealt with the crisis efficiently, but the tenderness accompanying each gesture Andreas had made would have been absent.

"It was nice," he said resolutely. "But not real." He sighed and stood up, placing the cup he had been holding on the tray. Unable to look at her, he moved to the door, speaking as he left. "I will check on you tomorrow—in the morning—and we will get Jason together."

The last word rang in her mind, echoed in her heart—*together*. It sent strange twinges of sadness and gladness and hope and despair cascading through her in a waterfall of emotion.

Andreas moved from her line of vision into the hall and would have been gone from her apartment in the next second if Kate had not called out. "Andreas!"

His footsteps halted; quiet prevailed.

She could still stop what had not yet actually been put into motion. It was as if she teetered on a precipice—a step forward and she might fall to her ruin, or fly, truly fly free for the first time in her life. Or she could turn back into the safe, miserable known.

"Andreas?" she called again, and it was done, the step taken.

"Yes?" He did not come back. Only his voice entered her bedroom.

She spoke hesitantly into the emptiness, wondering whether her decision would help her soar or bring her down. "I wanted you to know...that is, to thank you..." She paused. *Oh, God. Just say it.* "No, what it is, um, if you'd like to stay—I mean, I'd like it if you would stay. Tonight."

For a while she thought that perhaps he hadn't heard her, or maybe he had left anyway, and she had just been too self-absorbed to notice. At any rate, there was no response forthcoming to the tortured invitation.

Then, suddenly, he was standing within the doorframe, looking at her. His eyes were dark, no longer appearing green, but jet. Whatever reserve of control she had was dissolved in his presence.

"Yes," she whispered. "You win...I want you...."

Andreas nodded once, a downward slant to his head, much like the end to a prayer. "Then we both win. I want to make love to you," he said softly, without moving. "Love..." he said again, emphasizing the word.

"Not just..."

" I want to make love," he repeated with feeling. "This once."

And he was beside her in the next breath she took. His mouth pressed against hers as he held her face tenderly between both hands, thumbs moving softly against her cheeks. Kate shivered, feeling the reverence as if she were an object of infinite fragility, of beauty to be cherished. She was not just a sexual object, she was not...

"Andreas..." Kate breathed, rising against him as their mouths opened to each other, "I think I can fly now." And of course he could not understand; she could barely understand herself.

"You are so beautiful, so—" But his words ended there, for a fire seemed to erupt in him, burning away all thought but to possess her.

Still kissing her, his hands roamed the length of her body beneath the covers, pushing the material of her shirt aside, button by button, until her body was totally available to his mouth and the free play of his fingers.

His clothes were shed as deftly as hers had been removed, and with fluid grace, he slid beneath the covers. She lay against him, pressing full-length against his hard form, luxuriating in the heat and power of his body.

It was not just that she had been without a man for so long; it was more, so much more than that. It was this man, this one man, for whom she felt she had waited her entire life.

"The gods have sent you," Andreas said, pulling away to look into her face.

Through moist eyes, she felt as she looked into his magnificent face that indeed it was true: there were gods. For how else could this have happened, this fantastic moment?

"You are a god," she said, smiling and stroking the side of his face.

He laughed and kissed her. "Which one?"

"Um... Uh... Zeus!"

"Ah," Andreas said, "you have seen through my disguise. Do you know how a god makes love?"

"I want to know...." Kate whispered.

"But it is very serious, Kate...to make love to a god. You will never be free again...always...always," he said, moving his hand over her hip, downward to her inner thigh, "you will be bound to him."

"Then that's the price," she said, and closed her eyes to the exquisite sensation of a god and a mortal joining.

It felt like silk, the texture of their lovemaking; and their rhythm, now slow, building, spiraling, at last urgently claiming all senses, was in time to a silent melody heard through their souls. Trembling together, they became one, their cries mingling as they found release from the unbearable tension and yearning of their bodies.

"I never knew..." Kate said as their desire finally ebbed. She traced her fingers over the length of his moist back, wondering at the beauty of the male human body. "I never really understood before...about how it could be with a man and a woman." She kissed the hollow of his neck, tasting his skin.

"Oh...really? It's always like this for me," he said, and withdrew, turning onto his side to lean on his elbow and look into her face. Then he smiled. "I never knew, either."

Kate closed her eyes, relieved. "For a moment—"

"Kate," he said, and brought his finger to her lips, silencing whatever doubts she was about to voice, "it was different. With anyone else, it has never been the same as tonight."

Her eyes clouded over, and she looked away. "And tomorrow? What then, Andreas? Will tomorrow be different for you, as well? If the boats come and bring another tourist woman, will you—"

"Stop it!" Andreas ordered. He hurt her chin as he took it hard between his fingers, and turned her face to look at him. "Kate, I do not know any more than you what will happen. I will not go in search of a tourist woman, as you seem to believe. We had a night of love together. The morning is not only up to me...it is up to you, too. And it is up to the world if the sun will shine, or if it will rain again. Or if the boats come, or the planes leave. Kate," he said, "if the plane leaves tomorrow or the next day, and your son is well, what will you do?"

"I can't stay here," she said, as if to herself.

"Yet you want me to love you."

"Yes," she said. "It's how I feel, not how I know things have to be."

"And it is the same for me. I know how I feel, holding you, loving you...my beautiful Kate...but I also know how things have to be." He relaxed onto his back, and pulled her into the crook of his arm. "How can this feel so good," he asked the space around them, "so right...and yet not last?"

"It was a one-night stand with feeling, was all," Kate said, a catch to her voice.

"Maybe two nights, or a dozen."

He was being honest, and so was she, but she hated him for it. Had he told her it would go on forever, she would not have believed him—yet the lie would have served some purpose.

"I'd like it if you said you'd follow me..." she said.

"I will follow you."

"To the ends of the earth."

"Mykonos is the end of the earth, I sometimes think," Andreas said, laughing lightly but with little humor.

"Ah, then there really is nowhere for this to go."

"In my heart I will follow you, my love. In my heart, in my soul, in my dreams..."

"But if you were Zeus, you could make everything work," she chided.

"Yes," he said, "if I were Zeus."

"Be Zeus...be him, Andreas."

"To be him, then you must totally believe. And, my dear, American Kate, I do not think you can do that. To believe in our gods, you must be very young, or you must be born Greek."

"I am glad that tonight happened, Andreas. But I also think it may have ruined my life. Somehow I don't think a washing machine and a microwave oven are ever going to seem quite as wonderful to me."

"And someday, when I marry, I do not think my good wife, who washes and cleans and raises our children, will ever seem quite as wonderful as the American woman I knew on one rainy night."

Kate stared at him, stricken.

"What's wrong?" he asked, alarmed, and shook her shoulders as if the answer might tumble out on its own.

"Nothing. No, it's just that...well, I never thought about you being married."

"No," he said, "it is something even I rarely have thought about. But my parents do. They think of it all morning, all night, every day. And just as your plane will take you away soon, a woman will soon claim me."

"Couldn't you do what you want?"

"Couldn't you?"

"I don't know what I want," Kate said.

"I do. But I can't have her. I do not own a microwave oven, you see. Nor can I see one in my future." And he pulled her roughly against him, kissing her with a desperate passion, and in a moment entered her again, moving as if he might obliterate reality by melding his body into hers.

Chapter Six

The dawn arrived stealthily, in stages. There was the faint rustle of a sheet, a whispering sigh, not her own; then in the bedroom there was silence again, and Kate drifted half in and half out of the waking state. But before sleep could reclaim her fully, a gay, percussive beat of donkey hooves clop-clopping against the stone walk took up, and soon after the clatter of a motorized cart somewhere beyond the surrounding walls challenged the lingering shadows of night. A man's strident voice trumpeted, *"Kalimera!"* Good morning. And was answered in kind. All at once it was a new day.

For a moment after coming fully awake, Kate remained silent and still against her pillow while a tide of thoughts rushed in to fill the void left by dissolved dreams. The usual swarm of disjointed trivia intruded first, then came the heavier realizations of her divorce, joined by the familiar ache of her precarious emotional and physical status. She was about to go on from there to catalogue the remainder of her troubles, when her mind stopped.

Oh, God. She closed her eyes, shutting out the reality of the man she now saw in her peripheral vision. She was not alone.

Opening her eyes again, Kate turned her head to the side. Beside her, Andreas Pateras lay on his back still sleeping soundly. Even in this state, his presence was formidable, seeming to fill more space than his physical being inhabited.

The room had a single small window, covered with shutters on the inside in place of drapes. A slice of pale light pierced the center crack where the wood was warped and wouldn't join. More than one tourist had rhapsodized over the light of Mykonos. Even guidebooks mentioned the phenomenon. And it was true. There was a clarity to the atmosphere, a thinness to the air that seemed to flatten light, to refine it, so that whatever was touched became more distinct and so accentuated in detail that rather than appear real, objects became surreal. It was as if one's eyes had been suddenly cleansed, and for the first time it was possible to view the world as it had always been meant to be seen. Through this magical light, filtered as it was, she studied her drowsing companion.

Andreas's breath was even and gentle. The covers had dislodged, leaving him half-bare and probably cold. Carefully, Kate brought up the blanket to cover the smooth, muscular chest that rose and fell in a soft, rhythmic motion. One arm was bent behind his head, his fingers barely visible in the thick mass of black curls tousled about his face. She had to fight against the impulse to touch his hair, to run her fingers lightly along the side of the sharp, solid jawline, for fear of waking him. She wanted to lie upon him, to cover him with her entire being until they were absorbed into each other.

Would he want that? she wondered. Would he feel as she did now, wanting the experience they had shared during the night to continue? Or separated from the storm and the dark, exposed to the light of day, would he and she become strangers? She didn't know about these things, not on a personal level, anyway. All she knew she had assembled from the outraged complaints of world-weary single women who had crossed her path, and from the tersely written articles in newspapers and women's magazines, decrying the lack of intimacy possible with the modern male. But she doubted Andreas Pateras belonged to any category. With his jaunty, swashbuckling air, he might have been an eighteenth-century pirate. Then again, there was the man beneath the cavalier exterior, a man of brooding sensitivity, who, in spite of his rough clothes and careless manners, conveyed a concealed elegance. Behind the green gaze, she had noted the churning unrest of a man whose many parts warred within himself. If it were possible, he was even more beautiful in repose than in animation. Or perhaps, thought Kate, it was the Mykonian light. Or perhaps it was not; perhaps it was Andreas, just as he actually was. The sculpted, flowing form of his body seemed to glow from within, illumining and warming the surrounding space. He moved slightly, shifting his head to the side and the shaft of light caught the edge of one feathered curl. The lock ignited in a vibrant show of color. It seemed appropriate, totally natural, this explosion of light crowning him. The man himself was a brilliant burst of flame in her life. Which god was it who presided over fire? This man would be his human incarnation. Late last night she had experienced the molten force of his nature, she had felt for the first time what it meant to be fully a woman.

Memories of the night intruded, and with them came a mixture of emotions to torment her, from lust to gentleness to fear, and wonder that any man had the power to bring so much feeling into her life.

As if he had felt her thoughts, the eyes of Andreas Pateras fluttered open, at first without awareness, then with surprise, and finally with recognition. A slow smile accompanied the soft green caress of his gaze. *"Kalimera,"* he whispered in a sleepy voice. His eyes traveled her body languorously with unconcealed appreciation. Looking up, catching her eyes with his, his words were a melodious purr against her flesh as he said, "Ah, you are so beautiful...so beautiful to wake up to." He gave a quick, joyous laugh, and turning, lay on his side and traced his fingers lightly over her shoulders and down to the rise of her breasts above the bedcovers.

Kate shivered from his touch. A luxuriant heat built instantly from within. Yet, unsure of herself, and uncertain of the proper etiquette for the morning after, she was reluctant to offer an outer show of encouragement.

He had to sense her insecurity. Rather than remove the sheet, Andreas stayed his fingers, sensitively allowing her to maintain her reserve. His consideration made her feel small and foolish. She had certainly been responsive enough hours before.

"Andreas, I—"

"I know. Now it is morning and you are afraid." He paused, smiling with sad understanding. "But not of me—of you."

And it was true. At that moment she wanted him desperately. But she was also afraid of where such unchecked desire might eventually lead. She could not afford the foolishness of becoming a love junkie. She needed to go slowly into her new life, whatever it was to be. But here on

Mykonos, with this stranger—for he was really a stranger no matter that they had made wild love half the night—there was no time for candlelight and flowers and long soul-searching talks about the meaning of life. There was only time for the raw physical passion they had shared, or time for nothing at all.

"It's just that it's . . ."

"Not raining anymore?"

He had voiced her fears. His smile had become a crooked grin, the one reminiscent of rogues and testifying to many nights spent with many women. But in his eyes was a deeper wisdom, and it was this that made her tremble inside, for she knew there were depths to him in which she could drown forever. And perhaps not even care.

"Not raining anymore . . ." she echoed, and watched, amazed and somewhat disappointed after all, as he pulled himself out of bed and slipped into his pants. He was not going to press her for morning favors. Any other man would have, and she wondered if his gallantry was due to lack of interest or actual respect.

"Well, perhaps it will rain again before you leave," he said blandly, looking her way but without any particular emotion.

"There's not that much time." It was a reminder to herself.

"How do you know?"

"I don't . . . but, Andreas, what happened last night, well . . . it was—"

"Just one of those things?" This time his voice was cutting. He shot her a look located somewhere between disgust and hurt. "Is that it? Like your American songs about ships passing in the night . . . I forget the words. But I know them anyway. In essence." He turned his back to her and slipped his sweater over his head. "Come," he said as he marched from the bedroom and turned in the direction of the kitchen. "We will have tea and then go get the boy."

They were led to Jason by the doctor's wife, an attractive and surprisingly cosmopolitan woman, who, like her American-educated husband, spoke English fluently. "We have enjoyed him," she said to Kate, who had just voiced her regrets that Jason had inconvenienced their household.

"I'd say it was mutual," Kate replied as she stood in the bedroom door looking in at her son. He was surrounded by an assortment of sweets and books and three cats, all curled into balls at various positions on the bed. Rather than a wan and disoriented convalescent, Jason appeared to be a young and vital pasha, reigning over a delightful kingdom of delicacies.

Seeing Kate, his eyes lit up, but when he looked beyond and saw Andreas hovering off to the side, his expression changed from pleasure to ecstatic surprise. "Hi, Mom. Andreas! Look! I've got a book on Delos. And one on the Greek gods. There's one guy here who looks just like you—except he's got a beard."

"Which one?" Andreas inquired, stepping forward into the room with Kate.

"Here . . . here," Jason said, desperately flipping pages. "This one. Zeus."

"Ah," Andreas replied, studying the picture from the side of the bed, "you are right. The artist has caught me exactly. Perhaps I'm a bit more handsome, but the likeness is very close, indeed." He looked at Kate, a slight smile playing at the corners of his mouth. "What do you think . . . except for the beard, is it me?"

"Perhaps a minor physical resemblance," she admitted with a smile of her own. In fact there was a great likeness, although of course coincidental. "Tell me, what was Zeus famous for?"

"Everything," replied Jason. "He was the lord of the universe. There was nothing Zeus couldn't do."

"And the women were wild over him," added Andreas.

Jason chuckled delightedly and eyed Kate with one of his ancient looks that made her feel that he could X-ray her insides. Kate felt herself blushing. Could he tell about last night? Could he see into her heart and know that from yesterday to this morning, she was no longer the same woman?

"And, Jason," Andreas continued, "you must not speak of Zeus in the past tense."

Jason's face was alight with enthusiasm. "Because he might hear me. And get angry. Or sad."

"Exactly."

Jason looked to Kate, and his expression clouded. "But it isn't really true."

"If you believe in something it's always real." Andreas cast a side glance at Kate.

"What if I believe in Zeus, and my mom doesn't?"

"Then she'll be missing out on a lot." This time Andreas spoke directly to her.

The doctor's wife had left them, and now returned with her husband. "Your son is doing well," he said briskly. His office took up another part of the house, and in the background Kate could hear the squeals of restless children. "I checked him earlier. He has remarkable recuperative powers. Still, I advise against traveling. He must rest here for a few days before going on with your journey."

Kate sighed morosely. "A few days..."

"You don't want me to have a relapse, Mom!" Jason's voice was frantic. His fingers were white where they clutched the book with the likeness of Zeus peering boldly from the page.

For Kate it was not the words that wounded, but the tone. Once, not all that long ago, Jason had cried out to her in the same anguished voice, denying that Michael was no longer going to slam the door at night and call out to them "I'm home!"

Zeus was Andreas, and Andreas was the Michael who never really was, and all of them together spelled illusion and ultimately disappointment.

"But I do want you to eat," she said. She looked to the doctor. "I . . . well, I've really got to leave Mykonos as soon as possible." It sounded frivolous, as if her son's welfare was merely an outside consideration on a far grander personal agenda. "There's a personal financial matter to take care of in Athens." Now she sounded like a pompous jerk. Why hadn't she just said she was broke and be done with it?

"Andreas will feed us." Jason looked to Andreas for confirmation. "Won't you, Andreas?"

The texture of the room was thick with male conspiracy, from the doctor to Andreas to her own son. She was obviously not to leave this island without sanction of this coalition.

"Of course," Andreas said, taking up his line on cue. "And I will feed you American food. Hamburgers and soft drinks. An American friend taught me how to cook Macburgers. Something like that. And fries—we have many fries here on Mykonos. And I personally have never let one American tourist starve."

"Look, this isn't right," Kate objected, deeply humiliated by the offer of the handout, no matter how wellmeaning. "It's not that we're destitute. It's merely a question of—"

"Of course not," said Andreas expansively, which made her know he considered her a step removed from penury.

"I only have to get to Athens."

"Yes, so you have said." He turned to the doctor and his wife, explaining. "In Athens all her troubles will be solved."

The doctor laughed. He was checking Jason's temperature. "That is good to hear. For me, a trip to Athens always proves an aggravation."

"I only have one problem," Kate insisted defiantly. "It's temporary, and will be solved in this one trip." The conversation held the flavor of one of those check-is-in-the-mail dialogues. When Michael had started out in his real estate business, she'd heard him use the line often enough. And later, when he was making money hand over fist, the old dodge had been used on him. All pie in the sky and no money in the bank.

She hated asking for anything from anyone. She despised the helplessness of her position and the pity from others that went along with it. When Michael had left her for The Claw, everyone who knew had clucked and oh-so-sorried her into a state of desperate depression. She had vowed to herself when she left America that someday she would return as a new and improved woman. If conglomerates could do it with soap, she could do it with herself. She'd repackage herself from inside out. She would be in control of her own destiny and not dependent upon anyone for her sense of security, financially or otherwise. So far she hadn't quite put together the plan that would make her intention operational, but she would. Or so she had to believe. Her glorious unrealized future was one of those fictions that kept her forging ahead.

"Okay," Kate relented. "But the deal is this: I'll allow you to make hamburgers only if you let me pay you back."

"Mom," said Jason, almost leaping from the bed, "it's not like he's putting me through school. We're only talking a few hamburgers." The doctors wife pressed him back against the pillow.

"We're talking principles," Kate reminded, knowing the real issue was her big, fat ego.

"We have an excellent school here," said Andreas, a happy and mischievous grin turning his face into that of a handsome satyr.

"I'm interested in planes, not schools."

"But you always said good schools are important, Mom."

"I did, Jason. But somehow I think the school our friend means is the Mykonian school of life. And for that you aren't quite old enough."

"Oh," said Jason, turning slightly pink, meaning of course that he wasn't long for toy trucks and books on outmoded deities. But for once he didn't argue.

After strict instructions from the doctor, and with Jason bundled to the gills with sweaters and jackets Kate had brought, the three of them began their trip back to the apartment.

She had begun the trek home in poor spirits, thinking of the fool she was to have ever been born in the first place. But the walk was exhilarating. For the first time since Jason and she had arrived on the island there was scarcely a breeze, yet even though their path home took them through the back byways of winding streets, the slightest intake of breath brought with it the tang of the Aegean.

Here it was possible to imagine anything beginning anew. Whatever ailed one could be blown by the winds, washed by the sea, or energized by the dazzling sunlight. Maybe after a glass of ouzo, even she would be willing to believe in Zeus. Such was the power of the natural magnificence surrounding them as they made their way through the whitewashed paths.

All about, the world bloomed in innocent splendor after the rain. Walls and streets, and even the lined faces of old men and strained countenances of preoccupied housewives beating small carpets in the open air, absorbed the strange Mykonian light. In each black-eyed gaze was a dance, and in every voice a song, original and clear, piercing the soul with gladness.

As Kate moved along beside the two bantering males, her eyes were irresistibly drawn to all manner of minute detail, mining enchantment from the mundane, spinning fantasies out of the ordinary. Above, there was the richness of the sky—not any sky, but an infinite cloudless sweep of blue silk, the shorn garment of a goddess whose lover now held her in his embrace.

The world was alive with such magic! Nothing was as it seemed, but everything was something more.

Here and there, clinging to the stark white walls of the village's buildings, were lacy green tendrils with tiny buds beginning to erupt in preparation for the island's festival of summer activity. Kate's heart clutched from the delicate beauty she beheld. And, as the three of them rounded a corner, coming straight upon an old mule with two baskets of straggly wildflowers slung to either side of its flabby midsection, Kate's expansive mood converted the beast into a splendid steed and the pathetic blossoms into jewels of myriad shapes and colors.

Andreas hailed the man, explaining in Greek something to him about Jason. The man stared and looked from Jason to Kate, then at Andreas, to whom he rasped out a comment and followed it with a toothless chuckle. Tugging on the rope, the ancient man continued on with his equally decrepit creature. The old-timer's steps were side to side rather than continuously forward, as if he moved precariously along the rolling deck of a ship. Passing along the narrow thoroughfare, he croaked out his sales pitch with great gusto. A woman's sharp and crackly voice responded from a high window; from across the street another neighbor joined in with a fast tattoo of Greek syllables. Jason laughed uproariously at something Andreas said, and a small child shrieked as he tumbled down two stone steps. Yet amid all the pedestrian disharmony Kate heard the lyrical pathos of grand opera.

She had fallen behind the two males. Jason, sick as he had been the night before, jittered along beside Andreas, the two in constant communication. Andreas turned suddenly, his profile sharp and distinct in her vision, and she saw the power and beauty and magic of Zeus in the noble face. His shadow was long and reached back to where she lingered, drawing her along.

"Come, Kate!" called Andreas, his smile wide as he looked back her way. "Come walk with us!"

Her soul throbbed at the sight of him. God or mortal, she could not tell which, but she had fallen into a deep enchantment. She had fallen in love.

Chapter Seven

For Kate, the next three days passed as within a hazy technicolor dream. Events floated one upon the other, every new experience bringing with it a significant emotional revelation.

For one thing, she had never been happy before. Never, not one time in her entire life, had she experienced the kind of subtle elation at being alive that she did during what were actually no more than ordinary moments spent doing ordinary things.

The catalyst for this exceptional alteration in her existence was Andreas Pateras.

The first jolt of unmistakable happiness hit her on a picnic. The outing was arranged on the second day after Jason's dangerous tilt with death. He was becoming so cranky and rambunctious that with the doctor's permission, she and Andreas organized an adventure to another side of the island. The three of them took off near lunchtime in Andreas's rattletrap vehicle and, except for hitting a span of decent black-topped highway, spent the rest of the trip jouncing along dirt trails leading ever downward to the sea. Jason's glee increased with every direct hit of a rut or plummet into a pothole.

Their destination was Panormos Cove. Panormos Cove, or Pan's Cove, in translation, was a secluded piece of windswept beach. There were a few cacti, a few scraggly trees of indeterminable species clinging to the parched hillsides surrounding the basin of beach, and some ravaged grasses struggling to survive against the north wind. The area was totally isolated but for a small building on the sand that Andreas explained was a restaurant for bathers during the summer season, and another building, a bit more extravagant in design, situated upon a high bluff off to the left.

Jason ran off immediately in search of artifacts left over from ancient times. Andreas had mentioned obsidian arrows, unearthed some years earlier by a French excavation team. The find pointed to inhabitants from a prehistoric era having once ranged over the area. It made no difference to Jason that the exact location was a bit farther removed from the present site; he was convinced treasures awaited on every knoll.

"In the summer we come here for lobster," Andreas said. He made himself busy getting the picnic things from the car. Kate made herself available to help, but there was little to do. She stood silently by, watching and feeling awkward in the silence. They had not been alone since the night they had spent together, and without Jason as a conversational buffer, there was an uncertain intimacy to their company.

She thought she should say something to fill up the spaces, but her mind spun in dizzying circles, and what thoughts she had seemed to fly out in fragments. Her eyes followed every movement Andreas made. Graceful and completely masculine, he went about his work, seemingly oblivious to his own natural perfection. How could she ever be with another man after this man? To have lain with him once was a curse she would have to bear the rest of her days.

In desperation, she thought to pick up his last sentence. "Lobster? Really, I wouldn't have thought there'd be lobster here. In America it's terribly expensive."

"Here, too."

It was slightly inane, this emphasis they were placing on the lowly crustacean. Again, there was quiet, an infinite, expansive quiet that seemed to pulse in Kate's ears like a giant heartbeat. She tried to focus her mind on physical reality, lest she be absorbed into the sensual throb of her body.

Andreas was holding their basket of food and a bag containing a cloth on which to place their feast. "Oh, let me," Kate said, taking the bag from him. Their hands touched briefly. Both pretended not to notice, but a moment later Kate still felt the sensation of the casual connection.

Andreas was animated. He gestured to the higher of the two buildings. "The owner is Greek and his wife is French. They live upstairs, over the restaurant. In the winter they live in Paris." There was a certain longing to the last sentence.

Kate looked to where he pointed in the distance. There were only two tables remaining on the veranda, and five chairs scattered about. Vandals or the wind had toppled two of them to their sides and they lay there like helpless invalids waiting to be rescued. Stone steps led from the beach area up to the building. Everything appeared to need a coat of paint. Some thick, ropy vines grew up along the posts holding the roof of weathered reed matting.

Yet, in spite of the site's desolate condition, it was not impossible to imagine the charm of the place—abetted by Greek music, sunlight, flowers, and the laughter of patrons enjoying the gastronomic fare—as it would be during the summer months.

Now and then the wind whistled hollowly through the cove; otherwise, the entire terrain was cloaked in a benevolent silence.

"With an international combination like that their food must be very passionate," Kate said lightly enough to pass as a joke.

Andreas nodded, his green eyes twinkling behind the gentle upward curl of black lashes. "Ah, their fights are!"

They laughed together, she and Andreas, sharing not only the joke, but something more with each other.

It was all very subtle. The experience of that instant could not be defined easily, except to say that the satisfaction came from the mutual realization that they were of the same mind. Kate felt it, as surely as she felt the wind against her cheek.

As for Andreas, he looked at her, an expression in his eyes of startled joy. But the meeting between their souls was too intense, and he pretended interest in a jar tipped over in the basket he held.

Their experience had been the same, and there was a wonder in that recognition of their unity, a feeling existing independently of words.

Together they discussed the best place for their meal, and at last decided upon the perfect spot on the beach, allowing a full view of the cove. The sand was a pale beige and still slightly damp from the tide, which had gone out only a few hours before. They tried repeatedly to spread the cloth for their picnic. But the wind rose intermittently, like a bothersome, uninvited guest. At last, in frustration, they gave up trying to anchor everything down.

"Shall we try up there?" Kate suggested.

Andreas looked unsure. "Jason won't be disappointed? It's so civilized."

"He's in ecstasy just being—" And she was going to say "here with you," but didn't. "Just being able to go out."

Dogged by the wind, they retreated to the shelter provided by the bamboo windscreens on the patio of the higher restaurant.

Andreas went about collecting chairs and wiping off the table. Kate managed her part, but with less attention. It felt as if her entire soul was melting into the stark and magnificent scenery. Holding a few sticky stalks of wildflowers purchased from the flower peddler, she forgot the vase that waited to be filled, forgot even herself as she watched a gull circle and plunge into the shining mist of sea.

Overhead, the February sun was a flat, white disk against the blue canvas of sky. A few stringy clouds scuttered past like anxious pedestrians late for appointments, now and then casting a brief shadow over the earthly landscape. But the star of the scene was clearly the Aegean, the calm water of the cove seemingly cast of sparkling cerulean crystal. Shell wind chimes hanging from the reed-covered patio tinkled like fairy music against the cry of several more gulls newly arrived to the scene.

Then a boy's voice broke her reverie, and the gay banter between Jason and Andreas took up as usual, filling the magical spaces of silence.

Jason had returned to eat, filled with enthusiasm for the location that he claimed had to have been inhabited by a previous civilization. The hills, he insisted breathlessly, were not hills, but edifices covered by dirt over the centuries. Anyone could see that there was more to this place than what met the eye.

"Why doesn't anyone do anything here?" he asked Andreas. "Maybe there's treasure and temples, maybe a whole city is right under us," he suggested excitedly.

"This is Greece. There is always something beneath something else here. Anyway," Andreas said, laying out plastic containers of food taken from the basket, "when we Greek's discover something wonderful on our land, the British or the French or you Americans come and take it from us for your own museums."

"But why?" asked Jason, seemingly appalled by the piracy.

"They tell us it's for our own good. For the good of the world. We Greeks have little money to spend to preserve what is precious to us. Now we have barely enough to preserve ourselves from day to day." Andreas offered a square container of sliced tomatoes to Kate, then to Jason. "Once this land held the most important culture in civilization."

"What happened to it?" Jason wanted to know.

"When you have something beautiful, everyone wants it. They came—the Turks, the Italians, the Germans—at different times and many times over. They took our land, our culture, our money, killed our people, and mostly they killed our enthusiasm to build things up again." Andreas leaned back, seeing into the past. A gust lifted the edge of the cloth, and Andreas moved swiftly to stay it with a salt container. "Like a constant wind, they visited us here, and eventually we were worn down."

"Oh," said Jason sadly. "And now everything's gone."

"Not everything," Andreas said, with a kind of joyous, stubborn bitterness. He leaned forward to Jason, speaking secretively. "We have our heart left."

"And that can't be taken!" Jason crowed. "They'll never get that!"

Andreas sank back into his chair. "Not necessarily true. It happens. But we always have our pride," continued Andreas. He turned his face quickly to the side, away from Kate's view, and his words became more self-directed. "We try to keep something for ourselves. Maybe by not showing it to others, the little that we have left will remain safe."

Jason had noted the hurt. He glanced quickly at Kate, then on his own attempted to set things right. "I love Greece. I love your country. So does my mom."

"Everyone does," Andreas exclaimed. "They love to visit. And then they leave. We are too simple, too primitive here."

And Kate sat silently, knowing he spoke to her and not in generalities, knowing as he did, that what he said was entirely and sadly accurate.

"I would stay here," Jason said sincerely. "If I were older and could decide things on my own, I'd never leave Greece. When I'm big, I can come back someday."

A cat suddenly enlarged their small group. Hopping agilely upon the fourth chair at their table, it meowed plaintively, specifically eyeing Kate.

Kate offered the animal food. This was unacceptable. The cat refused and complained yet again, continuing to whine until it was taken into Kate's lap and she began to stroke its fur. When she looked up, laughing at something Jason had said, she caught Andreas watching her, his eyes as intense as that of the cat's when it had wanted her favors.

She wanted to make light of what she read in his look, tried to turn away and keep up the pretense that their relationship—but for that one night when they had fallen into each other's arms—was something transitory. In her own mind, she'd tried to place it as one of those adult, sophisticated encounters between men and women that meant what it did for the moment and in the next instant meant nothing. Of course she was not experienced in such matters. She had no way of knowing for certain if people were actually capable of such detachment, but she had heard and read about such emotionally freewheeling souls.

"So many cats here in Mykonos," she said, desperate to break the visual link binding her to him, but unable to look away. "Poor homeless creatures."

"She wants love more than food," Jason said. "Oh, Mom, that's sad."

Her body had turned into a liquid pool of desire. She wanted to be lying beneath Andreas, to feel his hands stroking her own form, to be one with him again completely and eternally.

Jason was saying something about the cat. She couldn't concentrate. She wanted love more than food. She was that cat. And Andreas knew it...he knew it as well as she did...in his eyes it was written.

They had not made love since that one time. Jason was always about. Then, too, there seemed to exist between them something else that held them apart. It was as if they sensed they had gone as far as was safe to venture: to pass that point would either shatter what beauty they had already experienced, or plunge them into a situation neither of them was prepared to deal with.

"In America they have places for cats to go when they don't have food or homes. People can come and adopt them. But sometimes," Jason added, suddenly understanding more than he wanted, "no one comes."

"Life is sad sometimes," Andreas said a bit coldly. Speaking pointedly to Kate, he said, "Have you had the chance to see any of our famed Greek tragedies?"

"No...unfortunately."

"Perhaps you will. Before you leave." He paused, letting the underlying message seep through. Kate lowered her eyes. "Anyway," he went on with more gusto, "on Mykonos you always find the best and worst of everything. The highest and the lowest. The sacred and the profane. Cats who get no food, and cats who get fed and petted by beautiful women. You will find here all the contrasts of life."

Kate glued her attention to the cat. The animal made deep purring sounds, and the warmth of its body was somehow comforting in her present state. She was confused by her need for Andreas and what her rational mind insisted was an involvement to avoid. There, another dichotomy.

Jason left his chair and asked if he might play with the animal. Allowing him his request, Kate followed the two with her eyes as they began a game of tag with a spindly switch of wood Jason pulled along.

"Kate..." Andreas whispered against the sounds of Jason's happy squeals. Only that: just the one word, "Kate."

She looked up, the softness in the word pulling her back into him against her will.

"I am happy now, this day," he said, the green eyes luminous with certainty. "It is what makes me fear for the future. And you? Are you happy, as well?"

And although she was filled with him, she could not even smile, nor could she utter his name, or any other word in response. The Aegean flowed through her veins, the wind was her mind, and the earth of Greece had become her body. Her whole heart had expanded into a joy so intense it seemed to render all speech superfluous.

"Yes, good," he said, and smiled, apparently reading whatever he needed to know in her face. He went on softly, choosing his words with care, as if each one was fragile. "I thought as much. It's enough...to know you are happy as I am. You can not hide everything always, Kate Reynolds."

Jason was back, annoyed that the cat had run off, and the picnic continued in an orderly fashion.

They ate a loaf of freshly baked bread. It was a variety indigenous to the island, and something similar to Italian or French loaves, but of a thicker texture and of a shape shorter and stouter. With it they had strips of lamb and heavily spiced Greek meatballs, roast chicken, and a salad of cucumbers and tomatoes, black olives and feta cheese.

As they ate, Kate's gaze would traverse the scene again and again, her heart expanding from the sight of the barren, hauntingly beautiful landscape. Now and then she would add a remark to the conversation being waged between Jason and Andreas, but mostly, floating in her bubble of pleasure, she was content to listen and observe.

For a Greek man, Andreas was unusual. Even in her limited experience with other of the country's male natives, she recognized his uniqueness. He was insistent always that he serve, organize and please—that he assume full responsibility for whatever occasion was at hand. If there was bread to be cut, it was he who reached first for the knife. If there was a decision to be made, it was he who assumed command; but not in a kingly way, merely in genuine concern that his guests were well tended.

Throughout the meal, whenever their hands touched—in reaching for a bowl, in catching a napkin, in passing the container of salt—an emotion that could only be described as a deep sob, full and sweet and painful and sharp, burst through Kate's being. When her eyes came to rest upon the face of Andreas, her breath would stop momentarily from the shock of such beauty. And when his glance would join hers, there was that feeling of drowning in warm honey and not caring.

They ate, the three continuing on with their small talk, and then Jason rushed again to find what treasures he might on the lonely beach.

For a moment the two of them sat in silence, Kate stroking the cat who had returned and curled into her lap. Andreas was pensive, facing outward toward the Aegean. He
gave the impression of watching Jason run along the stretch
of sand below them, but Kate knew he was not seeing. His
vision had gone within.

"I am so happy today," he said again solemnly, his voice
low and doleful.

"You don't sound it. You sound very unhappy," Kate
said, watching him with an aching heart that knew exactly
what he was feeling. This day contained a perfection—a
perfection that could not be held on to, taken away and
continued into another time.

He glanced at her, his eyes gentle. "It is not possible to be
happy without being unhappy. If you were Greek, you
would know this."

"But I'm not Greek. And I do know." She had tasted that
bittersweet joy. "I don't know if it's possible to be truly
happy until you've seen the other side. And the other side
of joy always casts a dark shadow."

"Yes," he agreed thoughtfully. "What is in your
shadow?" Andreas then asked, turning toward her with his
full attention.

Kate squinted into the sun, for the moment avoiding a
response. She didn't know if she wanted to share the past
with him. For one thing, he was of this time and place, and
she was feeling so good. She didn't want to contaminate the
present with the gloom of the past. Actually, on this day, the
experiences that had led her the long distance to this spot on
the earth no longer seemed that relevant to her life.

Tomorrow perhaps the nagging bitterness might return,
but now it was only a memory. The beauty around them
seemed to absorb her past and make the future inconsequential. But he was waiting and perhaps to discuss the

shadow that had accompanied her across the globe to this veranda would do her good. She felt momentarily brave, protected by invisible gods.

"You know already, don't you?" she asked, picking up an olive to examine rather than trust herself to meet his eyes. No matter what, there was still shame in her story of a cast-off wife.

"Trouble with a man," he stated outright, as if to name the topic to be discussed.

"Yes, trouble with a man."

"Always the trouble is with a man, with a woman." He was thoughtful. "Your husband?"

"My husband."

"And now you are divorced?"

"Yes."

"You were the one who left?"

"No." Kate swallowed hard. An image of The Claw came to mind. Maybe this wasn't going to be so easy after all. "It was because he got involved with another woman."

"He fell in love with someone else?" Andreas sat forward in amazement, looking as if nothing were more incredible.

At that Kate laughed. "No! No, indeed. He—Michael, my husband—isn't capable of falling in love. Michael just wanted someone different. Like he wanted a new car every year. It was for his image."

"I see."

But she saw he didn't. In a country where the general population thought in terms of keeping bread on the table, and nothing more, it would be hard to imagine trading in cars like people changed shirts—much less trading in wives to match a social style. "When we got married he had wanted the kind of wife he had seen on television shows when he was growing up. The kind of wife his own mother had been. Someone who stayed home and cooked and put flowers on the table from her own garden. All that.'' She stopped for a moment, letting the anger that had risen subside. ''It was chic then to have that kind of wife. Which I was. Once upon a time,'' she breathed wistfully.

''Didn't you like it?''

''Yes. No.'' Kate sighed, smiled with irony, and shook her head dejectedly. ''Well, I didn't know any better really. I had kind of vague ideas of what I was all about. Not to mention what the rest of life was all about. It seemed to stretch on forever, then . . . life did.''

At that, Andreas also smiled and nodded. ''Not only in America. Not only for women. Go on . . .'' he said, waving his hand for her to continue. ''I think you maybe need to talk about this.''

He was right. Of course she did. She could feel something in her loosening, a tight uncomfortable brittleness vanishing as she unraveled the past verbally. Strangely she wasn't minding unburdening herself. Before she couldn't; the time wasn't right. But she had come a long way, not only geographically but within herself. Inner as well as outer scenery had changed. It was as if she were speaking not of herself as she was now, but of another woman she had once known. Her sympathies were with this poor misguided being, but she could also feel peculiarly detached. There was even a certain gossipy enjoyment to her tale as she resumed.

''So, anyway . . . there I was . . . cooking and gardening and putting up new wallpaper every other year, when the style began to change for wives. Michael discovered the 'in' thing in women was to have a partner in business.

''He hired a woman. Her name was Sandra . . . Sandra Bloomfield.'' Kate closed her eyes for a moment, conjuring up her rival's picture in her mind. ''He had her over for dinner once. It was in the beginning when they had just met.

I should have poisoned her then. She was insufferably nice. Anyway, he fell for Miss Ice Blood. She's not younger, really. Actually she's thirty-five and looks every last month of it. But she never got stuck in the kitchen, so she doesn't have that telltale taint of Betty Crocker about her. Apparently she worked her way up from some minor job to learning the real estate business, became a whiz at wheeling and dealing, and then decided she wanted more than money and fame and glory in her life. She wanted a man. My man. Specifically. So she took him." Kate shrugged.

"She was that pretty?"

"She was very attractive," said Kate. "But she was more clever than attractive. Don't ever trust a woman with high cheekbones, blond hair, and cold blue eyes. I don't think that between the two of them they could come up with the components for one whole heart. Good riddance," she said, and took a swig of her wine. Maybe it did hurt still, just a bit. But she could handle the residue of pain.

"You do not miss your life with him?"

Kate thought for a moment. "Once I did. I thought I'd do anything, anything to get him back. But things have happened since then. That woman who wanted him back is gone now. She doesn't exist. And as for the kind of life I had, no. No, I want something more than a dust rag and a list of groceries to carry with me to the market once a week."

"And what will you do now in your new life?"

"I don't know." There it was, the real point to the conversation—the future. "Go back to America eventually," she said bravely, facing what had to be faced. She knew what she had really said: *there can be no future between us, my beautiful, beloved, sensual Greek man. This brief encounter is to be our whole relationship.* "I'll do something, find a job," she said aloud.

"I see." They were quiet for a moment. Then Andreas went on. "What work will you find?"

"Oh, you know . . . something to make me rich and famous and safe forever. Preferably within two weeks."

"To be rich and famous, perhaps that is possible. But there's no guarantee anywhere for a broken heart."

"I'm counting on American technology to come up with it. As well as a spray to keep out all women with high cheekbones, blond hair, and cold blue eyes. What do you want to do with your life, Andreas?"

"I would like to be rich and famous and safe forever, too."

Kate saluted him with her glass of wine. He nodded, but looked away at once. "But of course that is unlikely. Instead I will find a nice Greek girl to marry. In a year we will start a family. There will be my life."

"Coming from you that sounds pretty negative."

"Sometimes I break down. I become realistic."

She was going to admit that she liked him better the other way, but Jason's hollering interrupted her.

He dashed down the hillside, tumbling part of the way, picking himself up, and sprinted full-speed to the veranda. Even the cat opened its eyes to observe the commotion.

Gasping, he held out his hand, displaying a dark flat stone in the shape of a triangle. There was a chunk missing from one side, but otherwise it looked exactly like what it was— the tip of an arrow.

"You see!" he said. "I was right . . . I knew it, I knew I'd find something if I looked."

"Jason," Kate said, taking the artifact and examining it, "this is . . . well, it's great. I'm really impressed."

Jason took it back and held it out to Andreas. "Here," Jason said. "This is for you, Andreas. This belongs to Greece."

Slowly, Andreas reached for the small triangular stone. "Thank you," he said. He made no attempt to hide the tears in his eyes when he took Jason in his arms. His hand was clutched into a tight ball, his knuckles white as he held onto the ancient stone.

Chapter Eight

So! How were they?'' Seated opposite them in Kate's kitchen, Andreas surveyed their faces with anticipation.

Both Kate and Jason looked down at their plates. Collusively, each had managed to crumble and thinly distribute the remains of their hamburger repast over the china. It was an effort to disguise the fact that neither had touched more than four or five mouthfuls of the gastronomic disaster.

Jason giggled first, then Kate. Both were afraid to look up for fear of making matters even worse than they already were.

"Oh," said Andreas.

Kate collected herself and said with as straight a face as possible, "The hamburgers were really quite interesting."

But the attempt at diplomacy brought forth a gale of choked laughter from Jason. Andreas waited with dignified forbearance for the fit to end. "Perhaps you would like to explain the joke," he said finally.

When the spasm of hilarity was finally under control, Jason said, "I think maybe we weren't ready for them, Andreas. I've never had a Macburger before."

"And you did not like them," sniffed Andreas. He rose from his seat and began to whisk the subjects of scorn from the table. He still wore the apron over his jeans. It, like his shoulders, seemed to droop disconsolately.

Jason considered the statement. "I'll bet the military would go nuts for them."

Andreas turned from the sink, looking interested and a touch less despondent. He had been disposing of the Macburger scraps in a rubber bucket. One eyebrow was raised quizzically. "Really? The military?"

"Yup," said Jason, nodding importantly. "I can see Macburgers dropped upon enemy camps from thirty thousand feet." He made bombing noises. "The dirty whoevers wouldn't stand a chance."

"Especially if they ate them," Andreas enjoined thoughtfully.

"Something along those lines," Jason returned.

"Um," Andreas said, nodding. "Well, then, I guess I should tell you."

As he walked to the table, his expression was grave. Kate and Jason exchanged looks. For the first time, the hamburgers became a serious issue. Up until now they had really believed Andreas was in on it, that he understood it was all in fun. Perhaps, Kate thought, they had gone too far in their denegration of his efforts to give them an American meal.

"We're sorry if we made fun. It was really good of you to take the time and trouble," Kate said quickly, and with enthusiasm. "They were really quite unusual. Something different. Of course that's why people travel—to find something new and unusual."

"But these weren't supposed to be new and unusual. They were supposed to be American," Andreas said miserably.

"Yes, but anyway..." Things were really becoming difficult. "Well, you know how we Americans are. There's millions of jokes about us. We're laughed at and despised all over the world for...for..."

Andreas nodded. "I know very well how you are."

That didn't help her at all. "Then you know we're totally unadventurous. Hopelessly provincial."

"We mostly eat cardboard at home," claimed Jason, rushing in to rescue the situation. "That's what the French say about our food. You can't expect much from us. We wouldn't know great food if it bit us."

Andreas leaned down, both palms on the table, his head bowed in defeat. Raising his eyes, he said, "I have a confession."

The room was quiet.

Andreas drew in a long sigh, signifying suffering and shame. "I lied. I did not know how to make Macburgers at all. I had no such American friend to show me. Oh, over the years there were promises...but no one actually came through. So I invented my own. I added what I thought might be in a Macburger. I'm sorry. It was dangerous to play with lives that way."

And then he smiled wickedly.

"Ah, you rogue! I really felt like a worm. I shall never, never trust a man with a smile like that," Kate announced. At that moment she liked him better than ever before.

Jason giggled delightedly. "Don't you know it's because he's related to a spy! Being sneaky runs in his blood." Jason seemed positively enchanted by Andreas's latest scam at their emotional expense.

"Was Maria really a spy?" Kate asked, no longer willing to be gullible when it came to Andreas's tales.

"Almost. Our family tree is full of people who almost did this and almost did that." A dark thought flickered in his eyes. He picked up a bowl from the counter and pretended to examine a hairline crack on its side. "The war ended her career before it began."

"Okay if I go ask her about codes, Mom?"

"Go," said Andreas, putting the bowl down and turning back to them. "My grandmother knows more about secret codes and general skulduggery than any other old woman in Greece."

Kate agreed, too, and Jason rushed down the hall, yelling that he wasn't a bit sick, so they weren't to worry. The door slammed after him, and she and Andreas were alone together.

"My grandmother enjoys his company," Andreas said. "She made some cakes for him today, on the chance that he might pay her a visit."

"Jason really likes her."

"He has grandparents at home?"

"Michael's mother, is all. And she isn't much interested in her role. She plays lots of cards in Boca Raton—that's in Florida. Twice a year she sends gifts. For his birthday and at Christmas."

"And your parents?"

"Mine. Well, Dad died about five years ago in an accident at work. Some stupid freak thing with a forklift. Something that could never happen in a million years. Only it did. My mother just went into a decline after that. Then she had trouble with her heart, a couple of operations, and one night the valve failed, and she was gone. I'm all that's left—and Jason."

"In Greece the family is very important—the most important thing." He paused. "I liked this tonight."

Kate knew what he meant. The scene that night might have been part of an ordinary family's life. Only sadly, it wasn't. It was only make-believe and temporary, like a film. But then, so was her marriage that she had once thought was so perfect.

As he worked, Andreas washed the few dishes, humming something only marginally melodic, since it was in that strange minor key so popular with Greeks. But its disharmony made no difference: he was clearly happy, enjoying the domesticity.

That he did, made it all the worse for Kate, for it was a happiness that she was soon to shatter.

She watched him from the corner of her eye as she dried silverware and plates and turned the glasses upside down to drain, waiting for the right moment to do what had to be done. But there was no easy way to phrase goodbye euphemistically, and to say it outright seemed impossibly cruel.

"Tomorrow," she began, "the planes are going to fly again. I checked with the airline. It's about ninety-five percent certain. And the boats, too. I thought maybe the ferry might be more fun for Jason. Besides, it's much cheaper."

For an instant Andreas froze. Then his hand moved on, placing the towel over the back slats of the chair to dry. "You don't have to go," he said evenly, but there was a tight edge to his voice.

"I really do."

He tried to keep his voice light. "You've only just come!"

"Oh, Andreas . . . we've been here too long already. Jason's well enough to go on. I spoke to the doctor this morning and he said as long as we weren't going off to India or Africa . . ."

"Ah, the doctor said all is well. Good. Then you must pack tonight." Andreas's face, usually a canvas of expression, had become perfectly still. He couldn't look at her, which was just as well, because if he had, she might have given in to staying a year, or forever. He began to wipe the small squares of tile on the counter with a rag.

"I'm sorry," she said softly, her eyes filling in spite of her resolve not to let the scene deteriorate into unnecessary melodrama. "We both knew—"

Whirling around, Andreas slammed his fist violently into the wall, and immediately turned to her with eyes of green flame. "Macburgers!" he shouted. "Macburgers and microwaves—damn them all to hell!"

In a fast stride, he came across the floor and grabbed her by the shoulders. Gripping her with a force that made her wince, he said in a low voice filled with cold anger, "You come here and you take what you want. And then when you are bored you can fly off into the land of Macburgers and microwaves and cars that talk. And here we have nothing. We can only look at the television shows—shows your countrymen tell me that are not even your good shows! I would kill to taste a real American hamburger like I have only heard about or I see in magazines. I would kill to—!" He closed his eyes, trembling, and took in a deep breath as he gathered himself together. When he looked at her again, he said, "I'm sorry," and released his hold. Stepping back, he seemed almost to stumble. He rubbed his jaw, then self-consciously raked his hands through his thick thatch of black curls, much as if he had just awoken from a dark, confusing dream.

"So am I," Kate said. "I'm sorry it had to turn out this way. I had no way of knowing...you, either." The shoulder ached where he had held her, and she brought a hand up to rub it.

"There, I've hurt you," he declared miserably. "It was the last thing I wanted to do—to hurt you."

"I hurt you," Kate said with equal shares of distress and apology. "And it was the last thing I wanted to—"

"Stop," Andreas said. "There's no sense in this. What is, is. We don't have to draw out the inevitable. Even though perhaps we tried to do so these few days." His face had changed. His features had hardened into a mask showing no emotion. Coming forward again, he stood before her, but made no move to touch her this time. "I wish you well on your journey. I wish you well, Kate Reynolds, in your life in America."

And with that he left, the front door closing quietly, his exit dignified and final. If there was a curtain to destiny, it would have fallen softly at that moment.

Kate leaned against the counter, looking down the dark, empty expanse of hall. It had to be this way.

There were the usual faces in the bar. Andreas hailed this man and that, most were friends of many years, others were known but not well. These were the men who had come to Mykonos from the mainland to do construction during the winter. Since Greece had joined the European Economic Community, the island was undergoing a minor building boom. In general, there was little work in Greece, and if it meant leaving one's family for a few months at a time to earn a wage in a distant location, then that was what one did and without complaint.

In the winter there were rarely any tourist women in Mykonos with whom to dally for pleasure, and those who were Greek stayed in the home as was traditional. So the bar this night, as usual, was entirely made up of males talking and playing cards, drinking and arguing, a backgammon game in this corner, a game of cards over there. In one corner, attached by brackets high on the wall, a television set ran an old back-and-white American movie from the fifties, something with car chases and women wearing heavy eye makeup. The reception, or maybe the film itself, was grainy and the voices high, with a tin sound. Several men sat below the elevated screen, their chairs in a row as if they were in a theater, following the action with rapt interest.

Andreas moved through the room, seeing all of this through the thick haze of cigarette smoke that was a part of any setting in which Greek males gathered. Yet on this occasion he saw more than merely simple beings whiling away hours in harmless pleasures. He saw his past, his present, and his future written in the environment. He saw an endless procession of days and nights with no substance.

A friend stopped to inquire about some fishing gear he wanted to borrow from Andreas. Andreas spoke amiably, but inside...inside was a different matter. Within, his heart clutched in hopelessness and his guts churned in rage at his fate. Was there nothing more than this? This ridiculous conversation that he'd had a thousand times before, it seemed; a conversation with no consequence—yet look how involved the man's energies were. Did no one in the room see any of this but him?

Surely this was not meant to be his life, this meaningless parade of minutes into hours, and hours into days into years! Yet it was his life. And therein lay his distress, as he took a place at the long bar and ordered a beer.

For the time being he stood alone, without companionship, which was just as well given his mood. He tried to keep his mind off of Kate. Once, not long ago he could have brushed aside any woman who even remotely clouded his life. But now he could not. Kate's face, the smell of her, the memory of her skin, the voice...all of it haunted and tormented him to the point where he doubted a hundred beers could wash away her specter.

American rock music played from a tape deck behind the bar, the sounds blasting from overhead speakers and intermingling with the voices from the television. Andreas listened to the words, to the driving pagan beat, trying to imagine what existences those singers had come out of to be able to sound that way. What had they done and seen to give them that particular slant on life that would create those voices, that song?

He paid for his beer and turned, leaning his back against the bar's curved wooden lip, to watch the thirty or so duplicates of himself who unconsciously spent their lives in trivial activity. But that he was cursed to realize the tragedy of their collective existences, he was like any man there.

Of course the American would not want him. How stupid, how utterly asinine of him to have thought otherwise. His mind flew back in time, and he saw Kate as he had that first moment in the airline reservation office. Only a few days had passed. Oh, how innocent life had seemed then. He was still himself, the Andreas Pateras of old. Certainly there had been slight stirrings of discontent with his life, and that vague sort of longing to have a relationship with a woman that went deeper than a fleeting sexual affair.

But then, before seeing Kate Reynolds, he had only teetered on the edge of that dangerous, seductive world. Now he lived—and suffered—within this new realm in which feelings so soft he could weep, swept him into pastel dreamscapes of romantic harmony never to be realized.

Tomorrow Kate would leave. He had no address to reach her later. She herself had no place to call her own in the future. Ah, wouldn't he have given her a place to heal her wounds!

And the boy... clever and good-natured, always ready to seek adventure. Together they might have found hidden treasures. They might have sailed to Delos and fished and dove for the spiny black sea urchin, slicing the cavities in half and eating their catch then and there with vinegar and oil and spices only a Greek could assemble to perfection. Oh, yes . . . the boy and he might have done so many, many wonderful things together.

And together he and Kate might have found the only reason he could now see to remain on the planet. In a single word: love.

A man came up to him, joined by three more. They were bright-eyed, thrilled with news about a football game to be played in Italy soon. There was much speculation if Greece was to have a chance this time to win. More beer was ordered. Bets were taken. A fisherman, already teetering from too much whiskey, stopped by to say the caïques would be able to take to the sea again tomorrow.

And the planes would fly again.

Chapter Nine

Mom? Mom? Mom! Are you listening?"

The last "Mom!" broke through the sound of the wind and her thoughts. Kate put down the two duffel bags she carried and unkinked her joints that ached from the load. "How did we ever manage this stuff?" she muttered, looking down at the bags lying on the cement dock. A hundred feet ahead, the ferry loomed with its cargo doors open wide, taking on passengers and cars and pallets of containers.

"Where's Andreas?" Jason wanted to know. His voice was higher than usual and his face seemed redder than it should have been.

"Jason? Are you all right. Your skin's gone all—"

"Where's Andreas, Mom?"

"He's ... Jason ..." She had to stop and pull herself together. "Andreas is not part of our lives, Jason."

"He was part of my life," Jason said with defiance.

"He was a temporary part of your life—and mine, too. We've met lots of people on our trip. You never carried on like this before." It was hard to keep her voice from wavering. But she had to, both for Jason's sake and for her own. She had to be adult and realistic about the situation.

"Are you crazy, Mom? Andreas loved us! He didn't want us to leave. Dad wanted us to go—but not Andreas, Mom. Not him." Jason was crying. Jason rarely ever cried. It was just something totally out of character for him to do.

"Jason, please...don't..." She reached forward to comfort him, but he backed away. There was fury and betrayal written in his eyes but not for Andreas. Jason blamed her. And he had every right. She should have just put her foot down in the beginning, not gone on the picnic, the drives, the walks, had the dinners...oh, but God, she had been weak. And now she was paying for it—not to mention poor Jason.

"Jason," she said, allowing him to keep his emotional distance, "I know how it may seem to you. I also was very fond of Andreas, just as he was of us, but we come from different cultures, whole different worlds, and what can work for a few days, just doesn't have a realistic chance of survival on a long-term basis."

"Why?" Jason demanded.

"Because...because you and I come from a country that has so much more, and we would never be able to adjust to so much less. And—"

"Mom," Jason said, "we had a lot of stuff at home. And that didn't make anything good for you. And maybe Dad was my dad, but he didn't make me feel good, like Andreas did. So I think maybe you're real wrong about this culture stuff. Mom—I love Andreas!"

The boat gave a deep whistle. It might have been a moan coming from the bottom of her soul. "We've got to go, Jason. The ferry's going to leave."

Picking up the bags again, foolish and self-destructive as it was, she couldn't keep from taking one last look back along the dock. A few stragglers dragged suitcases and boxes along, but that was all. The shoreline held no sign of Andreas running toward them, green eyes filled with passion and determination to make her stay. But such scenes only happened in movies.

Twenty minutes later she was buying coffee for herself and some potato chips for Jason at the snack bar inside the ferry when the final plaintive burst of horn sounded their departure. The boat gave a slight shift, and they were under way, on their way into the future.

She paid the man, then turned toward Jason, who was just slipping through the door to the outside. Following him, she did what she'd promised herself she wouldn't. She stood on the outside deck and watched the town of Chora on the island of Mykonos disappear from her life.

Silently she spoke her heart, "Take care, my beautiful Greek man; take care, Andreas Pateras. Maybe somehow you will know that you were loved."

When Jason took her hand, they were both crying.

"If you can work the season, I'll give you a third more than the others," said the man to Andreas.

"Every night, I must work?" Andreas qualified.

"Every night. And in the afternoons you must unload the beer and other liquors."

"Every afternoon," echoed Andreas to the owner of Mykonos's most successful disco. Theo Asmanis had only just arrived that morning by plane from Thessaloniki where he owned apartment buildings. To Andreas, who had nothing, this man conveyed self-satisfaction along with a nervousness that all he had might be taken from him in the next second. But that was typical of all Greeks.

They sat together in the darkened room, drinking coffee from glass cups at the bar. The proprietor had a sheath of papers scattered before him. Ordinarily, Andreas would have admired him for his ledgers and notes, papers attesting to an existence of purpose, a life of forward momentum. But this morning Andreas could not keep his mind on the conversation. He knew it was important to secure work for the coming summer season. The winter provided merely a skeletal income. It was the summer income that created whatever financial solvency he could expect to support him through the leaner months of the year. Now and then he would tune in to the stream of words flowing from Theo Asmanis, but mostly Andreas was absorbed in an internal dialogue.

The ferry's horn had sounded, and within minutes the boat would sail from port with Kate and Jason aboard. After that, there would be no way to trace them.

"...into August. After that, we can let go of maybe three employees and—"

"Excuse me," interrupted Andreas. "There is something I forgot." Abruptly he stood, and without further comment, rushed from the disco, entering the bright light of the late morning just in time to hear the final blast from the ferryboat as it moved from the dock, bound for the open sea.

The port wasn't more than twenty paces down the hill from the disco, and Andreas made the distance at a run. His heart pumped wildly in his chest, vibrating like an enormous drum, and a tightness clamped his throat to the point that he was gasping for breath. It couldn't be! The boat usually waited several more minutes before embarking.

Helpless, he stood watching from the shoreline as the enormous ferry moved slowly but relentlessly away from the shore.

Oh, Kate... You'll never know. I loved you more than I shall ever love again. Oh, Kate... you were not just another woman. You were her... the one I loved... the only one. You were you....

The American Express office was located in busy Syntagma Square in the center of Athens. She and Jason had waited in line to ask for their mail, and just before closing time had been given the crisp white envelope with the familiar black imprint of her attorney's law firm on its upper left-hand corner.

Over the past eight months, varying emotions had accompanied the receipt of these periodic missives from her attorney. The main purpose of them was, of course, her support money from Michael. They had reached a legal understanding that he was to pay her support money every month via her attorney, who would forward the sum to her at specific times and particular destinations along her journey's route. There had been little foul-up with this method. Really, the support payments were her only means of livelihood, and they gave her a feeling of relief mixed with discomfort that she had to resort to what felt like a handout to stay alive.

She might have gotten a job, but at the time of the divorce, she'd been too emotionally shattered to face the commercial world, and she'd simply had no marketable skills. Her attorney had been the one to suggest the trip, claiming it would be a good transition for her to go from one life to the next.

Also, by the time she returned to America, the second half of the divorce settlement would be in financial effect. That is, Michael was to have refinanced his business holdings and would then be able to divvy up her share of their community property, now entangled in a web of complicated real estate transactions. This money would allow her to either return to school or find herself some investment property to provide a livable income.

It was rush hour when she stepped back onto the sidewalk outside the American Express office. Noxious fumes and the zoom-clatter-whoosh of every kind of vehicle from bus to motorbike assaulted her senses. Jason, by her side, wiped his eyes, which had to be stinging, as hers also were. "Let's go find a hotel," he said wearily, their bags on the pavement.

"Okay, right away." Kate looked in either direction. Off to one side were clumped the lofty hotels, including the King George and the stately Grand Bretagne with its international flags welcoming travelers from around the world through its refined portals.

"Jason," she said with a forced show of enthusiasm, "how about a splurge? Someplace luxurious, with a real bath and room service and toilets that flush without running all night and—"

Jason was not to be jollied quite so easily. He had been sullen and withdrawn during the entire voyage to Piraeus, and barely looked out the bus window from the port to downtown Athens. "Are we rich again or something?"

"Yes, as a matter of fact." She waved the envelope before his nose; then to make the proposed fantasy real, tore the end open and pulled out the letter.

But it wasn't the letter she had been so intent upon. The check wasn't there.

"Mom? What's wrong?" Jason asked.

She looked down at the pavement, lest the bank draft had fallen out without her seeing it. Then she checked the envelope again, the pavement once more, the envelope for a third time, looked on both sides of the letter, as if the check might have become invisible and reappeared miraculously. But the check was not there.

"Mom?"

"Jason . . . wait . . ." Opening the folded letter from her attorney, she began to read. As she did, her blood seemed to drain from her. She felt as if she had been transformed into a dried leaf and was incapable of withstanding the slightest impact from the outside world.

The letter began familiarly enough: "Dear Mrs. Reynolds."

After that, things started to fall apart.

He was sorry to tell her that there would be no check this month, nor did it appear that any additional payments to her support account would be forthcoming in the near future.

That much was recounted in fairly typical legalese. However, after this, the tone of the missive veered somewhat into a more colloquially gossipy tone.

Apparently, your ex-husband's new partner made some either intentional or unintentional disastrous business decisions that have forced your husband's financial holdings to collapse. There is some fairly substantial speculation that Sandra Bloomfield may have siphoned off large chunks of your former husband's estate and placed same into various accounts under various fictitious corporate entities. Whether or not this is true, and whether anything can be salvaged, is unclear as of this writing, and will take some time and effort to discover. Bearing in mind the court's calendar, I would see no satisfaction in this matter for at least three to seven years.

The letter then returned to the matter of the support money to be paid to her and Jason.

Mr. Reynolds has already been arrested for various other financial defaults and illegal business practices, therefore, prosecuting him for monies owed you will not have much effect on his already incarcerated state.

In conclusion, her attorney said that he was sorry to be the one to relay such disturbing news. He wished her well, and added that her account still showed a balance of fifteen hundred dollars due and payable as of the current date.

Stunned, she could not even move. Instead she stood rooted to her place, surrounded by fumes and vehicles and living, breathing, coughing, walking, running, talking forms—none of which could be real, just as the letter was not real. The whole thing was merely her imagination.

She was vaguely aware that Jason was pulling on her jacket sleeve and calling her name. But really, she hardly felt anything at all. She merely continued to stand there in the center of Athens, feeling disconnected to the entire scene, as tears gradually moved from inside to outside and all the people and cars and noise that seemed nothing more than creations of her mind swirled about her.

Out of the confusion, yet another symbol of her deterioration came into a blurry, surreal focus. A man looking very much like her Andreas was loping forward, emerging from the crowd just as if he really existed.

Chapter Ten

The man who looked like Andreas had come forward and stopped directly in front of her. Now he was saying something. Kate could hardly make out his face through the tears, much less make any sense of his words. Her mind reeled in total, abject confusion. She felt shaky, totally abandoned, no more than a small inconsequential spec of humanity adrift in a cold, busy, and unfeeling universe. With the ending of her marriage, the proverbial rug had been yanked from under her; but now the world itself had been whisked away. There was nothing left now. Nothing left at all.

"...a surprise to find you here at the same time. Amazed really. Pure coincidence. I had to pick up some papers at American Express for—No! No, that's not it at all. If you want to know the truth, I followed you here. I got on the first plane I could, and knowing you'd be here, I rushed as fast as possible to find you. The gods were with me this once! If I had missed you... Kate, I'm sorry for—" And here his voice broke off, his face miserable.

It was then, when he had used her name, that she suddenly came into the world of reality again.

Jason was jumping up and down, hugging Andreas, who was hugging him in return, and yet the green eyes were fully on her, intense, fiery with emotion.

"Oh, Andreas," she said, and all she could summon in response was a pervasive numbness. It was as if too much feeling had blown through her at one time, and whatever mechanism it was that allowed one to experience gladness and sadness and all the rest of the human spectrum of emotion, had shorted out. "I thought you weren't real."

"And I thought that perhaps you weren't—when you left me." He spoke sadly, but then his eyes brightened. "But here we stand, Kate...here we are again. Together," and he said it wondrously, casting his eyes upward to give thanks or to question whatever force had made such an occasion possible.

Her face was slick with tears and she rubbed away the latest batch with the back of her hand. Everyone was staring at her; in her mind each passerby had eyes the size of saucers. But mostly she felt Andreas staring at her. She had to have red eyes and a red nose to match, and God...there had to be dark tracks of mascara running down her face. Feeling foolish, she opened her shoulder bag and began to hunt for a tissue. Vanity died hard.

"We didn't think you'd come," Jason said breathlessly. "This is like...like a miracle." He was looking up at Andreas as if he were, in truth, capable of anything, miracles probably being the least of his talents.

Astonishment passed across Andreas's face. "Not come?"

"I was praying...praying you'd come," Jason said.

"Then that is what I felt..." Andreas pressed his hand lightly upon Jason's head and ruffled his hair affectionately. But his attention was really on Kate. The light banter was a necessary piece of business to cut the tension. The fun went out of his voice when he asked, "And you, Kate...what did you think?"

She could feel his soul straining toward her with a frightened desperation. She understood, for the hope and fear was hers, as well. "I couldn't think," she said quietly.

"You didn't remember," he responded just as softly. "Oh, Kate, Kate..." he said, taking a step forward, then stopping suddenly, as if monitoring his natural impulses. "I told you I'd follow you, always...in my heart, in my mind. But my body wanted to come, too," he said more expansively, a note of self-conscious awareness taking hold. A shadow of the Greek dramatist living within him reclaimed the stage, materializing to save him from losing all male dignity.

"This is despicable, what I'm doing. If another Greek man heard me, I would be thrown out of the country. Never breathe a word of this—you must promise," he asked in a voice much like a stage aside to the audience. "It would be my end."

"It sounds great to me," Jason said, with complete audience satisfaction. "I just don't know if she's getting any of it. I think her antenna's bent." He shook his head, and nodded Kate's way.

Andreas scowled, for the first time relaxed enough in his own emotional hysteria to notice Kate's state. "Ah..." he said, as understanding dawned. This time he did come the distance to her. Taking her chin between his fingers, he lifted her face and said, "Kate...Kate...what's wrong?"

When she didn't respond at first, he looked to Jason for the answer. Jason shrugged, signifying his ignorance. Then catching sight of the letter dangling from Kate's limp hand, he took it easily, like an experienced thief. Opening it before she could protest, he began to silently peruse its contents.

But Kate made a quick feint to reclaim the letter. "Jason, Jason...no." The letter was safely snatched back. She jammed it into her purse. "Don't ever do that again!" she snapped. "This is private...this is—"

"Bad news," Jason said in his small voice, his forehead wrinkled. His face had taken on that ancient quality again. Kate both admired it and found it annoying. Whenever it showed up, it was like a mirror being held out to let her see where she had gone wrong.

"I'll deal with it," she said defiantly.

Ignoring Kate, Jason looked at Andreas. "It's worse than bad news."

Andreas flicked his eyes to Kate. She remained stoic. "I can handle it."

"Tell me," Andreas said, his manner already empathetic to whatever the crisis might be.

"It's nothing," Kate responded with a sniff, and dabbed her face again with the tissue she had located and had already bunched into a tortured-looking wad.

"It's definitely something," Jason said to Andreas, "but it's about nothing."

"I'd like to see," Andreas said.

"I've just had a bit of bad news, that's all. Something unexpected."

"Sure," Jason muttered. "Like Pearl Harbor was a little bit of unexpected bad news. Mom," Jason said in a piqued tone, "what do you think? I'm some stupid kid? You think I'm not going to notice it when I start to starve to death."

"You aren't going to starve to death."

"There's no money, Mom. There's not going to be any money."

"Something will come along, Jason."

"Yes," Andreas said. "Your mother's absolutely right. I have."

Kate and Jason looked at Andreas, who stood with his legs apart, feet firmly planted on the ground. "There. Now you know...Zeus sent me. He wants you back on Mykonos. And so do I," he added. "His television show was not over yet."

With that he picked up the two bags by Kate's feet and gestured for Jason to do the same with his. "Come on," he said in a commanding voice, "we're going home. No chance to win in a tangle with the gods—especially Zeus."

It was like the first time, Kate thought as she walked along beside Andreas, only then they had been off in search of cheese pies. Now she was off in search of the rest of her life.

Three weeks later she stood facing a less heroic Andreas than the one who had shown up cloaked in romantic and chivalrous glory that day in Athens.

They were in the streets of Mykonos now, and this time she was not quite so emotionally wasted. In the middle of one of the island's two main foot passages, they glared at each other like two mortal combatants in a deadly arena.

It was the second week of March and the streets of Mykonos were slowly filling with tourists getting the jump on the crowded summer season. Now and then, someone would squeeze around the bulwark they presented to resume his progress.

"Why must you do this? You're eating, aren't you?"

"Yes. And it happens to be *your* food."

"So? Because it is mine, it doesn't taste good?"

To Kate, he seemed taller and broader and more impos- ing than at any other time she had known him. This was a new side of Andreas, a part of his personality with which she had not yet become acquainted. Looking at him, she often felt as though she were viewing a shifting pattern of clouds, each shape unique in and of itself, and a constant entertainment to her senses. There was his charming roguish persona, whose flip side displayed silences marking the depths of his feelings. There was the good-natured man who accomplished the fatherly ministrations that Jason so much needed to furnish his boyhood. And there was also the amazingly tender and passionate Andreas who brought to their lovemaking a quality that was primal, pure, uncom- plicated, and incomparably fulfilling.

And now facing her in the tiny avenue lined by shops, was this outmoded, totally unfashionable beast of Mediterra- nean machismo.

"The point isn't whether or not the food tastes good— which it does—"

"Fine," he said haughtily. "That's something, anyway."

"The point is," Kate sighed, "that you knew very well our arrangement was only temporary. You knew very well that I was going to have to eventually pick up the pieces of my life and do something to support Jason and myself."

"I'm supporting you."

"Yes. Yes! You are supporting us. Without you we'd be two bones lying on the shoreline by now. But that's pre- cisely the point. Michael was also supporting us. And when he got tired of doing so, then look what happened."

"I happened."

"Well, great. You happened. And don't think I don't appreciate you, and everything you've done. But it's time that I happened for once. Not you. Not Michael. Not someone else. But *me*."

Andreas cast scornful eyes from her to the large basket she carried. "And you think that by sewing clothes you'll be able to make a big difference in your life."

Both of them stared down at the large, open straw basket she held in her left hand. It was stuffed with several outfits she had designed and sewn herself, and it wasn't as if she were exactly adept at either skill. Everything in the bag was mediocre at the very best. It wasn't as if she were blind, or kidding herself about her capabilities. Oh, no... kidding herself just wasn't on her list of things to do anymore.

But she had to have something on her agenda, so she was casting about and this idea was one of the few she had hooked. Once, when she was younger—much younger—she had entertained the notion of a career in fashion design. But of course she had married Michael and then Jason had come along. And that was that. At this stage of the game, her old dream of being renowned in Paris and Milan was as likely to materialize as the notion of one of her friend's—a woman who had considered her own destiny to be that of a prima ballerina, and who still harbored these lavish fantasies even though her arches had gone flat and her hips had spread into the queen-size category of panty hose.

Andreas was making her mad, but he wasn't offending her—she was too realistic to have her feelings hurt. Besides, it was impossible to knock her down. She was already down. That was the great thing about having nothing; the possibilities for expansion from that point were infinite. If anything, she felt she owed others of her gender who had burned bras and marched on Washington a certain marshaling of gumption to defend her position as an independent, capable being. Even if she wasn't—there was always hope.

"Andreas, I'm not trying to put Valentino out of business. I'm only trying to make a few dollars to help pay for expenses. And in the meantime I'm thinking of something else I can do. I've been looking around here, and I've got a few ideas that I think, well, I think they may have a possibility of working out. Maybe even making a lot of money."

Andreas screwed up his face, as if she had just spoken the most preposterous jibberish. She half expected him to spit on the sidewalk. "This is pure silliness."

"Oh, really? Why?"

"You have no money for a business. That's one thing."

"I have a little money in America. It was part of my divorce settlement. I used most of it for my trip, but there's still a bit left for an absolute emergency. I figure my future fills the bill."

"In Mykonos you need more than a little money. You need a lot of money. And," he said with an air of pomposity, "you need to be a very hard businessman."

"Maybe," she said, "and maybe not." She transferred the basket to her right hand. "We'll just have to see, won't we?" With that, she passed Andreas on his left.

He spun around. "Kate!" he called after her. "Where do you go now?"

"To the dress store down by the harbor. The woman who owns it said to show her my things when they were ready."

"Fine," he said with a darkness of inflection. "Good luck to you."

"You don't mean it," she returned good-naturedly.

But Andreas was smiling again, only slightly, but his sense of humor had returned enough that he could see the struggle between the sexes in more global terms. "You make me look bad, Kate Reynolds."

"You're too handsome to ever look bad, Andreas Pateras."

"Then you make me feel bad!" he called out.

"You make you feel badly," Kate said, walking backward with her basket and laughing. "Don't lay your ego trips on me."

"All right," he returned, and looked quickly about to see that no one was near to catch what he next said. "Then come home now with me, and we will lay down together."

"Later!" she said, and skipped quickly away before she gave in to the handsome man whose expression plainly told her a tale of what pleasure she could expect in his invitation.

For now, she was off to the harbor to seek her fortune.

Andreas walked with heavy steps along the street. The conversation with Kate had greatly disturbed him, far more than he had let on. Oh, certainly he understood she perceived the encounter as one of those silly, modern battles of the sexes—what he knew the Americans called women's liberation and all of that. He was not a cretin; he believed in equality.

But equality was also a dangerous thing—at least it was when his side of the relationship had nothing to balance the other.

For over two weeks he had watched Kate sew her outfits. Most of them weren't very well made. Any Greek woman could have done twice as well with a machine. But Kate had borrowed Maria's, and had sat down for several hours at a time every afternoon, struggling with needle and thread and strange little silver mechanical attachments that she fiddled with interminably to make work, while Jason was in school.

On a few of the days when he had not found work doing construction, Andreas had sat there patiently and silently while she had blasted away on the machine with its motor going like a maddened swarm of busy bees. He hadn't exactly minded, thinking that it was something good for her to keep her mind off her recent troubles. Even he could tell there was no chance of her making a commercial success of such a folly.

Still, there was something original in her use of fabric and the choice of trim she had scrounged from this neighbor and that, assembling their scraps into unique decorative touches applied to a bodice or hemline.

But the real truth was—as he very well knew—he might have shown a bit more enthusiasm for her efforts if he'd had any of his own to engage his energies. But he had nothing going in the future department. For this reason, he resented even her feeble stabs at free enterprise.

To even think that she might come up with some real kind of business was more than he could bear!

He was a man—a Greek man, for whatever that was worth—and regardless of her American sensitivities, he had his own as well. Maybe it was not the fashion in America. But here still, a man was a man, and a woman was a woman, and if she had any doubts about that, he would banish them soon enough. When she came home, he was going to make sure Jason was otherwise occupied, then he would make love to her like no one had ever done before— not even he.

And then he would feel better.

Maybe.

"These are not made very well," the owner of the boutique said. She appeared to be a few years older than Kate herself and several centuries more sophisticated in terms of the world of commerce.

Her name was Despina and she, like other wealthy Mykonians, lived away during the winter months. She had just returned a week before, opening her store and receiving merchandise. During the off-season, she had lived in Paris with a French woman, a friend who was there the same afternoon as Kate.

The friend, Simone Z, had platinum-blond hair. It was cut shorter than any schoolboy's, the bangs coming down in spikes to mideye, and her eyes were large, round and blue, and they seemed to absorb everything they touched.

To Kate, this Parisian was at once enthralling and frightening. She was everything Kate saw herself as not being—immensely self-contained. Where, Kate wondered, did one acquire such assurance? What price did Simone Z pay for her powerful presence? Or was there any sacrifice to be made? Anyway, whether she sat silently in a corner, or strolled to run fingers through a stack of filmy scarves, the woman reeked of composure. To Kate there was something wonderfully tough about her.

Even as Kate stood despondently by while Despina examined the third of six outfits she had sewn, Simone Z smoked a short, thin cigar, exhaling luxuriantly after every puff. If she had stolen surreptitious glances at the Parisian, Kate now felt herself being observed with more than idle interest.

When the interview with Despina was over and Kate's devastation was complete—nothing of hers was good enough to hang in the boutique!—Simone Z finally stubbed out her cigar and stood. Her every movement was that of a languorous cat—a tiny one, Kate noted, for the woman was diminutive in both height and bone structure. She wore high heels and tight, black, Spandex pants with a startlingly attractive, oversize shirt having large shoulder pads and a brilliant starburst design in rhinestones arranged on the front.

Moving to Kate, she said in English heavily charged with French, ''My dear, this work is appallingly sewn. But it has a certain something—the designs. The fabric is *merde*, but that is not your fault. You are poor, *non?*" It was not worth a response from Kate. The situation was self-evident, and Simone Z continued with her monologue. "I will bring to you some good fabric. And you will have someone else here do the sewing."

Kate tried not to gape and act like some hick American housewife. "Really?" Kate said, clearing her throat in place of saying anything else that might render her ridiculous.

"Don't think I am a saint," Simone Z said with a laugh. "I am a very selfish woman. You see, I have almost no talent myself. My specialty in life is to see and use what other people have. You have something. It is a little something right now, but who knows? Maybe it will grow." The compliments were distributed as facts; there was nothing cloyingly gratuitous to any of what might have been construed as praise. "I want you to make me something very special. Something that no one else has. Of course I will pay you."

"Thank you," Kate said, almost disbelieving. She hadn't felt so elated since...well, she hadn't felt so elated since she had won the science fair award in her senior year. It was the only other thing she had really gone all out on, on her own behalf, that is, in her entire life. After that singular personal triumph, all of her creativity had been applied in making things nice for other people. She had enjoyed her years of flower arranging, decorating and cake making, but well, hell . . . she now realized she could become a true glutton for praise. Standing in the company of Simone Z, who was holding up something she, Kate Reynolds, had created out of her own passion to succeed, sure beat the pants off of carpooling screaming eight-year-olds to Little League games.

"Wait here, and I will be back with the fabric." She slunk through the room and out of the door, her small high-heeled shoes barely making a sound.

Thirty minutes later Simone Z returned. True to her word she came with some astounding fabric. For an hour they discussed the dress Kate was to design. Whether or not she succeeded, she would be paid well, and if the job was satisfactory there would be more commissionings.

"Who knows?" said Simone Z, her blue eyes as round as two magnificent full moons. "Some day you may have a famous fashion house in Paris."

"Ha!" Kate said, gathering her things together.

"One never knows," said Simone Z. "Have you ever thought, my dear, that all of the greatest, most important things in one's life just simply happen? One may plan, and one must...but the magic of life is that it happens to you—not, as some think, the other way around."

"Yeah," said Kate, nodding. "Life sure has happened to me lately. I would kind of like to kick it back a little now."

Simone Z's laugh was throaty and low. "When you do, give it a kick for me, too."

Andreas was waiting for her inside the apartment. There was a bottle of wine opened on a low end table and two wineglasses. A white flokati rug had been appropriated from some outside source and was spread upon the floor with pillows. Greek music, with its sinuous, Asiatic tonal nuances and erotic drumbeat, was spilling from a portable radio. The invitation could not have been more plain had it arrived engraved in gold leaf upon black velvet.

"Jason has gone with Maria to visit the monastery at Ano Mera," Andreas explained, referring to the tiny inland village. "And he has asked that I watch over you. He will be gone for at least four hours."

"It seems you take your responsibility very seriously," Kate said, looking to Andreas from the hallway. She held the basket with her failed creations and the new material that was her shining destiny—if she didn't blow it, that is.

"Love is always very serious to a Greek."

"Not only for a Greek," said Kate, moving into the living room. The excitement—good as everything had turned out—had cost her in energy and she sighed wearily as she at last abandoned the basket to the sofa. Some of the fabric spilled out from the top. The rich sparkle of the brocade cloth Simone Z had given her gleamed like a visiting prince in the muted surroundings. Andreas's eyes traveled to where it lay, spread out in casual and luxuriant folds. It might have been a lover she had brought home with her, such was the reaction its sight engendered in him. His eyes hardened, along with the set of his jawline.

"So?" he said, pouring them both glasses of wine. "How did it go with the fashions?" As he handed Kate her glass, his eyes probed her for more than a casual answer to the question. He was asking her much, much more than that.

She clinked glasses. "The bad news is that Despina thought my things were wretched. Hated them, absolutely," she said, and took a sip.

For a moment Andreas said nothing, and she knew it was because he was pleased she had failed but sorry for her at the same time. "You'll improve," he said.

Without appearing to, Kate watched him as he drank. His body had relaxed considerably. Still holding his glass, he put his arm around her and drew her to him. His lips caressed the hollow of her neck, lightly working downward to the indentation of her collarbone. Kate relaxed into the pleasure, permitting herself to go limp and yield to the slight pressure of his body bending her back, allowing his tongue access to her swell of breast as he parted the fabric of her blouse. And when her pulse quickened in response to his own state of excitation, she had forgotten about the shimmering fabric and Simone Z. She could think of no one and nothing, only the surge of desire wrapped in emotion flowing through her in undulating waves of pleasure.

Together they moved to the white fur carpet, sinking down to it, he upon his back, she over him, as he moved his hands along her waist, tracing the line of leg and buttock, his mouth open and devouring.

She felt him strain against her, and she moved slowly against him, her body spiraling in insinuative loops as if the music with its insistent, urgent beat had entered her. There was no world, there was no place, nor was there time in this universe of exquisite delight; there was only this need to merge into him and remain in the feeling they gave to each other.

Andreas rolled slowly to his side, undressing her as their bodies entwined again and again, never parting for an instant in their need for each other. For a time, it was he who enjoyed the secrets of her body, and then fevered, he stripped himself free of all restraining fabric and they lay locked together, their bodies hot and slick with the intensity of their love.

There was a difference to their union, a subtle shift in the level of desire, which had altered perhaps from its previous playfulness to what Kate experienced as a deep inner awareness of the other ranging far beyond the pure physicality of their pleasure.

Without a speaking a word, their bodies conveyed the truth of their souls. They had entered into jeopardy this day, and from here on, they would both walk a knife's edge in their relationship. How could they reconcile the overwhelming force of their desire to be a part of each other and their need to preserve what their very different pasts had made them?

Simone Z's shining fabric flew as a brilliant banner in Kate's mind, beckoning her to become at long last who she truly was—as she Kate Reynolds was, not someone's daughter or someone's wife, or even Jason's mother... but as her very own individual, unique and perhaps even glorious self.

But Andreas's mouth was hot on her belly, his hand stroking knowledgeably against her softness. Trembling, a violent hunger to have him enter her completely, absorbed all cogent thoughts of the future. She would be lost forever in this ecstasy... drowned in the bliss his body brought to her.

"Kate... Kate..." he murmured as she lifted into him.

Their pulses became one, the throb of him racing through her body, and with his entrance came an explosion. Again he took her, the thrill shaking her to the center of her being as she rose up, ever higher, to be tossed again and again into a place that had no name but was all experience. Love tore through the shining curtain of fabric offering to her the world on its other side. "Andreas..." she cried, her arms tightening as the spasms began.

"Kate, my Kate..." The words were hungry as he pressed into her. His own body trembled, yet he resisted his own satisfaction and slowed to bring her with him again.

"Andreas, I love you so... so," she breathed, and was silenced by his mouth opening against hers.

Like a floating white cloud, the long strands of the flokati carpet softly enveloped them. Lying upon it, his skin was a contrast in golden brown, a liquid sheen dotting the small of his back, his shoulders, his chest slippery against her breasts. There was a flowing, harmonious perfection to his body. Never separating from him, she gently guided him to his back. The hard, smooth lines of his shoulders melted into his torso, and seeing his beauty, her eyes and fingers traced lightly downward to the dark web beneath. He shivered as she found him with her palm, and sensing every desire as if it were her own, she pleased them both. His eyes closed from the slightest movement of her body, as astride she maintained his pleasure on the edge of ecstasy.

Then, together they moved. This time neither broke the mounting rhythms of their love, and joined, they entered the flame, finding each other a thousand times.

Afterward, holding each other, they drifted together in the world they had known in the luxuriant folds of the flokati, their kisses light, soft and adoring. They whispered words that sometimes neither could hear but were felt by either soul. Half-awake, partially drowsing, they were contented and amazed by their blessings. Through the single window in the corner of the room, shafts of ocher sunlight separated by the fronds of a palm, streamed through the glass and fell upon their entwined forms. Like their passion, the afternoon had expended itself.

The music from the radio was now slow, a stately and somber refrain. In some other dwelling, another song was played, and a man's voice rose in a haunting lament. Lying in the crook of Andreas's arm, she felt his breath change into an easy, deep relaxation.

She did not wish to sleep, not while the slow ebbing of desire was still with her. There was another kind of joy that came after the brilliant burst of flame, and it was this that she savored. There was a wondrous and sweet loneliness in realizing the miracle of being a woman. In that very moment, she experienced the splendor of loving.

Like that she lay, feeling herself riding on each breath Andreas took, imagining her spirit curled in his heart. Ah...how she loved this man...how she was a part of him, and he a part of her.

The light had deepened again, turning a mysterious indigo that further leavened the mood. How well the hue matched the plaintive call of the Greek singer. Now, against the white walls of the room, darkening shadows—flickering, indistinct—passed one after the next in a stately procession. They might have been the gods of daylight, finished with another day's meddling for entertainment. With heavy lids, Kate watched the wavering images creep from the mortal world to greet night in their own realm. When the wind died, the palms were still, and the last god had made his passage safely past the small apartment in which she lay so far from home—and yet home.

The light was violet just before her eyes closed, and all the gods departed.

Chapter Eleven

Kate was not a she-devil, and yet to Andreas, in his present mood, that was precisely what she seemed. She loomed as a beautiful *diábolos* in his mind. She was making him mad with worry. And oh, how small of him, how niggling and unworthy of him to resent her small success as a designer of fashions for the obnoxious Parisian.

Andreas stood in his small bathroom, letting the thin trickle of water from the nozzle play against his shoulders as he lathered soap over his chest. The bathroom's tiny, high window was open and a cool breeze mingled with the tepid flow of liquid. He felt two ways at once: impassioned with love for the woman, and frigid with indignation that she could not be as he would have her. For her very own good, he might add.

Andreas turned around and rinsed the soap from his chest, closing his eyes to the spray.

The image of a small creature formed in the dark space behind his lids. The creature was female, with ridiculously white hair and a tiny face with enormous blue eyes that showed no fear cf anyone or anything, and feet that clattered like busy little paws over the pavement in outlandishly high heels. It was the Frenchwoman. The meddler par excellence. The great troublemaker of Mykonos.

This Simone Z, to whom he had spoken on various occasions over the years that she had frequented the island, was the root of his misery. If there were a true devil in this, thought Andreas as he twisted each tap to its off position, it was Simone Z.

Through some nefarious means, the haughty Frenchwoman had appropriated his woman's soul in return for the promised fame and fortune.

Yes, his woman!

For Kate was his... in bed she was anyway. But it was beginning to seem that this was the only place where he could count himself as a significant part of her life.

Drying himself brusquely with a towel too thin to absorb the moisture on his body before becoming soggy itself, he thought back on that afternoon three weeks ago when they had made love. Ah, just the thought of that time was enough to make his body hot enough to evaporate a bath filled to its brim with water. Even this evening, after a hard day's work at not one but two jobs, the ecstatic memory of their lovemaking still clung to him like a vapor.

But that was a good three weeks ago—or a bad three weeks, if one wanted to be accurate—and a lot had occurred since that time.

Kate had changed considerably since that day when he had rescued her in Athens. She had made a modest success of the design enterprise, with Simone Z commissioning several more outfits for herself, and two more for a couple of her snooty French friends. The result of this was that Kate was beginning to harbor more elaborate notions of her future place in the world.

He did not know that much about design. He did know that Kate couldn't sew worth a damn, but that didn't seem to matter as she'd found some clever Mykonian seamstress to handle that part of her enterprise. Likewise, he had no idea of what the fashion houses in Paris wanted, much less if they could actually want Kate, as Simone Z had ever so subtly inferred. Damn the woman.

He only knew that he wanted Kate. He wanted to love her, to marry her, to take care of her and Jason until his dying breath, and God knew that even after that he would find a way to watch over their welfare.

But he wanted to be responsible for them—that was important, the most important thing of all. What better way to express his love than to provide for them completely? If he were a rich man now, then perhaps all would be different. He could easily and graciously allow her this conceited little hobby of hers, thinking that she could make an independent future for herself.

But it frightened him half to death to think she might actually do such a thing. In independence there lay the possibility that she would not need him and leave him for the glamor of Paris, Milan or New York. To even think of such a thing was terrible enough as it was. If it were to happen, it would be impossible to imagine the toll it would take on him.

Andreas hung the towel on the window's brass knob to dry, left the small room, and moved through the living room toward his bedroom to dress when he happened to pause at the open doorway. There was a sunset this evening, one that should have belonged to late summer rather than April. The heavens were splashed with colors so brilliant, the very air seemed to vibrate with light waves. Beneath the Aegean was a gentle pool of deep slate but for the shoreline where white foam came crashing into the triangle. If he could share this moment with Kate . . . if he could share his life with Kate . . .

If he were a rich man . . . he could.

For the next three weeks he worked himself to the bone. Unfortunately he made very little money doing so. Even though the physical exertion gave him the impression of movement, it was movement on a treadmill. He was going nowhere fast. On the other hand, he was wearing himself out to the point that he could not summon enough energy to continue the almost nightly disagreements he was having with Kate.

Oddly, the disagreements were not because her work was going well and he was resistant to her success. Her work was, indeed, progressing, but not fast enough to suit her. Simone Z had put other ideas into her head—lavish plans that danced like sugarplums before Kate. Simone Z had proposed that Kate leave Mykonos and come to Paris to open a small but exclusive boutique. Simone Z herself would fund half of the enterprise, and would ensure clientele through her upscale social network.

This might have disturbed him greatly, but it did not. For one thing, Kate did not have enough money to invest in such an enterprise, and for another . . . something else was horribly claiming his energies. Kate was seeking yet another means to make herself financially solvent. And this idea was not only on his turf, directly beneath his nose, but in an area that he could very well have made a success of himself—had he thought of it. But he did not. And Kate did.

"Andreas, I have an idea," she said one evening as she looked up from one of her latest sketches. She sat at a jerry-built artist's table Andreas had rigged for her. Three lamps surrounded her, but were still insufficient to cast enough light to properly see her work during the night. Jason lay on the floor doing some work from the Mykonian school he attended. He was learning Greek and now and then would ask Andreas for help, which Andreas loved to provide.

Andreas was lying on the sofa, too exhausted from. digging a ground well that day to do much more than reply to Jason's questions.

"You know all the restaurants that serve French fries with the dinners?" Kate asked.

"Yes."

"Well, they have to peel them and cut them up, and that takes a long time."

"Greeks have a lot of time," said Andreas wearily. "We have not much else. But time we have."

"That's just the point," said Kate, scooting off of her chair and coming to sit on the floor by his side. "If they used their time more wisely, they'd have more of it to advance. They're tremendously out of step with the modern world."

"That's why tourists like you come here. Because we're not like the rest of you. Where else can you come to see such chaos and inefficiency, and find such aggravation? It's our main charm."

"True," she said, and Andreas whacked her playfully on the head. "But really, I have an idea that I think could do some good—and make me a bit of money."

Andreas stopped breathing. He would have liked to have stopped time. Something in his Greek soul instinctively told him that what was next to come was to be the beginning of the end for him. He was not wrong.

"Andreas, I've sent away to America for information on this machine. Well, actually, I've called the company from the telephone exchange this morning. They'll send me all the specifics, and if I want it to be sent out, it can be shipped within two weeks. It'll peel and slice potatoes fast as can be. It will save so much time and money, everyone on the island who has a restaurant will come to me."

Andreas digested the information in one gulp and was immediately sick to his core. It felt as if he had been hit in the gut. Such a machine could alter the course of Mykonian history! And not he, but she . . . a lowly woman whose work should rightly consist of baking, washing and making love, would be responsible for this.

When he said nothing, she ran her hand lightly against his cheek and said, "You're angry?"

"Of course not," he lied through his teeth. "I'm thinking that it is a very good idea, and I'm only sorry that it was you and not me who came up with it. But how could I? I can't go to America and see all of these miraculous machines...I can only work myself into a grave!" He stood up and took a deep breath.

"Andreas," she said, looking up at him, "you've got to understand that I must find my own way in this world. I can't possibly go on not knowing who I am, outside of being someone's wife or mother. I want to know what I can do. I want to have at least the option of being free and independent, rather than be shackled to someone else's idea of me."

"And what happens if you become a millionaire with this machine? So what? Then what will you do? Who will you be?" He was tense with fury, and although he knew he was a totally ridiculous specimen of male insecurity, he couldn't stop the fear from rising.

"I won't possibly become a millionaire. But I could earn enough to start a boutique in Paris, like Simone Z—"

"Simone Z! That snake!"

"She's not a snake."

"She's odd, though," said Jason, who had been following the exchange from the floor.

"Great personalities are often unusual, possibly eccentric," Kate granted defensively.

"You know why she is doing this?" Andreas said. "Because she does not have a man of her own and she is jealous!"

"That's rubbish."

"Will you leave then?" Andreas asked, posing the dreaded question in one breath, steeling himself for the answer now, rather than lose more sleep over her capriciousness.

"Leave Mykonos? I don't know. I'll have to see when that time comes." She stopped, hesitating as if poised between saying something more that might cause a scene and keeping her own counsel. When she did go on, it was with careful deliberation. "Andreas, it's not at all what you think—that I don't care for you. It's just that I've got to do things for myself, too. Don't you see that I've come such a long way from when I left America. Not only in miles, but in feelings about myself and my place in the world."

"What about your place in my life?"

"And that, too. I want everything you want—"

"I only want you."

"No. You want more. You said so, didn't you?"

"You did," interjected Jason. "You said you wanted to travel. Remember?"

"But you can't," agreed Kate, "because there are things holding you back. And you resent it. Well, it's like that for me, too. I want to at least have the opportunity to try to do something."

"You can't have everything, Kate."

"Why not?"

"Because no one can have freedom and—"

"You? Why not?"

"Because . . ."

It was no answer, and he knew it. But it was all the response he could give her. How could he allow himself to appear even smaller in her eyes than he already did in his own? He made himself busy around the apartment, stalking here and there, doing nothing of importance but filling up a lot of space and making more noise than was really necessary. It annoyed him immensely that both Jason and Kate were engaged in projects. It bothered him so much that he made an excuse to leave early.

Kate walked with him to the door and was gentle and concerned as she said goodbye. That somehow was the final straw. As the recipient of her concern, he felt childish and weak. In return he was truculent, and left on a sour note to visit his grandmother.

And if it were possible, which it was, things got even worse there.

Chapter Twelve

Your parents are really coming?'' It had taken Kate a moment to actually digest the information. The question was really, "You actually have parents?" Although Maria was his grandmother in title, the elderly woman seemed somehow an independent entity in her own right, unattached to any particular family lineage. It was even more difficult to imagine Andreas as having strings to other mortals. Kate had come to imagine him as someone magically sprung into the universe arising out of some seashell or a pit of ashes like the phoenix.

"Yes. Yes ... they'll be here tomorrow." Andreas moved slightly to make room for a newly arrived group of diners to be seated at a table behind them. When he repositioned himself, his face settled into the same strained expression he had worn at intervals over the last few weeks.

Generally some bit of diversion would lift his mood, and he would regain his general bright spirit, but tonight the brooding humor clung no matter what topic was touched in conversation. Several times in the past, Kate had attempted to discover the reason for his radical change in temperament. Each time he had put her off, and she had come to believe its cause was related to her potato machine enterprise, which he still heartily opposed.

They sat at the edge of the water at the Sundown Restaurant. It was a pleasant June night without wind, although perhaps a bit chilly. Kate had worn a new jacket that she had designed and had sewn for her by her seamstress, a woman engaged full-time these days, as now even some of the boutiques were purchasing her creations. Music played softly from outdoor speakers, the melodies mingling with the rise and fall of conversations from patrons at other tables. Now and again there were bursts of laughter punctuating some remark.

There was no hint of celebration at their table, however. The dinner had been intended as a special occasion to mark the arrival of the potato machine. She was doubly excited because she had promises from several restaurants to purchase potatoes directly from her. In fact, the very establishment at which they now dined was to be her customer. She had not yet told Andreas of this latest break in her good fortune. This time and place was to have provided the right ambience, and bowing to Andreas's fears, she had practiced a nice little speech that she felt would allay all insecurities once and for all.

"You don't seem to be particularly pleased by your announcement," Kate said, feeling her way around his mood. "I thought all Greeks were devoted to their families."

"I am immensely devoted to my family," Andreas said. He stared out over the water, thinking something that caused his face to turn even more grim.

Beside him, the water lapped softly against the cement embankment on which their table and the others were placed. The restaurant was not merely a place to dine, but because of its location was also somewhat of a public thoroughfare for those who would take shortcuts along the water's edge. Its location also constituted one of the island's most photographed views, and for good reason. Nicknamed Little Venice, it was a section where buildings on tall pilings hung over the Aegean. At times the waves rose high and inundated the restaurants dotting the picturesque area and mortally threatened the stability of the dwellings grown fragile from years of constant assault. But like their mortal Greek counterparts, they clung steadfastly to their terrain, worse for wear but still sustaining.

"Well," she said, trying again to get something going in the way of conversation, "I'll enjoy meeting them."

"They're very simple people," he said absently, picking on his souvlaki without displaying much interest.

"I can take a bit of simplicity," Kate joked, trying not to let his mood affect her. "Where will they stay? With Maria or at your place?"

"My parents will stay with me."

He seemed about to add something when the restaurant owner appeared at their table. He exchanged greetings with Andreas first, and then turning to Kate, smiled and bid her a good-night. To Andreas he said, "Your friend is a very shrewd businesswoman. She has already pushed me into buying two weeks of potatoes."

"Congratulations," said Andreas, with no sign of jubilation. His entire face was expressionless as he looked across the table at Kate.

The restaurant owner excused himself, running off to answer a call from his wife, who stood on a high stoop, grilling fish over coals.

"He's spoiled it!" Kate said. "I was going to tell you myself. I've got several customers already, Andreas." She waited for some sort of reaction, either negative or positive. None was forthcoming.

Instead, Andreas took a sip of his wine, and when he put it down continued their conversation as if the man had never interrupted. "The others will stay with Maria."

Kate readjusted her thoughts to what they had been discussing. "Others?"

"Yes." For the first time he fidgeted uneasily, then made a show of being interested in the skewered lamb on his plate, reassembling the small pieces in a neat line by his rice. "My parents are coming to Mykonos with another family."

It was the way he said it, without any additional information, that alerted Kate that all was not what it seemed. Generally Andreas was expansive in his explanations, sharing with her the most minute details of any ordinary social transaction. It was one of his most attractive qualities. Michael rarely spoke to her of anything but the mechanics of running their household, or to inform her of some latest commercial triumph. Now Andreas was evasive. And there was a reason; she just didn't know it yet. "Oh," she said blandly, looking into her own plate in an attempt to match his casualness, "and I'll expect there'll be quite a celebration—family and friends all getting together."

"In a certain sense."

Kate put down her fork. "Andreas, you're being so mysterious. There's obviously something bothering you. So why not just tell me?"

Andreas had been cutting a piece of meat. He stopped, put down his silverware, and looking directly at Kate, said, "They're bringing me a wife."

Kate said nothing for a moment. The sentence had made no sense to her. To a son one brought a sweater or some cheese from home. One did not arrive to deliver a woman to his doorstep. Then she relaxed. *Of course.* He was telling her this because he wanted to get back at her about the potato business. "Andreas, really, there's no reason for this . . . this silly—"

"It's time I marry, Kate."

She stared at him, suddenly realizing he was serious. "I don't believe it . . . no one brings . . ." But of course it was true, preposterous, but a fact just the same.

"This is Greece, not your country. We have no microwaves in every kitchen here. We have women cooking over slow fires."

"An arranged marriage? For you, Andreas? For you?"

"You asked me if I loved my parents . . . yes, I do. Here in Greece, from the time a boy is born, certain things are drummed into our heads. Maybe not in Athens, but I come from a village. A small place, where tradition still remains. Your American boys are taught that they will go to college and become business executives. That is your brand of tradition. We are also taught. There's nothing so shameful, really. Nothing so archaic as you make it sound. It was the way the world was run all over until just recently."

"Yes. Of course, of course . . ." Where was her wonderful speech now? God, she had been so certain of herself, so sure he wanted her . . . would do anything . . . wait until the end of eternity if there was even the slightest chance of forming a permanent union. Her speech, her stupid, arrogant, wasted little talk was to have given him that hope. She looked down to the fried squid, something she always ordered when dining out, one of her most favorite foods. Now it held no appeal. "It's just that I thought . . . we . . ."

"We, Kate? We?"

"I know," she sighed.

Coldly, Andreas said, "You don't want me. You only like to have me around while you make yourself into this new person you always talk about. And when you do, you'll leave. And me, Kate? What the hell will I do then?"

"That isn't the way it is! You make me sound so self-serving and calculating." And of course she knew she was. But there was nothing else for her to be and do. She had no other choice but to find out about herself, even if it had to be at his expense and the whole world's expense.

"All right," Andreas said wearily. "Perhaps you don't plot and scheme. But I see it coming. I have watched more than one woman leave this island, with a man standing alone, weeping on the shoreline. No," Andreas said, "that's not entirely true. We Greeks never weep before a woman. We weep alone, telling our pillows our sorrows. But you'll forget I told you that. No one is to know that secret."

Kate was trembling inside. She wanted to erase what she had just heard. It had somehow never really occurred to her that she might actually lose him. They had come together with such passion, how could she ever consider that it would fall apart like this? Oh, of course they had their minor wars, but underlying everything was that love...that exquisite love they shared between them. How could any other woman slip into her place, into his bed, into his life?

"I'm sorry," he said, but sounded only partially so; the other part was slightly vengeful. She had driven him to this, and now not only he, but she was to suffer.

"How long have you known about this, Andreas?" she asked softly. "About them bringing you this wife?"

"For a while," he said flatly. "My grandmother told me when I left your apartment a few weeks ago. I was very angry that night—about your machine."

"I remember." If she had not been so adamant about her career...

"And it was then that she told me."

"And you said nothing? We made love all those times, and you said nothing about this?"

"I love you, Kate. But I can't have you. I can only have the girl from the village. I took what I could of you, just as you've been taking what you could of me. While it lasted."

"The girl from the village." Kate sighed. Her mind formed quick images of the other woman. Each face was beautiful, angelic, domestic and giving. Oh, God... She looked away from the lights of the restaurant and into the dark quiet of the Aegean. The moon was almost full. There was a silver halo surrounding its circumference. "Doesn't it even matter to you that you don't love her?"

"Maybe I will. Someday."

She had not expected this last cruelty, and looked back at him. "How could you say that?"

"It's realistic, isn't it?" Andreas leaned back, his face appearing much older, as if since the conversation had begun, lines had formed at his mouth, and creases had suddenly taken possession of his forehead. Beneath the shock of dark hair, the green eyes were pained but reconciled.

Of course he was calm tonight; unlike her, he'd had weeks to prepare for the inevitability of their relationship's end.

"So what happens now?" she asked, trying to remain dignified and adult.

"They will come, and there will be some dinners, talks between me and the girl's parents. And then—"

"Go on...and then?"

"Then I will say yes or no."

"Like she is a cow," Kate said scornfully.

"This is Greece."

"It's barbaric. And if you say you don't want her?"

"Then," said Andreas, "I had better have a damn good reason. A frivolous refusal would bring shame and dishonor to my parents. Just by bringing her all this way, there is a certain inevitability to the arrangement. I'm thirty-three. The girl, I understand, is nineteen. She is supposed to be attractive and a good woman. Her family and my family have known each other since they were children. Her family owns much land, and it would be a good match all the way around. No one expects there to be any problem.''

''So it's all but done,'' Kate said, her voice rising in restrained hysteria.

''All but the wedding.''

''I'd like to go home now.'' Kate stood. She almost knocked the table over, she came up with such abrupt force. The whole scene around her swam before her eyes, colors of lights and dresses and food and the moon and the sea, all bleeding into one jumbled picture. She didn't wait for Andreas, couldn't wait for him. Instead she began to walk rapidly through the aisle, then beginning to cry, she ran, not caring if anyone saw her or not. There were some times when it was pointless to be cool.

''Stop him from doing this, Mom!'' Jason was screaming at her. There was no eleven-hundred-year-old man of wisdom here. There was only a frantic boy with tears streaming over his freckled face.

''Jason...please...''

But he had thrown himself down on her bed and was weeping. It was so unlike him to succumb to hysteria that for a moment Kate could only stand where she was, amazed by the outburst. She was only half emotionally operable herself and his breakdown severely tested her strength, all of which she was going to need to get through the dinner.

She sat at the edge of the bed, rubbing his back and saying soothing things, which had no impact. Jason rose from his prone position, and with a face swollen with grief, pleaded with her to tell Andreas not to marry the girl from the village.

Kindly, Andreas had suggested to her that he speak to Jason himself, explaining the situation to him man to man. But Jason was not a man. He was a child, a little boy who had loved a man with his whole heart and was now being abandoned.

"Please, Mom," Jason implored. "If you tell him you'll marry him, he'll never leave us for that girl."

"But, Jason . . . don't you see that I can't marry Andreas now?"

"Why? Why can't you?" He looked at her accusingly.

"Because I don't want to be tied down to anyone now. It's my time to be me, me alone. And Andreas has some very definite ideas of how a woman should be. He'd never allow me to do my designs, or have the potato business."

"I love Andreas, Mom. I don't care about designs or . . . or televisions or . . . or anything. I love Andreas. We went fishing together and we talk about the gods, and he's teaching me to scuba dive. He let me drive his friend's boat."

"He'll still do that," Kate said. "Just because he doesn't have a relationship with me, it doesn't mean you can't be friends anymore."

"Sure," said Jason, a coldness replacing the heartache. Something traveled behind his eyes, a thought no longer belonging to the child he was, and Kate saw the ancient soul once again step into place. "When you and Dad split up, that was the end of it with him. Totally."

He stood and moved quickly, with dignity, from the room. From over his shoulder, he said, "Call me when you're ready. I'll be in the loft."

"We don't have to go, Jason," Kate called to his back. Suddenly the whole idea of being adult about the whole thing seemed stupid and entirely too much for her to fake.

That morning she had made a special point to seek Andreas out and explain that whereas she was certainly upset by his decision to marry, under the circumstances she could understand his position, and they would—she hoped—remain friends. It was a magnanimous gesture, she felt, considering her true feelings. But she did it partly for her own self; in a way it was like being dumped yet again. Not exactly, of course, but it had a certain similarity in pain if not in identical circumstance.

Jason returned, stepping in from the hall and facing her. "No," Jason said, "we do have to go."

"I can tell Maria we thought better of it. She'll understand."

"No," Jason said again, his expression one of adamant determination. "She doesn't have him yet. I'm not giving up. I'm going to be there." With that, he made a complete exit.

The dinner was an entirely grim experience.

The two nuclear families, including Maria, Jason and Kate, sat around Maria's dining room table. The food was marvelous. Maria had performed some last-minute magic in her kitchen and an astounding array of delicacies appeared as if by a genie's hand from the medieval kitchen. No matter how excellent the fare, nothing could relax the atmosphere.

The girl, Kate hated to admit, was lovely. She had long, dark hair that gleamed, as did the long black sweep of her eyelashes upon milky skin. Her eyes were equally dark and flashed brightly whenever she stole a shy glance at her intended. She spoke little, and always in Greek, so Kate could not venture an opinion of her personality, but her smile was nothing short of dazzling. The only thing Kate could think of every time she looked from Andreas to the girl was that they would have magnificent children.

It was impossible to summon hatred for the girl, whose whole demeanor radiated innocence. She was, however, quite capable of experiencing profound misery. Of course she hid it. She helped with the serving, and commented upon each dish, nodding and smiling to both sets of parents whenever there was an occasion that prompted a response. They did not speak any English.

As for Andreas, Kate watched him as often as she could without making herself look entirely obvious. Two or three times, however, he caught her in the act and a certain shock wave of understanding reached across the table. He knew her anguish, but in his glance she also read his rebuke and the message that this was the price that she must pay for having played with his love.

Well, she was paying. And dearly.

Jason was perhaps the greatest actor of them all. He was maddeningly adorable, helping with everything, and haltingly following the conversations in Greek. Whenever he saw the opportunity, he would insert some comment of his own, and be duly rewarded for his brave American effort with broad smiles and head nodding. But he was playing mostly to an audience of one: Andreas. If Kate would do nothing to lure him back, then Jason was doing his best to remind Andreas of the good times they'd had together.

Observing Jason's desperate attempts only made Kate's heart break more.

Dinner was suddenly over.

As if rehearsed, the men rose together and departed for the outside. Andreas glanced once at Kate before he left. She could not read his look, but Jason whispered a moment later to her, ''They're going to go talk about it now.'' As he spoke, he was white-faced and trembling. She supposed she was the same.

Chapter Thirteen

That night, Andreas tapped on her door. He did so stealthily, like a man with a secret to hide. And of course that was true. The girl's parents and the girl were at that very moment only steps above them.

Kate opened the door, letting him in.

"Oh, Andreas," she whispered with a sigh. She was as sorry to see him as she was glad.

"I know. I know... I should not be here."

He had been drinking. She could tell the moment she saw his heavy-lidded eyes.

"Kate..." he said, even the single word slurred. "I can't love her—only you."

But before she could protest that his sentiments were only the liquor talking, he curled her into his arms and pressed his lips against hers.

It was impossible to escape the passion that arose the moment their bodies were together. She didn't know how much he'd had to drink, but it had to have been a lot to have altered his speech. Regardless, it hadn't damaged his libido. She knew she was a fool and would wake in the morning to regret her weakness, but at that moment she could do nothing to help herself. She gave in to her desire, and with her finger placed to his lips, quieted him as she led him into her bedroom and locked the door.

For an instant, while she stood on the opposite side of the room, separated from him and the fire he elicited in her, a momentary flash of logic arose. "Oh, Andreas...for heaven's sake. What are we doing? You can't come here anymore, Andreas. It's not right. Not for any of us."

In the soft light of the room, he might have been a prince from some gloriously illustrated children's fairy tale. He still had on the same shirt as at the dinner—a yellow polo shirt with a tiny black crest embroidered over the pocket—and white slacks. Beneath the fabric was a lean and muscular body, tanned to a rich brown, a body she'd known so well and had loved so well. The thick chaos of black curling hair contrasted dramatically with the shirt's color, and standing before her, he looked luxuriantly sensuous. There was a sculptured refinement about him, a nobility of line in his straight nose and cleanly chiseled jaw and cheekbones—yet there was such softness to his mouth, and the eyes, ah...they glowed deep and dark in the shadows cast by his brow. The intensity of his glance promised an endless night of delight. God help her, but she was only flesh and blood.

"It's right, Kate," Andreas claimed passionately. "What's not right is that we will not share the same bed for the rest of our lives as man and wife. That, if anything, is not right."

He was slipping out of his clothes as he spoke, as if there were no chance she might reject him. But of course she wouldn't. It was impossible for them to resist each other. All night, she had wanted him, wanted him as never before, perhaps because she knew he was forever off-limits. Certainly she had believed that. It had never entered her mind that they would lie in each other's arms one more time.

But now he was here, after all, and she would not send him away. She would physically love him now with as much passion as she possibly could.

Slipping from the thin nightgown she wore, she stepped into the muted pool of light from overhead. She'd placed a thin, diaphanous kerchief in a paisley design around the bulb for a softening effect. His eyes moved hungrily over her body, taking in every part of her, as she had him a moment before.

This was her man, and she was his. There was nothing separate between them. This one night, this singular gift from the gods, was a time she would have to remember forever. Tomorrow he would be sober, and tomorrow she would have time to repent, but tonight . . . ah, tonight . . .

They came together slowly, in measured footsteps across the room. When he finally embraced her again, it was with a heart-wrenching moan. "My love!" he cried, and like a starving man moved his mouth over her eyes, tasting her tears, her mouth, lingering over her breast, lower to her belly, exploring every part of her until she thought she might faint from the aching pleasure he brought over her.

Falling onto the mattress, they pressed themselves into each other's souls, calling out the other's name, branding each other with a touch, a sound, a look that would last forever.

His body was demanding of hers. He sought and conquered; gently one moment and with a feverish domination the next. Time after time he brought her to heights she had not experienced before. And she, in turn, made him cry out in an ecstasy that was a mixture of pain and bliss, the love and loss merging in a delirium of desire that repeated itself until they both lay satiated in each other's arms.

The sorrow came with the first light of dawn.

"Kate...Kate?"

Kate opened her eyes slowly, hovering between the dream she had been having and the sound of Andreas's voice. "Oh..." she sighed, a smile curling onto her lips as first she saw his face, and then remembered their night of love. But the happiness faded with the realization that it was stolen passion, and in his eyes she read the same message.

"Kate...I must go," he said, an undercurrent of shame riding to the surface.

Once they would have lain together talking, then again would make love. They would have shared the freshness of the morning with each other, and planned their schedules for the day. But all would have been done "together." Now they were singular in their intents. And forever after it would be this way.

She turned her face away, biting her lip to keep from making a fool of herself and pleading with him not to marry the girl, but to abandon his family, his culture, and gamble his very life on her. But he would refuse. He had refused before, given the same conditions and the same information as she had offered to him. And there was no way to blame him; this misery was all her doing. And now it was even more impossible to reconsider the continuance of their relationship. His family was involved too deeply for him to back out of his commitment.

"Kate," Andreas said, turning her face back, "you know I love you."

"I know," she said, her voice hollow with the emptiness she was feeling throughout the rest of her.

"What will we do?" he asked of her, his voice begging for an answer, which they both knew was impossible to find.

"There's nothing to do. We'll have to go on," she said. "You in your way, me in mine."

"But we love each other!" He shook her by her shoulders, and a tear splashed against her breast. Furious with despair, he collapsed against the mattress, murmuring what might have been prayers or curses in Greek, "All right," he said wearily, and brought himself into a sitting position at the edge of the bed. "You're right. We will do what we must, each of us. We will each do what we feel is right." He said it with such darkness that for a moment Kate was afraid.

"Andreas..."

He laughed, reading her mind. "No, my darling Kate...you will not see me at the bottom of the Aegean conversing with Poseidon."

After the dramatic few days during which the girl and her family remained on Mykonos, life became much as it had before but for the knowledge that the marriage was inevitable if not immediate.

Although Kate and Andreas maintained a friendliness, they had not been involved physically again. Between them there seemed to exist a mutual understanding that to continue sleeping together would only make the ultimate withdrawal from each other more difficult. The level of their last physical encounter was too potent, so desperately intense that additional experiences on that level could prove shattering.

For several days she could not bring herself to ask Andreas about the details of the betrothal. There was a certain truth to the old adage "ignorance is bliss." Maybe it wasn't bliss, exactly, but not knowing precisely when and where the occasion would take place allowed her to maintain a certain denial of the situation.

In the meantime, her potato business was, in a word, booming. Almost every major restaurant on the island had become her customer. She had set up her machine in an out-of-the-way warehouse, once used as a barn, and had five employees working full-time, some working the machine, others picking up the potatoes from the produce distributor, and still others delivering the finished product to the customers. Besides this, she was working on more designs, the dream of her own Parisian salon beginning to take more concrete form. The money she was making on the potatoes was starting to add up to a nice sum. And Simone Z came by often, offering encouragement to continue her design efforts.

All of this gladdened Kate, but maybe not quite as much as she'd expected. The whole golden idea of her independence had become somehow tarnished now that she knew Andreas would not be a part of the final triumph.

It was Jason who finally brought her the details of the arrangement as agreed upon between Andreas and the girl's family.

"Andreas said he will not marry until he has something to offer his wife. So he's not getting married yet. He's still ours," Jason finished brightly.

"No, Jason, he isn't." Kate stood in their kitchen, stirring a pot of chicken stew, the recipe given to her by Maria. She and Jason were regular paying tenants now, yet the feeling of "family" still existed. "Here, taste this and tell me if it even remotely resembles something you've tasted from Maria's kitchen."

Jason opened his mouth and nodded affirmatively. But his mind was clearly not on food. "He's here with us, and not her. Possession's nine-tenths of the law. Remember? Dad always used to tell us that."

"But this isn't America. And Andreas isn't a car or an apartment building."

"Mom, don't you love Andreas?"

"That's not the issue, Jason. As we've discussed before."

"But do you love him?" he persisted.

"Yes. Yes . . . I love Andreas Pateras. But loving him and being able to live with him as a permanent, married fixture of his life is not the same thing. Jason," she said, piqued, "Andreas and I both understand that we have to go on with our lives." More gently, she added, "And you, too." Jason stared up at her, taking in the information, but by the look in his eyes she doubted he was filing it away under the right subheading. "What are you thinking, Jason?" she quizzed with suspicion.

"Nothing, Mom," he replied with too much innocence to be believed. "Mom, can I have some more of that stew?"

Andreas walked in long strides along the shoreline. He wore a black wet suit, goggles and a mouthpiece that reached upward. In one hand he carried an automatic three-pronged fishing spear, in the other the long, black flippers.

"You look great," said Jason, skipping happily alongside. "Like a devil!" Jason carried the bag that would hold their catch.

"I feel like the devil," said Andreas, stopping to examine their position. "Good," he said "we will fish here." It was late afternoon, and Andreas had borrowed his friend's speedboat to make the forty-minute ride to Delos. The water had been choppy, but they had managed to survive the trip and here on Delos the wind was down. Further on the other side of the island, tourists were still crawling over the ruins of temples, but where they had moored there was only the call of seabirds and the slap of the water against the large brown rocks jutting out of the shallows.

Jason cautiously waded in after Andreas. Each step was precarious, as beneath the water's surface the undergrowth was slippery. Eventually he came to a shoal deep enough to launch himself, and belly down, kicked off to join Andreas in the crystalline water. Andreas had given Jason his own small mask through which he examined the tiny marine life below.

Now and again Andreas would make a sudden dive and emerge a moment later with a fish on the end of his spear. Jason, dragging the catch bag along behind him, would float over and take possession of the booty, returning with it to the rocks where he would set about cleaning it the way Andreas had shown him. A small octopus was caught and, carrying out orders from Andreas, Jason slapped the limp carcass against the rocks to tenderize it for later consumption. In an hour, the bag was filled with enough fish and a good supply of the spiny black sea urchin, for the proposed fish roast they were to have that evening.

On the way home in the speedboat, Jason was allowed to steer while Andreas relaxed beside him, lost in troubled thoughts.

"Are you sad?" Jason asked as they came into the harbor at a reduced speed.

"No, I'm fine." Andreas made an attempt at good cheer, smiling broadly as he took over the piloting.

Jason scooted over, kneeling by his side.

Ahead of them were the lights of Chora, the white sugar-cube buildings rising in steps above the Aegean. Even in the distance, one could feel the island's vibrancy, and as they came ever closer, tiny moving specs turned into the forms of tourists parading past the harbor. Already some of the sturdy and colorfully painted caïques were moored in the bay, and bobbed gently in the calm sea.

"Do you love her still?" Jason asked of Andreas when they had landed on shore.

"Yes, of course I love your mother still," he replied, but without gladness.

"She loves you, too."

"But she loves this dream of her independence more," he replied.

"I know," Jason said glumly. "Women!"

Andreas ruffled him on the head. "Indeed. They are a magnificent lot, and full of trouble for us."

Together they passed the outdoor tavernas, now only partially filled. It was the off period, the time between late afternoon when people were returning from the beach, and night, when the discos and restaurants would be teeming with life. Still, there were many tourists gathered to sip iced coffee frappés, or indulging in pastries, or cooling off from the afternoon's heat with bottles of Greek beer. There were women so beautiful even Jason's head turned to follow the long-legged girls in their halter tops and scanty shorts. A group of long-haired Italian men in flamboyant attire bantered jocularly and loudly at a table. And always, always there was the music, Greek, American, English, filling the air with romantic promise.

Rather than incite good spirits, however, the resort atmosphere further depressed Andreas, who snapped at Jason when he continued to inquire about his feelings. They were just on the harbor's border, where the narrow paths began, turning into the inner village, when Andreas's spirit finally broke like a ferocious summer storm that had been gathering force for far too long.

Stopping, he turned sideways to Jason and in a harsh voice, never before used to the boy, said, "This is all about money, Jason. This whole rotten mess is because I have no money and your mother wants to live a life of luxury. Oh, she says she wants to do it herself, and that is admirable. That maybe I can understand—she thinks then she will be safe from having a man leave her with nothing to fall back upon. But even if she is successful, then what? Do you think that will matter? No. No, it won't matter one bit!" His face was clouded with misery long held inside. "Because I cannot be with her even then. Because I will not be a man in her eyes. The only way is if I have something of my own to equal what she has. And better to have more—much more. But there is nothing for me here. In all of Greece there is no chance for me to make something of myself."

"You mean," asked Jason, "that if you had something of your own then you and Mom might get it together?"

"Ask Zeus!" Andreas said angrily, and started away with the bag of fish. "Only the gods can know the craziness that is in a woman's mind! Who else can predict?"

Jason scampered after Andreas, his eyes upturned to the clouds drifting leisurely past like vast gondolas on which gods invisible to mortal eyes might lounge.

Kate's ultimate defeat came in the third week of July, just when things could not have been any better. The debacle occurred with the swiftness of the executioner's blade and finality of one's head rolling into the basket. She was finished.

The first hint of trouble came in the early morning when she received word from her largest client on the island that he was not going to be purchasing any more potatoes from her. She was on her way out the door of the warehouse to speak with him about the matter when her second most important customer arrived to relate the same news—no more potatoes.

"But why?" she asked, stricken and confused by the sudden rejection of her service, which only a day before had been lauded by both establishments as having saved them time and money.

"I am sorry," the man mumbled, offering no explanation, and backing away as if he himself had done some terribly embarrassing act for which he must feel shame.

And so it went, one after the next, her accounts canceled their business with her, all with apologies, but without any real explanation.

It was only when she approached the owner of a restaurant, who had not even had the guts to come to her himself, that she learned the truth.

"It is that Yiorgos, from Kos. He is the one behind it."

"I don't understand," Kate said. The only Yiorgos from Kos she knew was the man who owned the produce stand where she herself purchased potatoes. Even tomorrow she was scheduled to buy a week's supply to store in her place for her customers. What reason would Yiorgos have to sabotage her business?

"He said to us that he will not sell us any produce at all, if we are to purchase any more sliced potatoes from you. And he owns the only three places on the island where we can get our vegetables. We have no choice," the man said sorrowfully, his heart clearly disturbed by the unfortunate business.

"I see," Kate said. "But why? Why?"

"It is because he, too, has your potato machine. He thought he can make all the money himself. He does not need you. You need him. Go, you will see, you will not get any more potatoes from him."

Enraged, Kate said, "Then I'll get potatoes from the mainland."

"No," the man said, and shook his head. "It would cost too much to ship for you alone. This man brings in a great deal—all kinds of things. He gets bulk rates." Then he paused, and with a sigh, said, "Look, this man is very, very bad. This man does not just own the produce stands. He owns three hotels. And now he is going to buy a restaurant. He has bought land here. Always, he gobbles up things. And you can not fight him. He is too clever. He is an evil man, really. Once, when some farmers tried to bring in truck-loads of produce from the mainland—coming over on the ferryboat—this Yiorgos was so furious he paid to have the poor men beaten up by thugs from Athens. It was not just a lesson to those who suffered the beating, but for those who might want to come up against this *diábolos* from Kos themselves."

And there it was: in one day, her ruin.

Kate returned to the warehouse and explained the situation to her idle employees. She managed to remain cool throughout her short speech, announcing that her enterprise was no longer in operation. No one questioned her, but she had known there would be no third degree. By now she knew the efficiency of the Greek gossip lines. In speed of transmittal, the Greeks' social networking would rival the most sophisticated telecommunications equipment in the world.

At home she shut the front door, walked into her bedroom, lay down on her bed and wept. She must have fallen asleep because the next thing she knew, Jason was gently shaking her.

"Mom, Mom..." he said, "you were asleep, but you were crying and talking and ... what's wrong, Mom?"

"You can forget about your French lessons," Kate said, pushing herself up from her pillow to lean on her elbows. Her entire body felt leaden, as if she had been beaten like those poor farmers who had come to Mykonos with such hope. "France is finished for me. I'm finished for me."

Jason listened as she explained her woes, his face becoming more and more enraged with every word she uttered. "I'm going to kill him! This Yiorgos pig deserves to die!" He bounced from the bed onto the floor, and by the look on his face, Kate thought that he actually might try to assault the wicked merchant from the island of Kos. There was something in his manner, something in his choice of words, and the style in which he uttered them, that reminded her exactly of Andreas. It almost made her smile; but she didn't. She was entirely too sad and exhausted.

"I'd try to get even with the rat myself," she said, pulling Jason back, and holding his hand, as much for her own comfort as for his. "But it wouldn't do any good—bigger, meaner guys than us have tried to get even with that bum. We're just going to have to take our lumps."

Jason's eyes seemed to fold thoughts over and over, and with each turn his gaze became harder and older, until they bore a lethal hatred unthought of for a boy going from eleven to twelve. He pulled himself away, and as he did, Kate saw the child she had known drift from her arms and a male person face her. "I'm going to tell Andreas," Jason said. "Andreas and I will settle this."

"Jason! Jason, no!" But he had already slipped out the door by the time she had gotten there to demand he not involve Andreas. Anyway, she could not have stopped Jason. He was becoming more than a boy and more than just *her* son.

Chapter Fourteen

Andreas pondered the news Jason had just broadcast from his enraged eleven-year-old lungs. It was a masterful display of vengeful fury, in Andreas's opinion; what's more, he'd grant the dramatic outburst as being worthy of a genuine Greek in vocal timbre, gesticulation, and degree of pathos expended in the telling. Any more emotion and the whole thing would have become whiny and silly. But Jason had carried his part well, maintaining a delicate balance between too much and too little.

"So," Andreas said solemnly although he was, in fact, somewhat elated, "that snake in the grass Yiorgos has struck again with his greed." He shook his head. "One day, he'll own all of Mykonos."

"Then stop him!" demanded Jason. "Let's go and bash his brains in."

"And land in prison?"

"No one has to know it was us. We'll go at night when he's alone."

"That's not a good idea," Andreas said flatly.

"Then in the day!"

"No time is good. He has a dog. Even meaner than he is. We'd be eaten in five minutes." It was not the response Jason had expected from him, and Andreas could clearly see that he had gone down several notches in the boy's estimation. Ordinarily this might have upset Andreas, but his joy over the defunct potato business was so great nothing could dim his good mood. *The woman he loved would need him again.*

Jason had found him at an outside taverna by the harbor, sitting with several of his friends talking about politics. When the boy had arrived, something had lifted in Andreas's otherwise weary soul, a feeling of proud paternalism taking root in his heart as Jason approached. Andreas noted how the boy had grown in the last few months since he had arrived on Mykonos, and there were the beginning traces of the man he would become one day. In spite of it being foolish, Andreas looked instinctively for some traces of himself in Jason, as if by way of emotional contact he had infused the American child with his own spirit.

Andreas had excused himself from his friends, and moving to a corner table, the two spoke privately of the situation. There was the distinct, homey feeling of being father and son. Andreas liked the intimacy very much. The entire scene was much the way he had envisioned parenthood. Always in the back of his mind was the picture of he and Kate and Jason, a family. The rest of the fantasy was that perhaps one day Kate would bear him a child, but if not, Jason would fill that slot superbly.

In front of them, smoke from forty or fifty Greek cigarettes drifted upward like phantom bodies, and the surrounding sounds were deep and masculine, filling one with an expanded sense of camaraderie. This particular establishment for some reason—possibly its location off to the far side of the harbor—attracted more Greeks than tourists, and therefore more men than women. Greek women knew their places. They were home gossiping with each other, tending the children, cooking for when their men returned. Andreas lived half with this standard, and half with what he'd come to understand from the tourist women from less traditional cultures. Kate was a radical extreme from what he had been raised to expect from a female.

"You should see her," Jason said miserably. "You can't imagine how she looks."

At that disclosure, Andreas finally did feel badly. He had been thinking solely of his own position up until now, and realizing that the situation must have cut deeply into Kate, he felt the first pangs of sympathetic sorrow burn into him. He could imagine her devastation after having been so happy, after having worked so hard.

"Yes," Andreas said. "We must do something to help her."

"Then kill Yiorgos!"

"Something else."

"There's nothing else. He deserves to die."

"There's always something else," Andreas said. "We only have to think about it."

"Money. That's the only thing. She wanted money to start her own business, so she could be her own person...you know," Jason said. He sat with back bowed and his chest sunken in.

"Money," echoed Andreas, even more despondently. "Why couldn't she want flowers or candy, like other women? Why did she want to conquer the world?"

"Because she's crazy," said Jason.

"I know."

"So are you," Jason added.

"Of course," Andreas agreed. "I love her."

For a week, Jason and Andreas racked their brains for ways to raise Kate's spirits. They suggested picnics that she would not go on, and fishing excursions were turned down flat. Magazines and books purchased from the international bookstore were left unopened, and dinners cooked by Maria to cheer her up went uneaten.

"It's like she's dying inside," Jason confided to Andreas one evening at the taverna by the harbor where Jason had taken to meeting him after work. Andreas sat with a beer, Jason with a Coke. "Her body keeps going, but there's nothing in it hardly anymore. She just moves around."

Andreas lit a second cigarette before he had finished the first one. He had been doing things like that lately. This business with Kate had totally distracted him. He felt like he should do something, but couldn't find a single way to improve the situation.

His skin was a dark brown, making his eyes appear even more extraordinary than usual, and when he smiled he looked like the model on one of the Greek tourist posters over which females swooned. Even now women would linger as they paraded past and surreptitiously gawk, speculating on his availability among themselves. Andreas was somewhat aware of the dazzling effect he had on the female species, but he could not have cared less. His entire being was caught up in the problem of how to please just one woman.

He stared down at his hands, brooding over the situation. His hands were rough, with tiny cuts on them from pulling rope without gloves, as he had been working for a good part of the summer with four other men who were adept at finding water and digging wells. His shoulders had grown more powerful and his arms were impressively muscular. He was probably in peak physical condition. But it was his mind that would not work right!

If only there were a way to earn his own fortune. He could rescue Kate, thereby earning her respect and gratitude, and he would also have a future for himself—which would also earn Kate's respect. Everything he thought about, everything he did, revolved around this one single woman. It was a madness he could not shake.

"Do you want something else?" Andreas asked Jason when the waiter came to take an additional order. "Something to eat?"

"No. I'm not hungry."

"Eat. It will make you feel better!" commanded Andreas. "Tell me what you like." The waiter hovered restlessly over them, anxious to go on to other tables.

"Chocolate chip cookies," Jason muttered dolefully.

"What are these chocolate chip cookies?" asked Andreas.

"They're good. Especially when they're hot. On days I ended up warming the bench in Little League and felt real bad, Mom would make me chocolate chips, and I'd feel better. They're like vitamins or something. I don't know...there's something in them. They cheer you up."

To the waiter, Andreas said, "Bring him some baklava." To Jason he said, "We don't have chocolate chip cookies. Anyway, it's all in the mind. You can pretend with the baklava."

For a while they were silent, thinking their own morose thoughts. Then Andreas looked up at Jason and said, "How do you make them? These cookies?"

Jason thought for a moment, seemingly checking an inventory in his mind. "Flour, I guess. Butter or margarine or that white stuff that comes in a big can. Eggs. Uh, sugar...a lot of sugar. Yeah.'' He thought some more. ''Salt, maybe. Nuts and the chocolate chips...and, maybe something that's in those little bottles...vanilla, I think. I'm not sure. But it's a lot of stuff all mixed up and then you cook it and it tastes...'' His eyes became a bit unfocused, as if he imagined a heavenly scene. ''They taste really, really great.''

Andreas nodded, reviewing what he had just been told. ''Come,'' he said, and rose abruptly. ''We will go and find these ingredients. Maybe I can't bring your mother money to cheer her up, but I will bring her cookies!'' He slapped enough drachmas to cover their refreshments on the table, and they were off.

It was not an entirely easy thing, the accumulating of the cookie makings. In fact, it took two hours of walking from this market to that, until they finally had what Jason considered to be the main ingredients to put something together that might reasonably resemble the product that would cure Kate of her melancholy.

Together they worked in Maria's kitchen. It was hot as hell upstairs, and even with the window open they were still sweating with the oven blasting away. But when the first batch was taken out of the old black iron inferno and set on the table to cool, the smells emanating from the small room were reward enough for their creative efforts.

When the second batch was put into the oven, they tasted the first cookies.

Both Jason and Andreas chewed with deep concentration, neither of them speaking while the sampling was under way. Almost at the same time, their hands reached out for seconds. When their eyes met, they each nodded.

''Well?'' Andreas asked when he had sampled the second cookie.

"These aren't like the one's Mom used to make," Jason said, appearing mystified.

Andreas's face fell.

"Andreas..." Jason said, in a voice of awe, "these cookies, well...these cookies are something else. They're...they're incredible!"

"Incredible good or incredible bad?"

Jason was standing near the open window. As he went to gesture widely with his arms, he happened to catch sight of the street below. There were three groups of people down below, tourists kind of straggling as they passed by. They were looking up where Jason was looking down at them. The lot of them seemed to have their noses wiggling about, trying to get a fix on the aroma wafting down to street level.

Now preoccupied by what he saw below, Jason said, "They're great, Andreas."

Andreas moved quickly to view what had caught Jason's attention, and seeing the people, began to look himself for what the attraction might be. It dawned on him slowly.

He looked back to the cookies on the table, still warm but cool enough to eat.

"Ah," he said. "Ah..."

Acting quickly, he gathered a few samples onto a plate and took all seventeen steps down to the street on a run. Jason watched from the window, as Andreas smiled his old *kamaki* smile, utterly irresistible, and holding out the plate said with added Greek inflection, "You would like to try, please?" Foreigners loved that old Greek hospitality routine.

There was a sudden rush of hands and some laughing and bright remarks about the smell being enough to kill for, and then some silence as everyone chewed and swallowed, and Andreas waited through all of this patiently, and finally the words of amazed praise. "God, these are fantastic!" said one of the girls. "You got drugs in these?" laughed another guy. "You made these?" someone else inquired.

"Yes," said Andreas.

"Where'd you get the recipe?" asked one of the girls.

Andreas grinned, and looking up to the heavens, said, "Zeus!"

And everyone laughed. But not Andreas.

Kate was unsure of how she felt about Andreas's recent success with the cookie business. It was only three weeks old, his venture, and already he had changed to the point that she hardly recognized him. If he had shown up at her door in a three-piece business suit, she would hardly have been surprised.

Now, as she sat in the corner of her sofa, her feet curled beneath her, haphazardly attempting to sketch an outfit for one of Simone Z's friends—a Spanish countess who would be arriving in less than a week and expecting to pick up her finished frock—Andreas stood before her in a blue polo shirt and beige slacks, looking as if he might have stepped off one of the luxury yachts docked in the harbor.

"Why won't you go out with me?" he pleaded. "The night is wonderful—there's absolutely no wind."

"I have to do this," Kate said sulkily. It wasn't fair to take out her disappointment on Andreas, but she couldn't help it. Actually, she felt she was doing rather well just to carry on as well as she had since her potato empire had crumbled.

"Do it tomorrow. Tonight we will eat at Katrine's."

At this Kate raised her eyes. She chewed on the end of her pencil, and said, "Katrine's, huh?"

"I can afford it," Andreas said proudly.

"Your cookies are doing that well, are they?" She had gone back to her sketching, but was barely able to keep her mind on it. That Andreas was doing so well might have made her glad if the circumstances were different. For one thing, it meant that he was working hard in order to satisfy the requirements for his marriage promise. That didn't exactly gladden her heart. And for the other, it seemed a direct reflection upon her inability to achieve her own goal.

A few times over the past couple of weeks she had been out shopping and had run across the cookies being sold in various shops and restaurants, mostly as a favor to Andreas by his merchant friends. Also, both Maria and Jason were out with trays strapped around their shoulders, selling them to tourists as fast as they could be baked. All day and half the night, the aroma of the Zeus Cookies pervaded her apartment, as even her own oven had been appropriated by Jason to turn out the enormous quantities of product required to satisfy the voracious demand of cookie addicts.

"More than well," Andreas replied. "Today I have rented a shop of my own."

"Really?" Kate said, once again looking up in surprise. "So soon?"

"Soon?" Andreas said with self-deprecation. "I am thirty-three years old. This is not soon. This is an embarrassment. And even for this, I had to borrow money from my friends. If I fail, I will kill myself. But I won't fail. I believe totally in what I can do now." He sat down beside her, and taking the pencil away, placed her fingers in his hand. "Kate," he said, with shining eyes the color of emeralds, "I have dreamed of this happening for so long that when I wake in the morning and have, at last, somewhere to go and something to do, I half believe I am still dreaming. But this is real, my love—"

"Andreas, don't. Please." She withdrew her hand, and looking down into her half-finished sketch, said, "Don't call me your love anymore."

"You are my love, Kate." He reached up and pushed a strand of her hair from her cheek, anchoring it behind her ear. The rest of her dark hair had been pushed to one side. It was long enough to fall gracefully over her shoulder.

"You are going to be married to another woman soon." It came out bitterly, as an accusation. Immediately she was sorry, and felt foolish, as well. She was punishing him for what she herself had engineered. Since her business had fallen apart, she even felt more adamant that she not marry until she was totally and completely independent. It made no difference that she lay awake nights burning from the want of Andreas in her bed. What respect could either of them have for her now if she came crawling back? What a crock it would all appear: all her high ideals, her noble speeches of how she must be her own woman first, before she could be his—or any man's—woman.

"Not until I have enough money to give the woman I love everything she deserves and wants, will I take a bride. So we have time. I'm not nearly at my goal."

His eyes burned into her. They had not made love for so long, she could barely stand the proximity of his body to hers. It was agony not to press herself into his arms. To hell with morality, to hell with principles. But pride was the determining factor—base pride kept her from opening her heart and her body to him, as she so dearly wanted to do.

She struggled to keep herself aloof. If she gave him the slightest invitation and he took it, she would not be able to resist. "It sounds like you're speeding right along, though," Kate said.

"I have much to accomplish. But I will do everything very swiftly. I must," he said. "But, anyway, I have the gods on my side for once."

"Your gods again."

"Look," Andreas said, standing. He pulled a folded piece of paper from his pocket and flattening it, held it out for Kate's inspection.

It was a pen-and-ink sketch of the head of the god Zeus, rendered in a surprising and obviously deliberate likeness of Andreas. There was about the expression a forebearing nobility as well as benevolent humor. The head was cocked just slightly, and one eye was winking. It was impossible to look at the face without smiling.

"It's nice," Kate said, "really very captivating." Looking at it a bit longer, she finally handed it over to him again.

"It's to be my insignia...logo, you call it, I believe. Whenever this sign is displayed, I will have a shop beneath. My friend is making the first sign at this moment."

"The first sign, huh? And I thought I had big ideas."

"I have so many ideas, Kate...you can not begin to imagine."

"So did I, pal...so did I."

"I'm sorry for your troubles. But what may seem to be a tragedy now, may turn out to be a benefit later on. The tale has not been told in its entirety yet."

"Thanks, but I'm kind of through turning pages, Andreas. So I'll never really know."

The opening of the first Zeus Cookies shop was an enormous success. It was not the best location in Mykonos to attract street traffic, but that problem was overcome by Jason and a few of his friends who would go out every day with sample pieces of the delectable circles. A free taste was all it took to lure an army of new patrons back to the source.

Every morning Andreas would appear at the bank near the harbor and deposit the previous day's earnings. The amount of money he had earned in little more than six weeks was quite staggering. It seemed almost too good to be true.

Naturally, the more money he made, the more closed-mouthed he became. This was for two reasons, the first being that it postponed the marriage to the girl, and the second, that his success would not attract jealous competitors.

When he could, he visited Kate, who treated him with a reserve he would have found intolerable to bear, except that he kept before him the certain knowledge that in due time he would be able to win her back to him once he had made a success of himself. He had only to find an honorable way out of the marriage agreement. Of course, how this would happen, he could not even begin to imagine; nevertheless he had faith that he was, in fact, in the custody of the gods. At long last. The pieces of the dream were all coming together.

Then one day, he had a terrible shock.

It was that slime Yiorgos again, up to his old tricks!

Apostolis, one of Andreas's oldest and best friends, came to him like a thief under the cover of night, knocking on his door and rousing Andreas from a much needed sleep. The news he carried was horrifying. Yiorgos had been sticking his nose around, and through some source had discovered the amount of money Andreas was salting away in the bank. Yiorgos, himself, intended to launch his own cookie business, and because he had purchased a prime piece of property on the busiest street on the island, it would only be a matter of time before he had stolen away all of Andreas's business.

Andreas thanked Apostolis, who was also an employee of the rat-faced, vermin-hearted Yiorgos of Kos, and set about brooding over the threat.

When he confided in Jason, Jason again suggested murder. Andreas agreed it was tempting, but there was always the damn dog. They'd have to get him first.

And that was when the idea hit him. It was brilliant, masterful. A scheme worthy of the great god Zeus himself. Most of all, it was to be a suitably disgusting downfall to the unscrupulous Yiorgos.

Jason was delighted. Only the two of them would know—and their accomplice, Apostolis. Timing of course was everything, and for the next two weeks, Andreas bided his time with good spirits. Whenever he passed Yiorgos he would hail him with a hearty greeting. Yiorgos would glance slyly in his direction, never suspecting. Ah, sweet, sweet revenge.

And all the while, Yiorgos was preparing his own cookie palace, sparing no expense in the fixtures for his establishment. In two weeks of frantic work, Yiorgos was ready to open Heavenly Cookies. And on the very night he was to open, Jason and Andreas and Apostolis were likewise ready with their part of the grand opening.

The disaster hit within an hour or so after the first cookies were sold. One by one the customers of Heavenly Cookies experienced the uncomfortable indignities of stomach cramps, and in all directions that first morning, tourists could be seen galloping to the nearest public rest rooms. At first people thought it was a flu, but as the suffering victims conferred among themselves, eventually the topic of diets came up. The single common denominator in their affliction came out to be none other than the Heavenly Cookies they had consumed.

The police were summoned to investigate the contamination.

Yiorgos was astounded and protested innocence of any slovenliness in his sanitation procedures. Apostolis, himself, made indignant noises. After all, he himself had worked side by side with Yiorgos to ensure that everything was properly handled. In fact, the police could come and

look for themselves. And Yiorgos, showing good faith in his
own product, stood before them and ate half a dozen with
great relish.

Later, Apostolis was to fall on the floor clutching his own
sides in glee as he related to Jason and Andreas the piercing
wails of discomfort coming from the odious—now truly the
odious!—Yiorgos, after his product sampling.

Of course they knew that the greedy merchant from Kos
would not give up so soon, and the next day, and the day
after that, he again attempted to peddle his cookies to the
newly arrived tourists who were not yet onto the dangers
that came from biting into a Heavenly cookie.

On each occasion, however, the situation was the same.

No doubt Yiorgos would have continued his operation
preying upon new victims coming onto the island every day,
but that the police had become particularly nervous. Tourists were saying horrible things about the island's water
supply, about the sanitation, about everything...and it was
the income from tourism, after all, that paid the police their
salaries.

On the third day after his opening, Yiorgos was put out
of business, suffering a great economic loss when he had to
sell his new equipment to Andreas who was big enough to
help him out of his trouble.

And that afternoon, Andreas, Apostolis, and Jason went
together to Paradise Beach, which seemed a fitting place to
have their ceremony, and threw into the Aegean the small
vial containing the mild laxative with which Apostolis had
seasoned the Heavenly morsels.

Although on one hand they felt themselves to be heroic
champions of good against evil, on the other they were
pricked by their consciences. The three of them were truly
sorry for the fleeting and mild, although disruptive, discomfort caused to the innocent victims, and making at least

symbolic retribution for what they considered a necessary act, they offered a free Zeus cookie with every one purchased for the next three days.

People thought they were wonderful.

Chapter Fifteen

It was late August and the flavor of the island had again changed. One of the most amazing qualities of Mykonos was how within three days a whole new ambience could take hold. And the light! The strange and magnificent light had again altered in a way that Kate could swear had nothing at all to do with the sun. The light on Mykonos came from some other source, and shadows were not shadows but the overlapping of one dimension onto another, creating a density of molecules. Or so it seemed sometimes. For nothing here was ordinary.

From personal observation, Kate had come to believe that destiny brought certain groups of people together on the island at cosmically determined times, in order to experience whatever it was they needed in their lives to progress as human beings. Then, right on schedule, they'd all take off, having had their lessons, and the next bunch would appear. And for some reason the newcomers were all distinctly different from the last group to depart. The island was a kind of clearing house for souls.

Andreas had said it: on Mykonos there are no accidents.

Anyway, it made no difference that all these mystical attributes assigned to the island had no basis in reality. There remained something comforting to the idea that there was some grand and noble design to the universe.

Even the weather seemed to follow a unique pattern. The climate on Mykonos did not change gradually, degree by degree, as in most places. No, it changed radically, as if a hand, in ripping off a page on a calendar, established a whole new climate in one motion.

Now, on one of the last days of August, Kate ambled along a street with her basket. In it were three new designs to put on consignment with one of the boutiques. She wasn't making a fortune, but she was getting by.

It was cooler than on previous days and there were very few tourists about, especially compared with the hoards of Italians and French who had, only two days before, filled the island beyond its capacity. She had heard that the heat would return again, that the current temperateness was a brief respite for what was to come in September. Kate did not mind. Let the weather be what it would.

As she passed through the town, a stillness clung to the atmosphere, and in it Kate imagined she could still hear the raucous playfulness of the departed Romans and Neapolitans and Milanese. Now and then, on her stroll, she would be hailed by one or another of the Greek women who had come to recognize her as being a separate entity from the regular crush of revolving bodies to frequent the island. In spotty Greek, she would return their salutations.

She felt very good, very good indeed. Mellow, in fact. What other way to describe this pleasant sense of lethargy she had slipped into over the last month or so? Once her potato empire had collapsed and she had gotten over the initial despair, she had settled into her design work with far less compulsiveness. No longer was there any great pressure to succeed. No glorious goal loomed in the near horizon anymore. She simply took pleasure in her work. Of course she had made money, but not enough to open the kind of salon in Paris that she and Simone Z had envisioned.

She supposed that the end result of everything she had experienced over the last year, beginning with Michael's abandonment and ending with Yiorgos's sabotage, was that she was simply drained of all strong emotion. She was even too drained to experience being drained. And so she had reached a sort of contented balance in her life in which she lived each hour of every day without any particular expectation.

The only one situation she could not entirely resolve within herself was that having to do with Andreas.

Here there existed a definite problem.

With Jason so closely allied to Andreas emotionally, and also professionally—for Jason spent all his waking hours assisting in the Zeus Cookies enterprise—and with Maria living just overhead, there was no opportunity to put Andreas out of her mind. He remained a constant presence in her life.

She did not mind really, not anymore. She had somehow also learned to live with the inevitability of his arranged marriage. One could only live with denial or rage or self-pity for so long.

Oh, intellectually she knew she was insane to allow him to remain as part of her life. Their relationship was nothing more than a prolonged fantasy. With every week's passage, he seemed to become more successful, which was another way of saying the relationship was another week closer to being over.

Just a week ago, an Athens newspaper had picked up a story on him as being part of the new breed of Greek who could conquer the odds against success through hard work and by using one's head, and, doing so, rise to sudden glory.

"Of course," Andreas had said when he had sat in Kate's living room reading the article aloud. "Sudden glory! It's all so simple. Ha!" he'd exploded, half angry and half amused. "All it takes is a bloody miracle to do what I've done."

She had reached the boutique. She left the three dresses with the proprietor of the dress shop, then stopped for some Greek olive oil at a market, picked up a freshly baked loaf of Mykonian bread from a bakery, and still feeling good, began to trace her way back home.

En route, she passed her favorite home in the village. It was impossible not to stop for a moment to admire its charm. Unlike almost all the other houses in Chora, whose shiny green and blue painted doors were flat up against the streets, this dwelling was raised up several steps and positioned on a higher level than the street. It was also set back, with an open courtyard just barely visible to passersby. A low wood-slatted wall protected the property from intruders, which certainly there would have been—for one very good reason. The floor of the outside terrace was of deep red tile, and the overhead expanse was covered by a wood trellis from which groups of succulent purple grapes draped luxuriantly down. Without the wall as a reminder, who could have withstood the temptation to trespass?

Kate sighed regretfully, and as she turned, she collided into another body.

"Would you take this house as a gift from me?" asked Andreas, his hands coming up to steady her. In his eyes Kate saw tender amusement. He had clearly understood the expression of domestic longing in the sigh.

"How long were you watching me?" she asked, trying to cover her transparency with conversation. She pulled herself away. She was embarrassed at being caught admiring something so typically bourgeois as a "nice house in the suburbs" when not long ago she had made such an issue out of freedom and self-fulfillment through conquering the world of commerce.

"Long enough," he said. "You make a good view."

He was going her way, and they strolled along together, Andreas taking hold of the empty basket she carried. He smelled invitingly of vanilla and chocolate.

She had liked his compliment, but said nothing. Lately she had been spending a little more time on her appearance. She had gone to the salon and Leitsa had trimmed her hair a bit shorter, and after considerable discussion they had decided to give her a loose permanent wave—not enough to fry her hair, but with enough bend so her dark hair could be worn softer and fuller around her face.

She had also taken to walking in the afternoons after she had put away her sketches and had started something for dinner. Her skin had taken on a healthful tint, her cheeks pink and glowing. Today, because she was off to peddle her wares, she had added some eye makeup—just a touch of violet shadow, an outline of dark brown pencil along top and bottom lids, and black mascara to finish everything off. Maybe looking better was a sign of feeling better again.

She had put on a filmy, white, cotton dress, whose shoulders rolled down to become a strapless affair, slightly peasanty, yet with the élan of high fashion imitating the costumes of the masses.

Before she had set out on her way to the boutique, she had forced herself to undergo a critical self-examination in the full-length mirror she had put up in the bedroom. It had been important to remain objective. She twisted and turned, peered over her shoulder at herself, and faced the truth head-on. In the final analysis, she was pleased with what the mirror told.

If anything, she had improved in appearance since Michael had dumped her for The Claw. She had never been one to indulge in extended admiration of herself in any respect, but giving credit where credit was due . . . she looked damn good. In fact, judging from what she had seen in the latest and splashiest fashion magazines, she'd fit right onto a glossy page these days, what with her pseudo Gypsy look; her overall image bearing a sort of compromise between tastefulness and restrained wildness.

Yes, she was pleased that Andreas had noticed her appearance.

"Unfortunately," he said as they continued on together, "the house you like so much is not for sale. But don't despair. I'll get another one for you. And if you like that one, I'll have it duplicated exactly."

"And what will your wife say about that?"

"I'm not married."

"But soon you will be."

"The future is always unknown."

"Not this one," Kate said. "Why do you torment me?" she asked, her tone no longer light. "You're making a joke. I'm making a joke. But none of this is exactly funny, is it? Not really."

"Not really," he repeated.

"So why do you torment us both?"

"I'm Greek, we enjoy suffering."

"I'm not Greek. I don't like pain."

"I apologize," Andreas said. They walked on in silence for a while. "Since you want to be realistic...what will you do now that winter is coming?"

The winter. She had not even considered her life past the present evening. The days just came and went lately.

"I don't know. Go on, I guess. Back to America maybe." But she said it uncertainly because that's what she really was: uncertain. Over the past weeks she had honestly come to enjoy her life. Even in its uneventfulness there was a certain sweet rhythm to the sameness. She felt sometimes as if she were being gently rocked in a cradle.

But of course there was that nursery song, "Rock-a-bye, baby... when the bough breaks the cradle will fall...down will come baby..."

Ah, yes. Changes were due.

"And in the winter," she asked him, "what will you do?"

"I have some ideas," he said, but became silent, offering none of them.

"Which are?"

Andreas only smiled mysteriously.

Anyway, they had reached her place, and another situation arose immediately. Maria was sitting on her steps talking to a friend about some knitting problem. When she saw Kate, she rummaged through her apron pocket and pulled out a letter. It was from Simone Z. The postman had dropped it off earlier when Kate was out.

Andreas's face took on a dark quality as he watched Kate open the letter.

"Well, what is she up to now?"

"She says," Kate read, "that she misses Mykonos, but really the season is beginning again in Paris, and that if only I were there with her, I could make a fortune." Kate's voice drifted off.

"What?" Andreas said, sensing trouble.

"Nothing," Kate answered.

But something in her face did not correspond to her answer apparently, because Andreas followed her inside, not allowing her to skirt the issue.

"What is it?" Andreas asked, following behind her as she went to the kitchen to check the pot she had left simmering on the stove while she was out.

"I told you. Nothing. She's writing silly gossip, that's all. Girl stuff. You wouldn't be interested."

"I'm interested. Tell me."

"You have your secrets... allow me my own."

"So!" Andreas crowed, suddenly transforming himself into the injured party. "There is something going on!"

"Why don't you just cut it out, Andreas. You're so Greek sometimes, even you start to believe in your own petty dramas."

He abandoned the air of the severely wronged. "Fine, say what you will about my cultural heritage. Still, I want to know what the meddlesome Simone Z is now up to."

Kate sighed, and putting on an apron, began to stir the soup. "All right, if you really must know, she said that if I wanted..." She couldn't say it. It would only sow the seeds for an argument.

"Go on," urged Andreas. He commandeered the wooden spoon from her and took up her duty as stirrer, as if the physical activity interfered with her speech process. "Say the rest. If you wanted...?"

"It's nothing. She could arrange for me to have a loan. That's all."

"A loan."

"Yes, yes. You know. For a place in Paris."

"I see." His expression had hardened, and his green eyes turned cold as he looked at her.

"She's found a spot. A perfect location, she said."

"What a good friend." Andreas was stirring with so much force the liquid was lapping over the sides.

"Here," Kate said, taking the spoon from his hand.

He relinquished the utensil, but only to capture her wrist. Pulling her against him, he kissed her with a violent possessiveness. "I won't let you leave, Kate. I love you...love you..." he said again and again as he kissed her neck, her mouth, the indent of her collarbone.

"Andreas..." she began to protest, but to no avail.

He would not listen, and she could not—or would not—stop him. With one assured movement, he had slipped her bodice down and freed her breasts. While his mouth explored them, his hands lifted the material of her skirt, and running his fingers along leg, to upper thigh, to hips, he pressed himself hard against her.

"Jason will not be back until much later," he said, his voice ragged. "Oh, my Kate...you will never, never leave me. I can't live without you...can't live without this...no other woman..."

Deftly, he removed her panties, and made himself available to her as well. The thin, white cotton was like a billowy white cloud draped from her hips as he pressed her against the counter and lifted her slightly to accommodate him.

When they joined, there was no other consideration in the world—not Paris, not beautiful Greek girls waiting to be wed, not cookies or even the light of Mykonos for Kate; there was only sensation upon sensation of exquisite pleasure.

"Andreas..." Kate said, as afterward her fingers traced the curve of his cheek as they came slowly down from their passion, "if there are gods, then let them come forward now. They are needed, Andreas...they are needed so desperately."

Chapter Sixteen

Kate only half listened to Jason that evening as they ate their soup across from each other at the small kitchen table. "I've made a salad," she said. "Want some?"

"Mom? Are you all right?"

"Yes. Of course."

"We already had the salad, Mom."

Kate stared at him. "Oh. We did." She shook her head. "I guess I was just thinking."

"Yeah," said Jason as he tore off another hunk of bread from the loaf and stuffed it into his mouth.

In much the way Andreas did, thought Kate.

Oh, everything reminded her of Andreas now. She simply didn't know what to do. She didn't even know what it was that she was feeling anymore.

"I'll bet you didn't hear a word I said," Jason accused.

"What?"

"I said some Japanese man came by this afternoon and asked a lot of funny questions about Zeus Cookies." Jason shook his head sadly. "No offense, Mom, but you're becoming a real space case."

"That's nice," Kate said.

"Mom, never mind." Jason stood and clearing his dishes, announced that he was going to go down to the taverna to see if he could locate Andreas.

Kate remained at the table, lost in thought. The light was fading fast, and the fuzziness surrounding her seemed to match the thoughts moving through her mind.

The envelope with Simone Z's offer was placed to the side of the table. Again and again, her eyes moved to where it lay.

Oh, she thought, letting her head fall back and staring at the ceiling, what do I want?

But that was not the issue really: what she wanted. She knew what she wanted. She wanted everything. She wanted Andreas, and she wanted herself. A few weeks ago, maybe even up until a week ago, she knew that the choice she made had to be in favor of her own personal independence. She needed to explore her capabilities, test her range, experience life on her own, before she could again merge with another human being.

But now she didn't know. That was the problem. Before the issues were so clear, and now the lines wavered and the walls she had put up were starting to crumble.

Certainly she enjoyed her work, but that was just it: she enjoyed the work for itself. She was happy now. It didn't seem to matter all that much that she wasn't going to open the fashion house in Paris. It would have been very nice, but what she was experiencing in Mykonos on a daily basis, living with Jason, sharing all the mundane aspects of life with

Andreas, was fulfilling her in a way she had not envisioned as possible a few months before.

The terrible truth was she was happy as she was. Happy, dammit. Oh, why did such a thing have to happen to her? Happiness at long last, arriving just in time to mess up all her careful plans.

Reaching for the letter, she pulled it from its envelope and in the faded light, read the words Simone Z had penned. Even in the dark, there seemed to be a glowing promise inherent in the very ink. Fame and fortune. Independence.

With the pages still in her hand, her eyes moved to the spot where four hours ago she and Andreas had made love. She shivered, her eyes closing as she recalled the delight of that encounter. It had been abandoned, untamed sex, and yet every word, every touch was underscored with the certain knowledge of their love and respect for each other. In connecting with all parts of him, she was connecting with all parts of herself. Together they became even more than one whole, or so it felt—if such a thing could be possible.

When she looked again, the place where she and Andreas had made love in the sunlight of the afternoon was almost entirely darkened by shadow.

Before it was too late, she had to do something.

Standing, she brought her plates to the sink and dropped them into the plastic washbowl with those of Jason's. Her hand reached absently for the wooden spoon lying on the counter where it had been dropped from her hand when Andreas had taken her that afternoon. Feeling its solid, smooth strength in her hand again, it was as if they were still connected.

She started to drop it into the water with the other things, but her hand stopped in midair. Outside the small window, she could see the faint glow of the moon and the pink glow of the sky dying rapidly by degree as the sun retired. A feeling of infinite loss assailed her. She stood like that for some time, locked in a state of deep melancholia. Then, before the final light had left the sky, she decided.

Tomorrow night, she would tell Andreas. Rather than lose him, she would prefer to lose herself. If he still wanted her, then she was his to take . . . forever.

For Andreas the situation had reached seriously critical proportions. He sat in the taverna, surrounded by his friends—half of them married to Greek girls who were home with babies, probably discussing christenings with parents and in-laws, or what they would cook for the next religious holiday.

He was half-drunk already, yet nothing would dull the misery he felt.

Vassilis, to his left, was ogling a tourist girl walking past. He loved his wife, he said, but alas, he loved other men's wives as well.

But for Andreas, there could only be one woman. Kate absorbed him entirely, possessed his heart, his very breath. For him, no other woman existed, nor would any other woman be able to take her place in the future.

Today in the kitchen had been only a small sampling of the passion she aroused in him. He would take her like that, and a thousand other ways . . . passionately, tenderly; there was no limit to how he would express his love and desire for her.

And now what? He had been biding his time . . . no, buying his time, actually, as he sought to come up with some honorable solution to his plight. It had never once been his intention to marry anyone but Kate, if she would have him—and he was to ensure that through his success. His problem was how to make the money—which he was doing; and then, how the hell to tell his parents he was not going to be able to carry through on his word to marry the girl from the village.

Oh, he was a snake of the first order. He was a coward. He was a deceitful disgrace to the Pateras name and would be shamed as a son for all time on their family tree if he would break his word. For generations to come, members of the Pateras clan would gather around the Bible that listed the genealogy and shake their heads solemnly when they saw his name. Perhaps they would strike him out of the Bible, as if he had never existed. The humiliation his parents would suffer... dear God, thought Andreas, dying a hundred thousand deaths merely from the thought of what such a savage act of familial defiance might do.

In the background, the bells from a nearby church chimed hysterically. There was a madness to the clanging. Even the tourists who had no understanding of the reason behind the racket, stopped, seeming to consider the urgency behind the nerve-racking music.

But no one could have been more affected by the sound of the death knell than Andreas. The doom it broadcast of another Greek's passage reverberated throughout his body.

His hand shook as he downed a shot glass of ouzo, not bothering to cut it with water this time.

What, he asked himself, was life for, anyway? Was it to be wasted in rituals set up a thousand years before? Was it to please others, which he damned well knew was an impossibility when one really thought about it. Others were never pleased. Would he live out his days shackled to a life he had not chosen himself, but had had foisted upon him by the well-intentioned but outmoded beliefs of another generation? There was something to be said for tradition, of course; but there was so much more to be said for breathing in and breathing out—and having each breath be free and joyous.

He was thirty-three already. Soon enough the time would
come when the bells would toll their mournful announcement on his behalf, and others—like he and his friends—
would pause only briefly in their chatter of women and
politics and the rotten economy, to pay fleeting respect to a
stranger's departure from the planet.

He did not want to leave from this world without having
truly lived!

With a burning heart, he stared past the pedestrians
streaming past the taverna to the harbor in which four large
cruise ships were moored. Strings of tiny lights blazed along
each ship's outline. Once he had stood alone on the edge of
the port staring out at such vessels, and had ached to go
where their powerful engines could take him. Then he had
no way.

But now he did. He was his own engine, and with the
money he was going to make, he would be able to sail the
world; he would be able to give Kate anything and everything she might want to be happy; and, as he thought it, he
knew that he could not ever honor his parents' wish to
marry the simple and sweet girl from the village. He had not
yet left Greece physically, but in his mind and heart he had
voyaged far beyond the limits they had set up for him.

There was nothing else for him to do. Tomorrow he would
travel to his village. He would confront the issue directly. It
was the only way.

As he made the pledge to himself, the bells stopped and
around him he heard the laughter and song of the living.

Ah, he thought, and lifted a full glass of ouzo to Vassilis.
"*Viva*, my friend!"

It was a long journey, particularly so because it was one
that would forever alter his life. He first took the ferry to
Piraeus, as the planes were booked full and it might have

been a week before he could get passage if there were no cancellations. From the port, he took a bus into the city and bought his ticket to the village from the bus depot. There was no other direct form of transportation into the countryside. He might have driven, but his wreck of a car would probably have crumbled alongside the road.

Soon, though, when he and Kate were wed, he would buy whatever she liked for them. Well, he reconsidered, perhaps not whatever she liked—not at first, but eventually. He had such plans, and they would all work out.

He believed in himself totally. Nothing could keep him from succeeding. That certainty was in his blood these days. He could sometimes almost swear that he experienced the physical sensation of being carried along by some intelligent wind, or that he rode some invisible giant steed with wings and an inner compass to deliver him to his most heartfelt destination.

The bus ride took three hot hours. There were people standing in the aisles, and now and again packages of vegetables and meats would fall upon someone's head. They stopped three times in villages to allow people to get on and off, and to buy drinks and relieve themselves in the rest room.

The scenery became monotonous. Mostly it was gently rolling land, parched a golden brown from the summer's heat. Groves of olive trees appeared, and around more than one bend they encountered flocks of sheep sprawled across the road as a spotted dog and a young boy or old man herded them on their way to some other location.

In the front of the bus, the driver remained oblivious to the writhing discomfort of his passengers. He sat secluded in a tiny kingdom he had constructed for himself over the years he had driven the same route. It was so on all the buses. There was the typical small shrine with religious rel-

ics displayed, and above the tiny temple there were pictures
of loved ones. Off to the side, placards touting the suprem-
acy of a soccer team were hung. There was a gay, hand-
crocheted blanket strewn over the large hump in the floor
containing the gearbox and fresh flowers in vases attached
to the wall by brackets. And of course there was the radio
blasting Greek music.

At last Andreas came to his stop, and grabbing the few
parcels he had brought along that contained various gifts for
his parents and neighbors, and the few old friends who had
remained in their rutted lives, he stepped onto the ground
that had been home to him for the length of his boyhood.

Here the architecture was different than in Mykonos. All
the roofs were of tile and were slightly peaked. Now and
then it would snow in the area. There were some simple
wrought-iron balustrades outlining the few steps leading up
to front stoops.

It was going on early evening when he approached his
house. From fifty paces, he could smell the lamb cooking.
A flood of memories overwhelmed him and briefly under-
mined his assurance that what he had come to do was right
and necessary.

"Andreas! Andreas!" his mother said, her voice piercing through the small house as she turned to find him
standing in her kitchen. Even before she threw her arms
around him, she scampered to the hallway and yelled out for
her husband to come at once.

Andreas laughed, holding her tightly against him, loving
with his entire heart this simple woman whose life he might
very well be about to ruin with his own selfishness.

Although his mother wanted to make a big deal of his arrival and invite half the village to share in the meal that had
originally been prepared for only two, Andreas discour-
aged such lavish hospitality. He said that he was tired. That

was true. But mostly he knew it was best to keep a low social profile under the conditions of his visit.

He could not bring himself to ruin their meal with the purpose of his visit. Nor could he mention anything about it that night as the home began to fill up with neighbors, each one reporting to the next that Andreas Pateras had come home.

There was, of course, much jocularity surrounding his impending marriage to the girl.

"Where is she?" asked more than one friend, a question to which Andreas could make no educated reply.

Even he thought it strange that the parents and the girl had not come to pay their respects with the others.

The mystery was solved the following day, only moments before Andreas was to broach the delicate issue of his wish to back out of the marriage engagement.

It was going on eleven in the morning when the parents of his betrothed knocked lightly on the front door.

From the very first moment Andreas saw their faces, he knew something was wrong. They could barely meet his eyes and moved quickly into the living room, followed by Andreas's parents, who must have also recognized in their mannerisms that something was amiss.

There was a certain amount of throat clearing before the point of the visit was broached. The father and mother took turns explaining the situation.

It seemed that their daughter did not want to wait to marry. Of course she thought that Andreas was a very fine person, and would have liked to have been his wife, but in the meantime—while he sought his fortune, which they all agreed was admirable—she had met another young man who was ready immediately to settle down.

There was considerable handwringing. Such a thing had never happened before in their family. Both sets of parents were almost beside themselves with grief. They repeated over and over again to Andreas how sorry they were. But their daughter was incorrigible, demanding to lead her own life as she saw fit. They said they were as surprised, shocked and wounded as Andreas. They hoped that he could understand and forgive them all this terrible injustice.

Andreas felt sorry for them. He would have liked to have confessed that he was delighted to be set free, but felt it would not have been in anyone's best interest to do so. It was kinder all the way around to let everyone think he was the castoff, rather than let them know he had not wanted the girl.

He did what he could to look grave and dignified throughout the discussion. At its conclusion, the two sets of parents bid each other a stiff goodbye. Andreas looked properly crestfallen when he asked them to convey to their daughter his wishes for a long and happy marriage.

He was a tragic and wonderful figure.

Ah, thought Andreas the next day when he rode the bus back to Athens, the gods were indeed watching over him.

Kate had perhaps never in her life felt quite as giddy, quite as romantic, quite as hopeful—and nervous—as she did that morning when she awoke with the certainty that by the evening's end, she and Andreas would be firmly and finally committed to each other for the rest of their lives.

Jason had slipped out too early for her to have told him the news. She would tell him later that evening when he returned. It seemed altogether right that before she told Andreas that she was going to accept his proposal of marriage, she should discuss the matter with Jason. Of course, the mother-son discussion was a mere formality. Jason had made no secret of the fact that he wanted Andreas as a father.

This was going to be the single most beautiful evening of their lives. Every detail of it was to be perfect, and would be, for she was going to plan everything out with all the love in her heart.

She decided where to tell him—the romantic choice was to go to the first little taverna where they'd eaten cheese pies on the day they'd met. Yes, that would be perfect! Andreas would be amused and touched.

Then she thought of what she would wear. She wanted to look more beautiful that evening than Andreas had ever seen her look. After thinking about this for some time, she decided upon a dress being finished by the seamstress for one of Simone Z's friends in Paris. The woman was the same size as Kate, and they had, in fact, fitted it to her proportions. There was no rush on the outfit, and another could be easily made up with no one the wiser that Kate herself had worn the original.

It was a deep, royal-blue jersey dress, with puffed sleeves, a low, scooped neckline, and a bodice that clung to her body. The fabric fell softly over her hips, molding itself to her form, and ended in a tulip flare. The color was magnificent, and complimented her totally.

When her outfit had been arranged, she took off for the jewelry stores and found a beautiful gold chain, masculine and rich, which she'd give to him, along with her little speech about how she wanted to be joined together with him forever.

Oh, it was going to be such an evening!

She was still in high spirits when Jason came dragging home at three o'clock.

"What's wrong?" she asked, mystified as he moved past her in the hall and continued through the living room and started up the ladder to his loft bedroom without even acknowledging her presence.

"I'm not going back there anymore," Jason said.

"It can't be all that bad, can it?" Kate said, catching up with him and ruffling his hair as he stepped onto the first rung of the ladder.

Jason whirled around. "I hate Andreas!"

"You had a fight?"

"He's not there! He's gone back to his village. He told Vassilis he was going to get married!"

Kate didn't move. She knew she had heard correctly, but she didn't want to accept the words. Tears were streaming down Jason's face. "Vassilis said that?"

"Yes! He came this morning to help in place of Andreas. He told me that Andreas had to settle everything once and for all. That he could not go on with his life, living half here and half there. He had to make a decision. And he had. He was going to the village to tell them that he was ready to get married. That's exactly what Vassilis said. And I'm not like you, Mom—I listen!" Jason gave her a hard, blaming look, and then turned and climbed up the ladder.

For a time she could only stand where she was, her hands gripping the ladder for support. Tears did not fall. She was wounded far too deeply for any display of emotion. Upstairs, Jason sobbed enough for both of them.

In Athens once again, Andreas went directly to a jeweler where he spent an hour looking at wedding rings for Kate. After considerable deliberation he selected a beautiful filigreed gold band. Someday he would take Kate to Paris or Rome or Switzerland and buy her the most splendid ring there was. It would have a diamond as big as a sea urchin! Ah, the future, the future...it gleamed before him as brightly as the gold band the jeweler placed inside a small box lined in silk and covered in dark blue velvet.

After his purchase, he took himself to the office of an attorney.

"I would like to make the son of the woman I am to marry a half partner in my business," he announced. The office was very plush. Perhaps even six months ago, he might have felt intimidated by the sophisticated surroundings. Today he was not. He had a lot of money in the bank. And with the dreams he would soon turn into reality, he would soon have a great deal more.

"Very generous of you," was the reply when the details were discussed more fully.

"You realize he's only eleven. That shouldn't be any problem, should it?"

"Eleven!"

"He works very hard," said Andreas. "And it was Jason who originally inspired the whole enterprise."

"That's good of you. Still . . ."

"And most of all, it's a wedding gift to my future wife. I want to make some enormous gesture . . . something so big there will be no mistaking my commitment."

Behind the large desk, the man smiled knowingly. "And this way you reduce your risk of being turned down?"

"Yes, something along those lines," Andreas admitted. "I've come to believe that when you want something, then you do everything necessary to obtain it."

"Not a bad philosophy. And I believe Onassis did much the same when he himself married an American woman. You realize that the woman will be the executor of the estate for the boy until he is of age."

Andreas smiled.

"Ah," said the other man, "so in this way you are all linked together."

"If you could write a contract to bond us together through eternity, I would buy it."

"You love her very much," declared the man, nodding.

"She is my whole life. She is life itself to me."

"It's dangerous to love so much."

Andreas shrugged. "Sometimes you haven't any choice. It happens."

The papers were drawn up to Andreas's satisfaction. They would be presented to Kate on the day he asked her to marry him. That would be tomorrow, when he returned to Mykonos on the ferry.

He was in a taxi, on his way to visit a friend, when he saw the sign. "Stop!" he commanded the driver. "Wait here," said Andreas as he left the cab and wrote down the address of the shop with the sign announcing the building was available for lease or purchase. There was a telephone number to call if there was interest.

Four hours later Andreas had agreed to buy the place for a third less than the owner had asked. Within a month, he would have a new sign over the building's door. It would be a large winking head of the god Zeus.

And this was only the beginning for what was to come.

Chapter Seventeen

Perhaps if she had not involved herself in such frenetic activity the day after she had learned that Andreas was to be married, she might have collapsed completely. But as it turned out, the misery propelled Kate to act with compulsive haste in order to avoid any further pain. It was over, finished between them, and she had to get away. What memories she had were sweet; it was these she would take with her when she left Mykonos. She would remember Andreas as hers. To see him again, a man who belonged to another woman, would stain every image she had of their own relationship.

"Do I have to leave everything?" Jason asked as Kate threw her clothes into one of the old duffel bags. All of life might fall apart, but the ugly, green canvas bags remained. It was part of some universal law.

"Sorry, yes," answered Kate, remorse seeping through the efficient resolve to do what had to be done without any emotionalism attached. Jason leaned against the wall, watching her pack. "For now, anyway. But I've already spoken with Maria, and she's agreed to supervise the packing of our other stuff. I hired those two sisters—you know, the ones who sometimes help with the sewing when my seamstress can't handle everything. They'll ship everything to us." Kate glanced at Jason. Even through his summer tan, his face looked much paler. She thought instantly of when he had been so sick that first night they had stayed in the apartment. And of how Andreas had helped. Oh, Andreas! Even the name brought on agony. Would she ever be able to see anything that would not remind her of some magical moment they had shared?

And poor Jason. He was paying a dear price for her foolishness. They had both lost the best man either of them would ever know in this world. But losing Andreas was all her fault, as they very well realized. She had dillydallied so long that even Andreas had lost patience with her. How could she blame him for going on with his life? She couldn't blame anyone for anything. This was all her doing. And now she was paying the consequences.

Her eyes fell on the blue dress she was to have worn the previous night. Lifting it, she held it in her arms, experiencing it as the limp, pathetic corpse of the only great love she would ever know in this world. Folding it then, she placed it gently in the duffel bag along with all the other items that would remind her of Andreas. In her mind, the bag took on the image of a crypt. "I know things seem kind of bleak now, but—"

"*Kind* of bleak?" Jason droned incredulously.

"Okay, a lot bleak."

"Try rotten. As in stinko."

"We'll get through this," Kate said, without sounding very convincing.

"I'm tired of getting through stuff."

"I know. Me, too. But I'm going to make this all up to you," she promised. She turned, facing him with what she hoped was an expression of enthusiasm. "Simone's always talked about the good schools, and I'll see that you'll get into the best. You'll be able to learn French. And we'll see all the great art museums. The Louvre! And the food, Jason . . . the food's superb in Paris! You'll see, this is all going to work out."

Jason said nothing. He merely turned and left her with her own feeble verbal baloney echoing in the room.

In four hours she had packed the belongings they'd need to get them started in Paris. As soon as they arrived, she'd call Simone Z from the airport, and Simone would help them to begin their new lives. As best they could, anyway.

They were lucky in one thing. They were able to get two cancellations on a plane to Athens. Kate was particularly grateful for this small gift from fate, as she doubted she would have been able to stand on the boat and watch the island slowly recede from her miserable life.

As it turned out, she did not entirely escape the agony of reflection. As the plane banked sharply upon takeoff, it was impossible not to look down upon the arid piece of land mass that had so completely rearranged her entire being.

Tears came on their own. To hide her embarrassment, she kept her forehead pressed against the window and looking out, looking down, said a silent goodbye to a time of splendor in her life that would never come again.

Simone Z had been a good friend to her in Mykonos, but she proved even more devoted to her welfare once she and Jason had arrived in Paris.

For the first few days Kate allowed Simone Z to act as hostess. Her hospitality was lavish. The flat was large and overlooked the Seine. Flowers were delivered every three days, and arranged by a maid who arrived in the morning in time to bring coffee and croissants to their beds. In the evenings there would always be some event to attend, dinners at marvelous restaurants, theatrical productions to enjoy, a small party.

"You're knocking yourself out to keep me from thinking, aren't you?" Kate accused one day when they were having lunch at home.

"No, of course not!" Simone Z protested. "Well, I'm not knocking myself out, anyway. I enjoy your company."

"You know I can't stay."

"Well, not forever..."

"Not any longer, Simone," Kate said. "I've got to start doing something with my life."

"Fine. We'll find a location for the salon, and—"

"And an apartment for Jason and I. I've enough saved to pay for something modest." Kate glanced longingly around Simone Z's opulent dining room. Beyond the window, she could see the spires of Notre Dame Cathedral. "I'm afraid if I don't leave now, I'll get used to this, and you'll have to pry me out of here."

"I'd like you to stay, really. But, of course, I'll allow you to decide your own future." Simone Z became reflective. Then she said, "Kate, in France many times women are mistresses to married men."

"I'm not French. I'm American. I'm not judging anyone's standards, but I know I couldn't live with that. Even if Andreas would consider such an arrangement."

"But you two love each other!"

Kate looked pensively out the window, her eyes tracing the intricate patterns of waxy-leafed ivy growing up the stone walls of an ancient building across the river. "He'll be married soon—if not already. There's bound to be a child immediately. And with family life comes an attachment that'll dim any passion he once held for me. That's reality, Simone. You know it, and I know it.''

"Still, many men are married and still love another woman."

"Andreas is not many men. He's Andreas. I know him. He couldn't split himself in half that way. It's all or nothing. That's why I'm sure that there isn't any doubt in his mind that what he did was right. He knew as well as I that we couldn't go on like this forever. When he returned to his village, he severed our relationship. It didn't take a long letter of goodbye to explain. And it didn't take a speech. Anyway, we'd given each other all the speeches already. He knew I'd understand, and I do. It's over Simone. It's finished.''

A week later Kate had located an apartment, sublet at a ridiculously low rent from a wealthy friend of Simone Z's, and Jason had been enrolled in a fine private school with classes taught in English and French.

It took another three weeks of searching, however, until a building had been located for the dress salon. It was in the sixth *arrondissement* off the boulevard Saint Germaine. After much deliberation, the name selected for the fashion venture turned out to be Impulse.

By the end of each evening, Kate left the salon in a virtual stupor. There was painting and wallpapering, which she did herself, and the supervision of men who hung mirrors and shelves, not to mention the priceless Austrian crystal chandelier that was picked up for a pittance from an ancient French countess who was bailing out of one of her country estates. The floor was parquet and required refinishing. Amid all of this, Kate also had designs to create, from the conception to the finished product.

But the opening came off in less time than she would have thought possible, and it was, in a word, stupendous. The French totally embraced her as one of them. Of course, being Simone Z's friend was an added boon. The trendy wealthy were ready for something fresh, and Kate was there to give them the benefit of her original flair.

Several men attempted to date her; all were turned down.

"You are never going to forget him," clucked Simone Z, "unless you replace him with another man."

"Not yet," Kate said. "I'm really too busy."

"Too much in love, you mean."

And of course it was true. No matter how tired she was at the end of the day, she would find herself wondering what Andreas was doing that moment. It was the end of October, already two months since she and Andreas had parted—parted without ever really saying goodbye formally. Perhaps if they had, things would be different for her now. But sometimes it seemed as if there was still an unsevered cord binding them to each other. It was a ridiculous, self-defeating thought, of course. The truth was, Andreas was by now married to the pretty young Greek woman, who would no doubt be carrying his first child.

Jason had grown two inches since they had left the island and was now twelve. He had become slightly rude, which Kate took as normal and healthy for the age, and had begun to study piano seriously, as well as to play football seriously. He seemed to have a natural aptitude for languages and besides French was learning German. In his spare time he was building something in his room out of scrap metal, string and wire that closely resembled either a medieval torture chamber or a space ship. Clearly he was going through his Renaissance phase.

On two separate occasions, Kate found half-finished letters he had written to Andreas lying on his desk. She tried not to look, but couldn't help herself, and it occurred to her that Jason had left them there intentionally in an effort to spark in her the same idea of contacting Andreas.

The letters began in a light, enthusiastic vein, but as the paragraphs continued the tone became darker, and Kate easily read into the sentences the sadness Jason was still experiencing over his separation from Andreas.

The letters were never mailed. Later, she found both torn to shreds and lying in the bottom of his wastebasket. And in conversation, his name was never mentioned between them.

One afternoon, a month before Christmas to the day, it began to snow. The snow had begun early in the morning and by noon, the news was terming it a blizzard. By one that afternoon, cars were unable to get through the streets, and Kate knew that if she was going to get home by taxi, she had better leave at once or she'd be destined to a freezing walk home. There would be no customers that day anyway.

She turned off the lights and secured both the front and back doors, then, bundling herself into the first fur coat she had ever owned—a full-length red fox, purchased through another designer at great discount—she set off for home.

The snow was coming down in huge, white, fluffy balls, not drifting, but dropping from the sky with precision force. No matter that it complicated life, there was still an immense and awesome beauty to the swirl of white crystals.

Kate stood on the edge of the curb, looking down the street for a cab. The neighborhood had become strangely vacant in the last twenty minutes. The snow made rustling sounds, like voices whispering, as the flakes from above joined those on the ground. Cold and wet, the frozen crystals hit her nose, clung to her lashes, fell into her long, dark hair. Her feet were damp already and beginning to freeze. But somehow amid all the beauty everything was all right.

Down the end of the street, a taxi turned in, crawling slowly in her direction. A couple of times, it skidded. Kate stepped forward and raised her arm. Shivering, she waited for it to arrive and save her from frostbite and pneumonia.

It took a moment more for the driver to pull to a stop. She was smiling in gratitude as she opened the door, and was about to lower herself into the back seat when her eye caught sight of a figure moving slowly along the sidewalk across the street. Her first thought was that she might want to offer to share a ride, as it didn't seem likely that too many more cabs would be out for much longer.

And her second thought, as her smile was lost in bewilderment, was that she had gone mad.

Chapter Eighteen

The five men were a strange group. There were the two Japanese—one of whom had originally contacted him in Mykonos—one Swiss, and the Arab. And of course, there was Andreas himself, the lone Greek, but clearly the man to whom the others deferred. They didn't like it, but they had no choice.

They sat together at a table in the dining room of the Athens Hilton, having a celebratory dinner after seven and a half hours of hard negotiating. But it was decided. They were, in fact, a partnership. They had a master plan to dot the entire continent of Europe with Zeus Cookies within two years. A few shrewd Americans had populated their United States with cookies, to great economic success, and in Europe their own group would do likewise.

Of course, as Andreas had found out on his own, his new partners had originally thought to begin their own cookie enterprise. They had worked with several chefs in developing a recipe, and had market-tested it against the Zeus samples. No matter how great their greed, eventually they had to bow to the statistical data: nine times out of ten the public preferred Zeus Cookies to any product the consortium's chefs could concoct. What good would there have been in investing all their money in a product that would fail if put up against Zeus. And if they didn't tie up the Greek cookie king themselves, eventually someone else would. Better to join him if they couldn't beat him.

As to what ingredients made the cookies so special, no one could say for sure. "A little of this and that," said Andreas whenever pressed for a response.

"Exactly what is this and that?" the Swiss interrogated.

"A bit of mythology, a dash of magic, a lot of belief, and the blessings of the gods."

"You are full of it," muttered the Arab, who had spent the last eight years in America living in Beverly Hills.

"And that, too," agreed Andreas with a rascal's grin. He loved annoying them. They were a ruthless, money-grubbing lot—rather like high-classed versions of Yiorgos. He understood them; therefore, he would be safe. In fact, he would triumph. But they did not understand him, and would forever be off balance in any negotiations.

Indeed, he also had a great deal to grin about. He had gone from the one cookie store in Mykonos, to three in Athens and now would begin his pilot program out of Greece. He would own fifty-one percent of the Zeus stock, and having controlling interest not only guaranteed him a lot of money, but it also made his vote count for more.

"Paris," he announced, as the place where the first Zeus Cookies would be placed outside of his own country.

There were a few feeble protests that they might think in terms of West Germany or Austria, perhaps Italy...but the men had already learned that Andreas Pateras would never give in or give up if he got an idea into his head.

"In my life, gentlemen, I have given in and given up enough times for a thousand men. No longer will I do so. What I want is what I will get. Understand this and life will be a lot easier for all of us."

No one said anything.

And Andreas smiled his charming rogue's smile yet again.

However, in the privacy of his own quarters, which were now in Athens, he did not smile very often. It was true that he had already made more money than he had ever dreamed possible. And this was only the very beginning of the projections for his company. Not only that, but there would be other investments to come from the proceeds of what Zeus Cookies generated in the way of capital.

No, he did not smile often because his mind was obsessed with one thing...one woman...Kate Reynolds.

When he had returned to the island to find her gone, he had plunged into such a depression that for five days he did not eat or leave his house. Kate had left no note for him. All he knew was what Maria knew. Kate had decided that it was best to go to Paris, to open her own boutique, just as she had spoken of doing with that blasted Simone Z. He had always known that the French woman would cause him grief! Kate would discuss nothing with Maria. Her things were eventually sent to an address in Paris she had left with his grandmother. Andreas had stared at the address, the letters burning into his mind like lit coals. The few words were his only link with the woman he had loved more than his own life.

After the worst of the depression had lifted, and he could function again, at least marginally, he went into a cold rage, cursing the day he had ever caught sight of her. He spent hours walking through her apartment, fury radiating from every cell of his body as he reviewed their relationship. He saw himself as a fool, a duped, love-lorn jerk. The rage was much better than the initial sorrow, and he found particular satisfaction in the fact that this time he would not be sentenced to the usual fate of the jilted Greek lover standing on the shoreline watching the woman sail off into safe boundaries.

No. Because this time he had the money behind him to ensure that he would be granted a visa to America. Or any other country he cared to visit.

The country he would visit was, of course, France. And the city, Paris.

She had not escaped him.

It was this sense of furious honor, a kind of low-level Greek revenge, that propelled him to work like a maniac during the first few months after Kate had left him.

But later, the anger again altered into yet another feeling. The emotion was positioned somewhere between sorrow and love; but basically it was an indescribable, pervasive ache that filled his body, his mind, his soul, his days, his nights, until every breath was a bittersweet reminder of the woman he had loved and lost.

He would go to Paris. And he would seek her out. Why, exactly, he did not know. Rationally, he understood that it was over between them. If she had truly loved him—as he did her—she never would have gone off that way without even so much as a goodbye between them. Yet it was precisely this unfinished business that made him still feel attached to her. There were nights when he would lie awake reviewing all the positive and negative points of their relationship, when it seemed that she had somehow slipped into his mind, and with him rode each wave of thought.

The idea that they were still joined was so compelling on an emotional level that he began to walk around with the golden band that was to have been her wedding ring in his pocket. He carried it like an amulet, worshiped its power as if it were a magical talisman, believing that it bound them together.

On the twenty-fifth day of November, he had the ring in his overcoat as he walked in Paris on the boulevard Saint Germaine.

In rapid French, the taxi driver asked Kate if she was to get in the taxi, or if she was going to freeze to death on the street, and probably take him with her to the grave if she did not close the door of his vehicle at once. The snow was a blinding screen of white.

Although Kate's French was from high school, she understood enough of the tirade to make an effective response—but she couldn't. Her mind was locked in a state of disbelieving shock.

Across the street stood a man, even now looking directly at her, who resembled Andreas in every way but for the fact that he was wearing a long, expensive-looking coat and was standing in the middle of Paris.

As if laser-borne, the eyes, which from the distance appeared to be a brilliant green, pierced through the thick, white curtain of snow separating them. She was unable to move—the eyes held her with their power, as surely as if he had physically taken hold of her shoulders.

The cabdriver was shouting at her again. He was going to drive off if she didn't get in at once. But didn't he understand? She was unable to move. Just as the car started to roll slightly forward—the cabbie making good on his threat—the man across the street turned and headed away. She was released from the spell.

She yelled quickly to the driver and plunged into the back seat of the automobile, shaking from more than the cold. For a moment she had honestly thought it was Andreas.

By the time she had arrived home, she was convinced it had to have been someone else, some handsome Frenchman who had perhaps mistaken her for someone he knew as well. Or maybe he was simply a man on the prowl, and had been gauging his chances of picking her up and decided against it in the end.

That night she cried herself to sleep.

Andreas felt like exploding. He paced his hotel suite like a wild beast. If he had been home, he might have picked up a piece of furniture and smashed it against the wall. But he was not home. He was attempting to play a man of civilized sophistication. But he *was not* a man of civilized sophistication. His feelings were base and masculine, primal and real. Totally raw.

Only two hours ago, he had seen her. He had stood close enough to call to her from across the street, and yet he couldn't. He had stood there frozen in fear. What if he had called out to her, and she had turned away from him? No, he could not bear that. If something like that had happened, he doubted he would have the fortitude to hold his daydream together that some day, in some way, there would be a reconciliation.

Had she seen him? He couldn't tell. The snow had been so thick it had been impossible to read the expression on her face. Ah, that face... that beautiful, tantalizing, exquisitely expressive face. His Kate.

Andreas moved to the window of his suite in the George V and stared down to the traffic below. He was surrounded by luxury, but all the money in the world was nothing to him without the woman he loved. And he could only love one woman.

"Simone... Simone! I don't know what to do! Look across the street. I can't believe it. Do you see it? Simone... it *was* him I saw. What do I do?" Kate was beside herself. Beyond the window of her store, almost directly across the street, an enormous sign bearing the winking countenance of the god Zeus, was being hoisted above a shop by a crew of workmen.

Several times Kate moved up to the window to peer out, and then would whirl around and dart back out of view into the safer regions of her boutique. The store was officially closed for lunch, and only Simone and she were there.

Sitting at the elegant cherrywood table eating one of the finger sandwiches she had brought to share with Kate, Simone said, "He'll come again. When he does, go and talk with him. Clear the air between you and then get on with your lives."

Kate's face was white. "I couldn't, Simone. I couldn't go up to him." She sank into a chair and stared forlornly at the plate of sandwiches. "I would rather die first."

"You are acting like you're half-dead anyway."

"But don't you understand? If he had wanted to speak with me, he would have stopped me that day in the snow. We were alone. It would have been so easy. Just one word..."

"And why didn't you say one word if it was so easy?"

"I wasn't certain it was him."

"*Merde.* Your heart told you it was him, even if your eyes tried to play with your mind."

"But it wasn't up to me to make the first move. It was Andreas who made the final decision to give up on our relationship. And now he's married, and I just can't trust myself to meet him face to face. Simone ... Simone, I love him. I will always love him. Nothing will ever change my feelings. Nothing! And I can't bear to see him and not be with him. He belongs to another woman now. Can't you understand? It hurts so..." And with that, Kate lay her head on the table and sobbed.

Simone rose from her chair and moved around to Kate. She placed her hand lightly on Kate's shoulder and with her other hand began to stroke her hair. "Tell me something, my dear friend ... why do you think this man has opened a shop directly across from yours?"

For a moment Kate kept sobbing. Then slowly she lifted her head, and turning to Simone, looked questioningly up at the older woman.

"Yes," Simone said. "It was a purposeful choice. It was not any accident."

"But why? Is he trying to torture me?" Kate asked, her eyes traveling to the window.

"Do you think the man you loved is so cruel?"

"No ... no. He was not cruel. Clever and sometimes manipulative. But never was there anything deliberately mean or small about Andreas." She smiled, even through the pain, remembering all the sweet moments he had brought into her life.

"Then perhaps this shop across the street is meant to bring to you another kind of message. And if you respond ... well, that is for you to decide."

On the fifth day of December it was bitterly cold in Paris, but the skies were a clear, if weak, blue. The heat had not yet been connected in the new shop, and Andreas stood behind the glass front of his store in his long gray overcoat. The coat was from London and had cost a small fortune. Even the long white scarf draped over his lapels cost as much as two weeks of his former Mykonian wages. And the Italian shoes he wore...he still quaked when he thought of the price! After so many years of forced frugality, being careful was second nature. He resented spending the money on himself; yet he was now in a position that required him to appear affluent. To appear shabby worried the investors who were everyday purchasing stock in the company. It seemed, as he stared across the street to the shop marked Impulse, that his recent monetary good fortune was a snowball that, once begun, kept rolling and growing by itself.

Impulse. The name of the store seemed to invite him, to urge him forward. Impulse. And what, he wondered, would happen if he were to walk now, straight across the street and face her? Longing as he did for another chance to be in her presence, he might sacrifice the pain of rejection for just one moment of blissful proximity. He might do something like that if he were not careful. He might...upon impulse.

"Do you want these lights hung now or later?" yelled a worker to Andreas. "Hey, these things are heavy, you mind?" the man called again when Andreas did not respond at once.

"Now," said Andreas in a low voice. "Do it now." But he was not speaking to the man as he moved to the door and, swinging it open with sudden force, entered into the frigid air.

From inside her shop, Kate watched him coming across the street. She observed the scene with all the amazed horror and fascination of a woman standing on the shoreline watching a tidal wave rolling in to obliterate her. She was dimly aware of her customer's voice asking her how the dress fit around the hips. She might have said something, murmured a reply, but she couldn't be certain of anything at that point. If someone were to have asked her name, it would have been impossible to say. Her eyes glanced at the clock over the mantelpiece of the small fireplace, but all the numbers were blurred.

He was coming across the street. His stride was as she remembered: long, powerful and purely masculine, the slight sway of his body exclusively his style of movement. Oh God . . . she loved the man . . . the sight of his body, even in the long coat, made her weak with desire for him.

And then it was too late for any plans. He was at the door and then in the shop.

The tiny bells over the door jangled pleasantly as he stepped in. A burst of astringent air accompanied his arrival. Three of the customers and her one saleswoman paused in their activities to eye the handsome stranger who had just joined their small group.

It seemed to Kate that the world had stopped spinning. She felt faint, light-headed, totally out of control of any of her physical or mental faculties.

For a moment the two of them stood staring at each other in much the same way as they had during the snowstorm. Then they both moved slowly together, stopping three feet from the other.

"Hello, Kate," Andreas said simply. One hand was covered by a black leather glove; the other glove was held in his bare fingers.

"Hello, Andreas." Her heart was beating as fast as a hummingbird's wings. She thought she might faint, might truly pass out from fear and elation and uncertainty.

"You've done very well for yourself," he said, the green eyes moving about her place with curiosity and admiration.

"Yes . . . and you . . . you've also . . ." Her eyes went past him to the window, where beyond she could see his store.

"I've done well," he agreed. "More than well."

"I guess the gods were on your side," she said, feeling her eyes filling with tears. "After all."

"Not entirely," he replied, and a note of bitterness surfaced. Then quickly, he asked, "How is Jason?"

"Jason...oh, Jason's fine. He's getting so big now! You should see him, he's—" She stopped, realizing she had made a mistake. She had overstepped the boundaries of what was meant to be a casual social call. The moment was pregnant with embarrassment for both of them. She understood, of course, the reason for the visit. He was playing out one of those infinitely civilized scenes that take place between ex-lovers, little vignettes between people who want to tie life into nice, tidy, little packages. It was like setting out the garbage in an attractive little parcel so as not to offend anyone. But her mind shouted something else, something contrary: to behave so wasn't the way Andreas played the game of life! Not her Andreas, anyway. He was passionate and to the point. There were no petty ruses in his repertoire.

But this man standing before her was not her old Andreas. No, indeed. This man before her was a man she felt she scarcely knew anymore. His hair was shorter and his clothes gave him an air of sophistication, one might say an aura of power, he had lacked before. This man was not her old Andreas.

The momentary lapse in conversation was finally filled by Andreas. "I'd like to see him again. I was very fond of Jason."

"Yes, and he, too. He was fond of you, too," Kate said stiffly, trying to gather her composure after almost making an enormous fool of herself.

"Then...maybe I could take him for dinner..."

"No," Kate said hurriedly. By Andreas's expression, she felt she owed an explanation. "I think it would only confuse him—make it more difficult for him to..."

"Yes, of course," said Andreas. His voice was tight. He transferred the black glove to the other hand and then back again, the actions of a man preparing to move on.

A panic seized Kate. Even as she stood before him, he was slipping out of her life again. There was no guarantee they'd ever meet a second time. If she were to, as Simone had suggested, abandon her morals, her standards, become his lover if not his lawful wife.... Oh, she did love him that much! Once she had thought she had to love herself more and him second. But now she knew that wasn't true. Guiltily her eyes traveled to his hand, looking for the ring he would wear. His glove covered the ring. And she couldn't do that to another woman anyway. There was no way. Besides, he had given no indication of his interest in her sexually. He had only asked for Jason. *Stop, Kate. Do not make a pathetic fool of yourself.*

"It was good to see you again, Andreas."

"And you, Kate."

They both managed slight, insincere smiles. Kate warned herself not to cry, not to beg or plead for one more chance in his arms, not to make a spectacle of herself. In a moment, he would be gone.

And then, he was.

Andreas was fortunate. The cab was cruising by just as he left the boutique. He hailed it and quickly got in. Leaning against the upholstered seat, he took deep breaths in an effort to stop the trembling. He was a man, a Greek man, a grown man, dammit, and he wanted to bawl like a child. His eyes stared straight ahead but saw nothing through the moisture gathering in his eyes.

My love, my love, my eternal love... I have played my hand and lost. You did not offer me any hope at all. You were so cool, so in control, while I fell apart before your very eyes. I begged... I asked to see Jason. And of course I wanted to... I love the boy as I would my very own son—which I will never have, because I will never marry if I cannot marry you! But Jason was my link to you, Kate. He was a thin thread connecting my dreams of you to the reality of you.

At the George V, he paid the cabdriver and tipped him too much, not caring about anything as he stumbled numbly to his suite. There were messages waiting for him, but he put the stack of papers down on a table, unable to think of anything. He was overcome by loss. As he moved through the suite, going to his bedroom, it was as if he had fallen into a dark, endless well. There was no light left in the world for him.

He lay on the bed for some time, staring up at the ceiling and willing his mind to shut down forever, if that was the only thing he could do to end the torturous despair. He stayed like that for what seemed like several lifetimes and eventually, mercifully, sleep claimed him.

In the middle of the night, he was roused by a horn blast several stories down on the street. Shocked awake, his mind was clear for a moment before the memory of his loss of Kate intruded. But before the overwhelming sadness closed in to obliterate him again, he had a thought.

He was not quite done yet. True, he had played his hand—all but one card. He still held the trump.

Chapter Nineteen

The letter was addressed to Jason, in care of his legal guardian, Kate Reynolds. The envelope looked forbiddingly official and Kate was almost beside herself before Jason returned home from his piano lesson that evening.

"It's yours," she said, handing over the mysterious envelope. "I've been going crazy wondering about it."

"You could have opened it."

"I was respecting your privacy."

"Just like all the books on how to raise teenagers advise, huh?"

"Exactly. So open it now...before I kill you." Kate waited. It was taking him forever. "You haven't beaten anyone up, have you?"

"What?" Jason asked, wrinkling his nose.

"Beaten someone up—as in broken limbs...smashed eyeglasses...as in nasty civil lawsuit by outraged parent?"

"Ah," Jason said expansively, understanding, then muttered while still reading, "Just the guy who said he didn't like Americans. He's out a couple of front teeth, is all."

"Jason!"

He looked up from the letter and grinned. "Only kidding, Mom." And maintaining the smile, he handed her the letter.

It was from an attorney in Paris. As representatives of Andreas Pateras, they were hereby requesting the presence in their office of Jason Reynolds and his custodian, Kate Reynolds, in order to settle a financial matter of considerable importance to both parties.

Their client, the principal shareholder of Zeus Cookies, felt that in order to establish his legitimacy and gain clear title to his holdings in the firm, he was morally obligated to make financial restitution to Jason Reynolds for services previously rendered, in the order of twenty-five percent of the firm's stock.

"I'm going to be rich, Mom," Jason said without any particular awe.

As for Kate, she was clearly stunned. Also suspicious. "Jason, do you really think that you deserve twenty-five percent of Zeus Cookies? Do you honestly believe—"

"Of course not, Mom." He shook his head, looking at her as if she could not see the obvious.

"Of course not? Then why, tell me, are you looking so pleased?"

"Because, Mom, it's Andreas's way of telling us he wants to see us."

"No, Jason..."

"Yes, Mom." He came to where Kate was standing and wrapped an arm around her shoulders. It was the first time she realized he was almost her height. A couple of times in the last week his voice had skidded into foreign registers and careened back just as recklessly. "There's no way I deserve anything at all, the way I see it. I made up a batch of cookies, and they tasted good. But Andreas put together his own recipe. And when I worked for him, he always paid me double what I was worth. He doesn't owe me a thing."

"Good, then it's settled. I applaud your integrity. We aren't going."

"Maybe you aren't, but I am. I've got no problems with accepting a gift if someone wants to give it to me."

"Jason, it isn't right. Besides, you're defying me."

"Look, Mom . . . you did what you had to do, and Andreas did what he had to do, and now I—Jason Reynolds, a person in my own right—am going to do what I have to do. For me. You'll find *that* in your book on how to raise teenagers, too."

Then he marched into his room. A few minutes later she heard him in the shower. He was singing very loudly.

Of course in the end she had to relent and attend the meeting. Otherwise there was no telling what might happen. Jason had suddenly become possessed of a new and forceful personality. And if that wasn't enough, it was a fairly level-headed persona he had adopted. In the presence of such logic, it was almost impossible to get away with being irrational anymore.

Kate followed Jason into the office after the attorney. Andreas was already there, waiting. He was standing, looking at some books in the floor-to-ceiling bookshelves when she entered. "Here we all are!" said the lawyer, and at that Andreas turned slowly around.

Their eyes met briefly, but this time there was no green fire sparking out to reach her. Instead there was the cool reserve of a business magnate. He was dressed impeccably in a dark gray suit with a thin, maroon pinstripe. His silk tie was a paisley design in dark, rich, vibrant shades, and the shirt was a light gray. He was, thought Kate, as dazzling in his new persona as he had been in his other incarnation of the island *kamaki*, as lover extraordinaire ... as her old Andreas.

She sat down in the chair offered to her by the attorney, and Jason took his place beside her. Nervously, she crossed and recrossed her legs several times, then tugged at her skirt, rearranging the folds of silk. It was a dress of deep violet with a white border ranging around the V-collar and a large white belt at the waist. It was her own design, both feminine and chic. A large producer of American fashions had asked if they might offer her a contract to gain permission to produce the outfit in mass quantities. She had decided against the offer. She enjoyed what she did and did not need more money than she had. It was enough. More than that ... she was enough. That was the best part.

Andreas arranged himself in the fourth chair, slightly to the side of the desk behind which the attorney sat going over his documents.

"How are you, Jason?" Andreas asked, his voice deep and rich and level, a man totally in control.

"Very well, thanks." Jason's voice slid slightly, taking in two different vocal registers. Rather than being embarrassed, Jason grinned.

And so did Andreas. For a moment Kate saw her old love returned as she had known him. The recognition of all she had lost pained her. It was as if a wire tightened around her heart.

"I'm growing up," said Jason. "Pretty obvious, I guess."

"You're growing up well."

The two males locked eyes. There was a union between them, a bond that would always be there. Even then, on the first day they had met in Mykonos, Kate had realized she had lost a part of her son to this man, and that fact was reconfirmed again. Whatever her differences with Andreas, the love between the other two was still there. All one had to do was to look at them.

She was thinking this, and smiling inwardly as she did, when her eyes touched upon Andreas. She took a quick breath as he caught her staring at him, and looked away. When the lawyer began to speak just then, she still felt Andreas watching her. She wanted to look back, but couldn't. She was afraid—afraid that she might be wrong, afraid that she might be right. Either way, she would hurt when the meeting was over.

The conditions of the contract were fairly straightforward, and basically followed the details as presented in the letter. Jason was to get twenty-five percent of the fifty-one percent of Zeus stock owned by Andreas. This, of course, was generous to a fault, as Kate pointed out to no avail, but it also clearly—as the attorney pointed out—left Andreas as principal shareholder.

"And you must also realize, madame, my client has many other financial interests. Zeus Cookies is merely the foundation on which several other ventures have been formed. There have already been expansions to the nucleus venture. My client is a good and generous man. But he is not stupid."

And there was something in the face of Andreas Pateras, when these last words were spoken, that made Kate realize that there was much more to this generosity than met the eye. Or at least her eye. Jason seemed to have other, deeper insights into the arrangement.

When the matter was concluded, with Kate having to accept the obligation of administering Jason's holdings, they all stood and shook hands.

When she clasped Andreas's hand, it was as if an electric jolt passed between them. But neither of them said a thing.

Three days later, the first notice came that Kate was to attend a special dinner for the principal shareholders. As it was on a school night and would be too late for Jason, it was decided that Kate would have to go alone.

"I don't like this, Jason," she said as she dressed in a black jersey evening dress with a modestly scooped neckline. She wore a thin diamond necklace that she had purchased recently, and Simone Z had made her an extravagant gift of matching earrings, saying that Kate had done much to add glitter to her own life—which of course was a major lie as Simone was a thousand watt bulb by herself. Simone was just plain generous.

"Mom, don't you want to look after my own best interests?" Jason wheedled. "I'm your only son. Your only beloved son. Remember?"

"The fact that we are related hasn't slipped my mind, Jason."

"Good, Mom." He sauntered toward the hall, but then turned before quite to the door. "Oh, and Mom . . . I think you should wear your hair down with that dress. It makes you look . . . well, you know . . ."

Kate stared at him. He beamed back, and then was gone.

She had expected the principal shareholders. Instead there were only two seated at the restaurant table: she and Andreas.

"I don't understand," she said.

"Understand?"

"Why aren't there more of us? Will the others be late?" Of course she already knew the answer.

"No," Andreas said unconcernedly. He picked up the menu. "We're all here."

"But the principal shareholders—"

"Are Jason and myself. Pity," said Andreas, "that Jason couldn't make it. He'd probably love the steak Diane."

"Andreas," Kate said, sinking against her chair's silken upholstery, "is this for real?"

"Absolutely," he said, and brought up a folder with a sheath of papers to lend credence to his claim. "Would you like to get down to business immediately? Or shall we order wine and then tackle the small print?" He looked directly at her, his expression one of total sincerity as he waited for her decision.

"Wine, I guess." There was no sense in being a total hard-nose.

While he ordered, her eyes drifted to his hand, and she noted the ring. It was a striking design and simple. The gold band was wide and inlaid with a blue gemstone. The color reminded her of the Aegean on a clear day. It did not look like a wedding ring, not at all; and yet, as her hopes rose, she told herself to be realistic. Andreas was too unusual a personality to wear an ordinary wedding band.

The slight burst of happiness she had felt warned her to be on her guard, and for the rest of the meal she remained remote and aloof. The only responses she gave were of a professional nature.

At the end of their meeting, Andreas asked her if he might drive her home. She said she could take a cab.

"I'd like to see you home safely," he said.

"It's not necessary."

"I know. Kate . . ." He stopped speaking, yet his eyes relayed feelings she didn't want to know about. He desired her, wanted her. Frightened to the core, she rose and tried to escape, but he reached out and took hold of her wrist.

"No, Andreas . . . no."

"You still want me."

"Yes! Yes! But it's over between us. You chose! I chose," she said forlornly. "And now we have to live with what we've done." This time she managed to pull free.

She saw him leave the restaurant just as she got into her cab. With the window glass separating them, they stared at each other.

Jason was still up when she arrived home. He took one look at her face, and she saw understanding enter his own expression. "Doesn't look like the meeting went too hot," he commented blandly.

"It was fine," she said, and threw her coat on the sofa.

"How was Andreas?"

"He was fine." She began to remove her earrings, anything to distract herself from thinking.

"How are you?"

"I am fine."

"Your hand's shaking. Mom...you're still in love with Andreas."

"Jason," she said, looking at him with what she hoped was an adult's condescension, "what could you possibly know about romantic love?"

"This is Paris. It's part of my education." He smiled.

"All right. Maybe there's a little something...a lot of something...still there. But he's married."

"He can get a divorce."

"No," she said adamantly. "Greeks who marry girls from their village because the parents want them to, do not ever—and I repeat—ever get divorces."

"But he loves you, and you love him. None of this makes sense. With all that's going for you guys, there's got to be a way."

"The way is to accept the situation as it is, and to go on with our lives. Time and distance and new people will even-

tually erase the past. Now, just be a normal kid and go t
bed and let me be, Jason. Let me be—"

Jason closed his books. Looking down at the cover, h
asked, "Have you ever thought of at least talking it out to
gether?"

"I don't want to talk about it. I don't want to think abou
it. I don't want to know about her, or him, or what thei
problems are, or what their dreams are. It isn't something
want to hear."

Three days later another meeting was set up between th
business partners. This time the meeting was in the late af
ternoon and Jason and she were both going to attend. Sh
liked that idea, as it saved her from any intimacy with An
dreas.

They were almost ready to leave when Jason remem
bered he had to go back to school to pick up some book
before they locked up for the night. If he didn't, he'd fail hi
final examinations that he had meant to study for over th
weekend.

"We'll get them on the way," Kate said desperately.

"No...because I think I've got some at school, and som
are at Jean-Claude's and there's no time. No," he insisted
"you can go for me, Mom."

And in the end, she did. This time there were three othe
partners attending the conference. The whole meeting wa
perfectly legitimate. Andreas did not once address her in an
way that could be construed as personally presumptuous
Obviously the other night was just a play for a little physi
cal excitement on the side. Everything was going to be purel
business from now on. Good. Very good.

When she left, she returned home and found Jason wait
ing with his books spread out on the table.

"So?" he asked, eyeing her with interest.

"So it looks like you're going to own an empire. The guys have big plans."

"Did Andreas bug you again?"

"No." She moved to the window and pulled the drapes apart to look out. It was already dark and the streetlights gleamed. Ordinarily she might have found it a cheery night. But not tonight.

"Then how come you're acting so rattled?"

"I'm not," she said. Letting the drapes fall closed, she turned around and started quickly for the hallway. "I'm going to bed," she said.

"At six?"

"I'm tired. I'm just tired, okay? And stop looking at me that way! It's over between us! Andreas and I have separate lives now. So just stop looking at me like that!"

"Sure, Mom. Whatever you say."

Two days later, there was another meeting.

"I'm not going," Kate declared to Jason.

"You've got to. You're my guardian. I'm too young. I can't sign the contract, and this is about signing a contract. It says so right here in the letter." He waved it in the air.

"I know what it says."

"Then you know you've got to go with me, Mom."

Kate glared at him. She felt as if she were a hooked fish, and she was slowly but surely being reeled in by some master fisherman.

She dressed in a severe gray suit with black boots and a white blouse. There was nothing frivolous, nothing romantic in her attire. Her hair was tied back into a little knot at the nape of her neck. She was ready to leave twenty minutes early.

However, five minutes before it was time to go, she decided upon a red suit, sleek and fitted at the waist, and some high, black pumps. Her hair was fluffed out and worn long.

"Wow, Mom..." Jason commented approvingly when he caught sight of her. "What happened? You looked like a funeral five minutes ago."

Kate felt herself coloring. "It's almost Christmas. Red's seasonal."

"Oh, yeah. I almost forgot." He put on his jacket. "Like your perfume, Mom.... It's enough to make an elephant lose his memory."

"Knock it off, Jason."

"Sure, Mom..."

The letter had said they would be fetched by a driver and at precisely the right time they were picked up in a long Mercedes limousine with a uniformed chauffeur. Within fifteen minutes they had left the city's boundaries and were headed in the direction of the country.

"Excuse me," Kate said, "but are you certain we're to be taken out so far?"

"Yes, madame," came the clipped reply. "I'm quite certain."

It took an hour before they pulled up to a palatial estate located at the end of a mile long drive formally flanked on both sides by magnificent old oak trees. According to the driver, the château had once been the summer home of a king's favorite mistress.

It was now the residence of Andreas Pateras, who was waiting for them in the vast living room. There was a fire blazing in the hearth and a giant Christmas tree decorated with what appeared to be a thousand twinkling lights.

Andreas was standing by the fireplace, sipping brandy. His back was to them, but when he heard them approach, he turned around with a smile of welcome.

"I'm glad you could come," he said, walking toward them. He shook Jason's hand warmly. To Kate, he said, "I hope the ride wasn't too long."

"Why didn't you tell me?" she said.

"I wanted to surprise you," Andreas said without defen-iveness.

"Is this really about business?"

"Yes. Very, very serious business." And although he said t lightly, there was a lack of humor in his eyes. "But first, 'd like to offer you some refreshments. I'm afraid the cook s not in just now... but if you'll come with me, we can dig something up ourselves."

"This is great!" said Jason, keeping pace with Andreas while Kate kept a reserved distance behind them, signify-ing, she hoped, her disapproval of their presence in his home.

"The place isn't mine," admitted Andreas. "I'm only leasing. But one day I might settle into something. It's all been modernized, though. The actual owners live in Spain a good part of the time. They have a castle there, they're also refinishing." And on that they stepped into an enor-mous space gleaming of aluminum. Even Kate was im-pressed.

"Microwave," Andreas pointed out. "Another micro-wave," he said. "And the walk-in freezer, plus the elec-tronic stove, these four ovens..." It took him several minutes to show them all of the kitchen's features.

"Does it remind you of America?" Andreas asked Kate as they walked back to the living room with a tray of pâté and crackers, some smoked salmon and oysters, and for Jason, a few special pastries and fruit.

"Not of an ordinary kitchen," Kate laughed.

"Ah, you mean this is even better?"

They exchanged glances of understanding. Once a mi-crowave had been a necessity in her life. Now it was a dis-tant memory. And now he had even more than she had once thought she could not live without. "You've done very well,

Andreas. You have every right to be proud of your accom
plishments."

When they were again settled in the living room, Kate
broached the subject of the visit. "The letter from your
attorney said our meeting concerned the signing of a contract."

"Yes, but I thought..." He looked to the tree, to the
fireplace, and the food.

"Andreas, please..."

"Very well." He rose from his chair and returned a few
seconds later with a typed document of several pages, taken
from a desk. "If you care to read it through...but I'll explain to you that the terms set forth in the contract call for
a merger of Jason's shares and my own. That would make
one block of fifty-one percent single ownership once again.
The purpose is that one of the partners has sold out to another partner and has controlling interest in Zeus Cookies.
I don't think Jason and I want to see our enterprise fall into
the hands of other than the immediate family."

Kate was trying to make sense of what she had just heard.
She got the part about the percents, but the last statement
wasn't quite clear, unless of course he was speaking figura-
tively of family.

"I'm sorry. I don't quite understand what you have in
mind..."

"It's a merger, Mom," said Jason. His face was flushed,
and his eyes were very bright. For a moment the budding
man was gone and a very young boy sat beside her on the
velveteen sofa. "Mom, don't be so dense. Andreas wants to
marry you."

For a moment Kate was too stunned to speak. Then, only
trusting herself to look at Jason for fear that she would
burst into tears at the cruel joke being played on her, she
said, "That's not funny."

She attempted to rise, but her legs weren't solid beneath her. She felt as if she might start to cry uncontrollably, as if she would never stop this time.

"My mother loves you, Andreas," Jason said with a long-suffering sigh. "Like all females, she's just difficult sometimes."

"I know," Andreas replied, watching her.

"Stop it!" Kate cried. This time she did stand. "This isn't a joke! This is a hateful, rotten thing to do! You're a married man, and you're a rotten kid!"

"I'm a rotten kid, Mom. But Andreas . . . are you a married man?"

"I'd like to be . . . if your mother will have me."

"She will," Jason said, while Kate stood between them, her eyes still holding tears.

"You're not . . . ? But I thought . . ."

Andreas reached into his pocket and brought a small, gold, filigreed band. "This ring was bought for you the day before you left Mykonos."

"For me?"

"For you, Mom. I kind of got things wrong, I guess. That's the trouble with gossip."

"Kate . . . do you think I could have lived my life without you? Do you think that I would have cared about any of this if you weren't a part of it?" Andreas swept his arm in a generous arc, taking in the luxurious surroundings. "You're my whole life, Kate . . . you and Jason are. I want you always to be my whole life."

"Mom, say something . . ." Jason pleaded. "I can only do so much here. There's some things you've got to do for yourself."

Now the tears were escaping. Large, hot tears slipped down her cheeks, making the lights of the tree blur, making the tapestries on the wall blur, making Jason blur. The only thing that remained distinct was Andreas, perhaps because she saw him not with her eyes, but with her entire heart.

"If you've got those papers ready to sign...I think we really should...you know...merge," said Kate. It was hard to get it out because she was choking down sobs again.

There came an explosive cheer from Jason and a cry of joy from Andreas.

Her eyes closed as Andreas took her into his arms, holding her against him as if he meant never to let her go. When she looked into his eyes, her soul swam in pools of endless green, and she knew she had entered a world of endless love.

On a perfectly beautiful day in February, which just happened to be a year to the day Andreas and Kate had originally met, a wedding was held on the island of Delos. Many people came from Mykonos, and Andreas's family from the village. Simone Z and a group of her friends arrived on a chartered jet from Paris. There were seven members of the international press there, snapping pictures of the poor Greek man who made it big overnight and the beautiful American woman who had captured his heart.

It was, as several journalists were to write later, a fairytale story, and Delos—that ancient isle of mystical power—was a particularly fitting locale to launch the marriage of the remarkable couple whom it seemed fate had blessed.

After the ceremony there was a lavish feast—Greek style—and the wine, music and song all flowed in one continuously sweet stream. Hardly anyone noticed the boy who had slipped away and climbed the ruin said to have been dedicated to the great deity Zeus.

But Andreas turned just at the moment the sun's rays burst for one last second at the horizon. Kate, in his arms, followed his gaze. They were both in white for their ceremony, Kate in a lacy dress and Andreas in white pants and shirt. Yet all around them, the world was aflame in brilliant color. And silhouetted against the magnificent sky, stood the lone figure of a twelve-year-old who looked wise and satisfied with the scene he observed below him. When his parents waved, he raised an arm and winked, much in the way Zeus might have done—had he been there in person to claim his triumph.

*   *   *   *   *

ATTRACTIVE, SPACE SAVING BOOK RACK

Display your most prized novels on this handsome and sturdy book rack. The hand-rubbed walnut finish will blend into your library decor with quiet elegance, providing a practical organizer for your favorite hard-or soft-covered books.

Only $9.95

Approximately 16" x 8" when assembled

Assembles in seconds!

To order, rush your name, address and zip code, along with a check or money order for $10.70* ($9.95 plus 75¢ postage and handling) payable to *Silhouette Books*.

Silhouette Books
Book Rack Offer
901 Fuhrmann Blvd.
P.O. Box 1396
Buffalo, NY 14269-1396

Offer not available in Canada.

BKR-2A

*New York and Iowa residents add appropriate sales tax.

Silhouette Special Edition

COMING NEXT MONTH

#433 ALL THE RIGHT REASONS—Emilie Richards
Crack attorney Brett Terrill wasn't looking for love—just an obedient
wife who'd bear his children. Meek, maternal Olivia LeBlanc seemed
the perfect match . . . till she developed her own case of ambition.

#434 HEART OF THE TIGER—Lindsay McKenna
After her marriage failed, Layne Hamilton vowed never to get
involved with a CIA man again. But agent Matt Talbot had a
mission . . . and enough charisma to hijack Layne's heart.

#435 ONCE BURNED . . .—Karen Keast
Morning Skye Farenthall and Brandon Bear Hunter had once pledged
eternal love . . . then betrayed their youthful vows. Now a raging forest
fire reunited them, and their burning passion—and blistering pride—
threatened to consume them.

#436 SAY HELLO AGAIN—Barbara Faith
When Miguel Rivas met his high school heartthrob, Brianna Petersen,
at their fifteen-year reunion, the old feeling was back. And this time
he wasn't looking for a prom date, but a partner for always.

#437 CANDLES IN THE NIGHT—Kathleen Eagle
For practical Morgan Kramer, falling in love with idealistic dreamer
Mikal Romanov was sheer insanity. Driven by his humanitarian
causes, would he ever notice *her* very human needs?

#438 SHADY LADY—Patricia Coughlin
On Diamond Cay, Kara McFarland found the privacy her past
demanded. Celebrity Max Ellis sought precious solitude himself. But
as they trespassed on each other's turf, proximity led to dangerous
passion.

AVAILABLE THIS MONTH:

Silhouette Romance ™

Legendary Lovers Trilogy

BY DEBBIE MACOMBER....

ONCE UPON A TIME, in a land not so far away, there lived a girl, Debbie Macomber, who grew up dreaming of castles, white knights and princes on fiery steeds. Her family was an ordinary one with a mother and father and one wicked brother, who sold copies of her diary to all the boys in her junior high class.

One day, when Debbie was only nineteen, a handsome electrician drove by in a shiny black convertible. Now Debbie knew a prince when she saw one, and before long they lived in a two-bedroom cottage surrounded by a white picket fence.

As often happens when a damsel fair meets her prince charming, children followed, and soon the two-bedroom cottage became a four-bedroom castle. The kingdom flourished and prospered, and between soccer games and car pools, ballet classes and clarinet lessons, Debbie thought about love and enchantment and the magic of romance.

One day Debbie said, "What this country needs is a good fairy tale." She remembered how well her diary had sold and she dreamed again of castles, white knights and princes on fiery steeds. And so the stories of Cinderella, Beauty and the Beast, and Snow White were reborn....

Look for Debbie Macomber's *Legendary Lovers* trilogy from Silhouette Romance: *Cindy and the Prince* (January, 1988); *Some Kind of Wonderful* (March, 1988); *Almost Paradise* (May, 1988). Don't miss them!

SRT-1